Schiller, Friedrich; Hart, James Morgan

Schillers Die Piccolomini

Schiller, Friedrich; Hart, James Morgan

Schillers Die Piccolomini

Inktank publishing, 2018

www.inktank-publishing.com

ISBN/EAN: 9783747797488

Schillers
Die Piccolomini

EDITED

WITH AN INTRODUCTION, COMMENTARY, INDEX
OF PERSONS AND PLACES, AND
MAP OF GERMANY

BY

JAMES MORGAN HART.

Was die Natur auf ihrem großen Gange
In weiten Fernen auseinander zieht,
Wird auf dem Schauplatz, im Gesange
Der Ordnung leicht gefaßtes Glied.

NEW YORK
G. P. PUTNAM'S SONS
1875.

PREFACE.

THE text here presented is that of the *Historisch-Kritische Ausgabe,* the orthography being conformed to the rules laid down in the preface to *Hermann und Dorothea.* I have modernized also the punctuation. It was a mannerism of the eighteenth century to make lavish use of the dash. I have retained this sign only where it seemed justified by present usage, namely, to indicate a parenthetical clause or a certain abruptness of construction. I take the opportunity of calling the attention of lovers of German literature to the Historical-critical edition of Schiller's works. It is the collation of all the best editions with Schiller's manuscripts and with the critical emendations that have been proposed from time to time in literary reviews. The editor-in-chief is Karl Goedeke, and with him are associated Ellissen, Köhler, Müldener, Oesterley, Sauppe, and Vollmer. The edition is a monument of German industry and scholarship. It is to be regretted that *we have not a* similar edition of Goethe.

A few words in explanation of the nature of the
Introduction and Commentary. I have had throughout
a twofold object: first, to show how the drama came,
in Schiller's hands, to be what it is; next, to put both
teacher and pupil in possession of all the collateral
information needful to a complete understanding of
the drama, and also to a legitimate correction. Schiller
comported himself as a true artist, he took the materials
as he found them and fashioned them into shape to suit
best his purpose. He accepted, rejected, curtailed, expanded, invented, and altered at will, although never
without a motive. In thus rising superior—from the
artistic point of view—to the subject-matter, he showed
his excellent good sense. But, on the other hand, we,
as students, may not forget that the Thirty Years' War
was a veritable epoch in history, that Wallenstein was
no mythical character like Wilhelm Tell, but a per-
sonage as real as Gustavus Adolphus, Richelieu, or
Cromwell, that his so-called conspiracy, whatever view
we take of it, was a crisis in the political affairs of
Germany, that the names Colalto, Colloredo, Gallas,
and many others, still figure on the rolls of the Austrian
nobility.* We should be guilty of culpable remissness,
were we to suffer the poet's genius to beguile us into

* *The male line* of the Piccolominis became extinct about the
close of the eighteenth century.

overlooking the claims of history. Much, very much, can be learned from Schiller's 'Wallenstein,' if it be only rightly studied. The lines that stand as motto upon the title page,—they are taken from Schiller's poem *Die Künstler*,—seem to me to state the case with singular conciseness and precision. What Nature, and the historian toiling painfully after her with his historic method and his original documents, give to us in disjointed fragments and broken lights, the artist re-creates for us as a symmetrical, harmonious whole, with forms that move and colors that seem to speak. Only, let us not confound fiction with fact. Let us not mistake the drama for the history, but let us rather read the one hand in hand with the other, assigning to each its rightful place.

I venture to express an earnest wish. It is that the time may speedily arrive when the study of German, and also of French, shall be raised to a higher plane. May the acquisition of the two great languages of Continental Europe be regarded as of intrinsic value, not as a mere appendage to Latin and Greek, or as the price to be paid for the ability to read text-books of chemistry and physiology. Especially, may the study of continental history, this Pariah of our college curriculum, be regarded as at least equal in dignity and value to the study of the *institutions* of Greece and Rome.

If the present volume be found contributing to such a result, I shall regard the minute and often irksome labor spent upon it as not spent in vain. I have shaped everything to the end that the teacher may teach not only the German language and literature, but also German history and geography. The map has been kindly furnished by Messrs. Scribner & Co. from their edition of Gardiner's History of the Thirty Years' War, a work which I take the greatest pleasure in commending. It supplies a long felt want. In connection with Gardiner should be read Bryce's Holy Roman Empire and the excellent manuals of German history by Bayard Taylor and Charleton Lewis. The teacher and pupil who venture upon this formidable looking course of reading, will never have reason, I am confident, for regretting their enterprise.

J. M. H.

NEW YORK, June, 1875.

INTRODUCTION.

THE following works have been used in the preparation of the notes to " Wallenstein ; " they will be cited by the abbreviations :—

B. S.—Boxberger, *zur Quellenforschung über Schillers Wallenstein,* &c. (in Gosche's *Archiv für Litteraturgeschichte,* 1871, pp. 159–179, and 402–431).

D. W.—Düntzer, *Erläuterungen zu Schillers Wallenstein.* Leipsic. (The year of publication is not printed, but the work is very recent.)

F. W. B.—Förster, *Albrechts v. Wallenstein Briefe,* &c. 3 vols. Berlin, 1828. (A valuable collection of letters and documents of all kinds, connected by a continuous thread of historical and biographical narrative.)

G. T. W.—Gardiner, *The Thirty Years' War,* 1874.

H. W.—Herchenhahn, *Geschichte Albrechts v. Wallenstein,* Altenburg, 1790.

M. B.—Murr, *Beyträge zur Geschichte des dreyssigjährigen Krieges . . . nebst Urkunden und vielen Erläuterungen zur Geschichte . . . Albrecht Wallensteins,* Nuremberg, 1790.

R. W.—Ranke, *Geschichte Wallensteins (zweite Auflage)*, Leipsic, 1870.

R. P.—Richter, *Die Piccolomini* (No. 201 in the *Sammlung gemeinverständlicher wissenschaftlicher Vorträge*), Berlin, 1874.

For an account of the causes and origin of the Thirty Years' War, and for the progress of events up to the year 1634, the student is referred to Gardiner's history. The present Introduction is of necessity restricted to sketching briefly the career and downfall of Wallenstein.

Albrecht Wenzel Eusebius v. Wallenstein * was born in 1583. His father was the possessor of a single baronial estate, Hermanitz, in the Königingrätz district of Bohemia. As the father left five other children to share in the inheritance, young Albrecht's portion and outfit in life was a mere pittance. But the family, although poor, was connected with some of the most influential noblemen of the kingdom. Adam v. Waldstein, an uncle of Albrecht's, was Chief Burggrave of Bohemia. Another uncle, on the mother's side, was Albrecht v. Slavata, Baron of Chlum and Koschumberg. Another of his uncles, on the same side, was Johann Kavka v. Ricam. The Waldsteins and Slavatas were at that time Lutherans, and Albrecht was brought up in the Protestant faith. He was sent by his father to the school in Goldberg, in Silesia. At the

* The more correct spelling of the name, and the one followed by the general himself, is Waldstein. But the usual form has taken such firm hold, that it would be pedantry to attempt to change it.

father's death, Albrecht was taken by Albrecht v. Slavata into his own family, and his education continued under the charge of the Bohemian Brotherhood. In 1599 and 1600 we find him at the university of Altdorf, near Nuremberg. Although the story of the naming of the university *Carcer* after Wallenstein's dog, *Lager*, vii. 466, is to be rejected, yet there can be little doubt that Wallenstein's student-life was brief and inglorious. He appears to have been of a quarrelsome disposition, and was cited more than once before the university-court (M. B. 301). By Ricam he was placed at the Jesuit academy at Olmütz, but whether before or after his stay at Altdorf is not altogether clear. Neither is it known precisely when he became converted to Catholicism; most probably at Olmütz. Gualdo Priorato, in his *Vita d'Alberto Valstain*, and Herchenhahn after him, narrate that Wallenstein entered the service of the Margrave of Burgau, son of Ferdinand of Innspruck (afterwards Ferdinand II.). One day, while sleeping in an upper window of Ambras castle near Innspruck, he fell into the courtyard below, but escaped injury, as by a miracle. Ranke makes no mention of Wallenstein's having been a page at Innspruck, and the story is probably a legend invented in a later age. Schiller has repeated it, however, in *Wallensteins Tod*, IV. 2. 2545-2565, but has erroneously laid the scene in Burgau instead of Innspruck. We next find Wallenstein at the university of Padua, where he acquired some knowledge of law and astrology, and a taste for Italian culture. In 1606 he took part in Basta's campaign against the Turks and *Protestant* Hungarians. Gualdo Priorato

states that Wallenstein traveled extensively in Italy,
France, the Netherlands, and even in England.   To this
list of countries Herchenhahn has added Spain.   Von
Janko, in his *Wallenstein, Ein Charakterbild*, 1867, p. 8,
states that he traveled as companion of a rich nobleman
of Moravia, Licek v. Riesenburg, and that the third
person of the party was Paul Verdung, subsequently
Kepler's friend, and the one who probably awakened in
Wallenstein's spirit the fondness for astrological research
(see also F. W. B. I. 9).   Ranke makes no mention of
Wallenstein's travels.

But the most important event in Wallenstein's early life
was his marriage, about 1607, with a wealthy Moravian
lady, Lucretia Nekyssova v. Landeck, a widow and much
older than himself.   Her death, in 1614, left him the sole
possessor of her large estates.   Henceforth Wallenstein
occupies a conspicuous and independent position.   He
appears in state at the court of the Emperor Matthias;
as soon as his ready money is exhausted, he retires to his
country-seat, to accumulate a fresh supply (R. W. 9).

In 1617 Ferdinand of Grätz, soon to become emperor,
was involved in war with the Venetians.   The latter laid
siege to the important town of Gradiska, in Bosnia.   In
the successful attempt, under Dampierre, to throw supplies
into the town, Wallenstein, at the heat of a mixed force
of cavalry and infantry that he had raised and equipped
at his own expense, took the lead and thereby laid the
foundation for his future military career as Ferdinand's
generalissimo.   It was the time when the intrigues that
brought about the deposition of Cardinal Klesel, Mat-

thias's prime minister, and the adoption of Ferdinand's reactionary measures were in active preparation. The chief men of the anti-Klesel party at Vienna were Molart, Meggau, and Trautmannsdorf, and with them were allied Ferdinand's immediate retinue, Eggenberg, Mersperg and the Counts Harrach, father and son. Eggenberg's daughter was married to young Leonard v. Harrach, whose sister, Isabella Katharina v. Harrach, became Wallenstein's wife in 1617. This second marriage was the turning-point in Wallenstein's life. He was made count and imperial chamberlain, and became a member of the military and political clique that controlled for the next fifteen years the policy of the Austrian court. At the age of thirty-four he had raised himself from obscurity and comparative poverty to a position second only to that of the ministry. He had won the personal friendship of his sovereign and the confidence of the War and Privy Council, while he had attracted the hearts of the multitude by his engaging manners, his profuse liberality, and his reputation for daring and energy.

In 1618 broke out the Thirty Years' War. Although his estates lay in Moravia, and therefore were at the mercy of the Protestant insurgents who rapidly gained control of that province, Wallenstein did not hesitate to declare himself in favor of Ferdinand, who had been elected King of Bohemia and was emperor in fact, if not yet in title. Then in command of Moravia, he was deserted by his troops. Nevertheless he succeeded in carrying off the army-chest, with 90,000 thalers, and *bringing the money to Ferdinand.* With part of this

money Wallenstein speedily equipped and sent into the
field a regiment of cuirassiers, that took part in several
sharp skirmishes and that made the reconnaissance which
precipitated the battle of the White Mountain, in 1620.
Wallenstein himself was not present at the battle (R. W.
22). From 1620 to 1625 he took but little part in military operations. While Tilly, Mansfeld, and Christian
of Brunswick were winning barren laurels, he had found
a more profitable field for his activity and could afford to
bide his time. It was the era of the Restoration of
Catholicism in Bohemia. The battle of the White Mountain had crushed the Protestant party. All who had par-
ticipated in the insurrection were proscribed as outlaws,
and their estates were confiscated and sold at auction.
Neither Utraquist, Lutheran, nor Calvinist found mercy.
At this juncture Wallenstein, who had carefully amassed
his revenues, stepped forward as purchaser by the whole-
sale. Förster, in his *Wallenstein als regierender Herzog*,
gives the nominal value of the estates thus acquired at
seven million florins, but adds that the real value could
not have been less than twenty millions. In 1623 the
wealthiest proprietor in the land, Wallenstein was created
Prince of Friedland. His possessions comprised nine
towns and fifty-seven villages and villas (*Schlösser*). In
1627 he was created hereditary Duke of Friedland (R. W.
102), with the right to confer titles of nobility, to coin
money, and to conduct the government and administer
justice. The emperor reserved only a few causes of
appeal; but in most respects Wallenstein was practically
independent, he owed to the emperor nothing but feudal

allegiance. In the same year, 1627, he acquired also the principality of Sagan, in Silesia.

The year 1625 was a crisis in the fortunes of the House of Habsburg. Although Frederick had lost, through the battle of the White Mountain, not only Bohemia but also his own electorate, the Palatinate, and although the Catholic Reaction was apparently in the flush of success, the elements of the Protestant opposition were rapidly assuming formidable coherency and shape. The Spaniards in the Netherlands could do little more than hold their own against the Dutch Republic, the Catholic League under Maximilian of Bavaria, which had decided the fate of Bohemia five years before, was unable to resist the coalition which had been formed among Lower Saxony, Mecklenburg, the disaffected minor princes of Germany, the free cities, and Denmark, while the Turks and Transylvanians under Bethlen Gabor menaced Austria itself with a most dangerous flank-attack from the east. It became evident that there could be but one instrument of deliverance for Austria, a powerful army independent of the League and Germany proper and subject only to the orders of the emperor. But the imperial treasury, as usual, was empty, the imperial credit was at its ebb, and the best generals were either scattered over Europe or deficient in talent for organization. In the very nick of time, we might say, neither too soon nor too late, Wallenstein, who had demonstrated his capacities as a soldier and as a financier, came to the relief of the emperor. He volunteered to do what no one before him had undertaken, *to raise and equip* an army of 20,000 men at his own expense, and to lead them wherever the emperor might direct. After some hesitation and doubt, the offer was accepted and Wallenstein created generalissimo. Popular imagination has exaggerated the figures of the original offer to 50,000, for which there is no contemporaneous documentary evidence (R. W. 36). In the autumn of 1625, Wallenstein's army, about 20,000 strong, left its recruiting stations in Bohemia and marched through Franconia to Magdeburg and Halberstadt, where it went into winter-quarters. Like a snow-ball, it grew as it rolled. It was in anything but battle-order; if we may believe a contemporary report, some of the men were not even supplied with arms. But the general displayed, even at this early day, his skill as a strategist by avoiding battle. The army was supported by contributions levied upon the occupied provinces. Yet, unlike Mansfeld and the other irregular leaders of the day, Wallenstein suppressed plundering. His policy was to exact supplies sufficient for the support of the army, but without ruining the farmer and the crops. At the same time he enforced discipline to an extent that had been hitherto unknown. By the beginning of the next year he had brought his men under perfect control and had converted his disorderly and motley rabble into a formidable army. The Danish-Saxon coalition found itself confronted with a new power for which it was no match.

It will not be necessary to enter into the details of Wallenstein's subsequent campaigns. They should be familiar to every reader, and moreover Schiller has given *their leading* features in his drama. Suffice it to say that in four years Germany was overrun and conquered. The Dukes of Mecklenburg were dispossessed, the Danes driven from Sleswick, Holstein, and Jutland, Pomerania occupied, Brandenburg put under contribution, the electorate of Saxony overawed, the minor principalities crushed, Silesia rid of invasion, Bethlen Gabor checked, Tilly and the Catholic League thrust contemptuously into the shade, as an ally of no consideration. From the Alps to the Baltic and the Oder there was but one emperor, and Wallenstein was his lieutenant. The general's designs reached still farther. Not satisfied with the dominion of the land, he wished to make himself master of the sea. In laying siege to Stralsund, he hoped to acquire a port from which to attack the navies of Denmark, and especially of Sweden, then becoming a great power under the genius of Gustavus Adolphus. But Stralsund was saved by the Swedes, and the Baltic remained free.

Ambition of a more personal nature, however, was gratified. Wallenstein, although Prince and Duke of Friedland, and Generalissimo, was still the emperor's subject. But in 1628 he demanded of the emperor the duchies of Mecklenburg. The dukes, Adolphus Frederick and John Albert, had been dispossessed because of their alliance with the King of Denmark against the emperor. Wallenstein's demand was unprecedented. To appreciate its full purport, one must bear in mind the constitution of the then German Empire. The emperor, although the nominal head and superior, was not in strictness the feudal and hereditary lord of the other German princes; he was *only primus inter pares.* The emperorship had never been other than elective; from the American point of view we might almost say that he was a president among governors. The electors, dukes, margraves, counts, and other princes of the realm looked upon themselves as the equals of the emperor in blood and sovereignty. The elevation of Wallenstein to the dukedom, accordingly, was nothing less than making him the peer of the reigning houses of Europe, the "cousin" of Orange, Bavaria, and Toscany. Charles V. had indeed forced John Frederick, in 1547, to abdicate the electorate of Saxony in favor of Maurice, and Ferdinand himself, only a few years before, in 1621, had deprived Frederick of the Palatinate and given it to Maximilian of Bavaria. But both Maurice and Maximilian were princes of the realm by birth, whereas Wallenstein was originally a simple nobleman, a Bohemian adventurer, a *condottiere*, as his enemies were wont to style him. Around this Mecklenburg question, then, centered the opposition to the emperor and his general.

Wallenstein's request was granted. He was invested with the duchies, at first only provisionally, as security for his expenditures in the maintenance of the army, then, in 1629, definitively and in full form (R. W. 108. 141). He had the administration of the land and was entitled to ducal honors; at the conference held in Brandeis, the emperor bade him be covered. Schiller mentions this incident, in the *Lager*, XI. 860.

In July, 1630, the emperor convened the celebrated Electoral Conference of Ratisbon, with a view to obtaining the election of his son (subsequently Ferdinand III.

as King of the Romans and his presumptive successor in the empire. The emperor himself attended the conference. No sooner had the electors met than it became evident that Ferdinand had evoked a storm upon his own head. The Catholic Electors of Menz, Trier, Cologne, and Bavaria (Palatinate), secretly backed by France, refused to listen to an election, and, on the other hand, inveighed in the sharpest terms against the emperor and his policy. Remonstrances poured in from all quarters against the arrogance, the exactions, the brutality of Wallenstein and his army, which then numbered over 100,000. Germany was represented as exhausted to the last degree, law and order at an end. Threats were even heard of forming an alliance with France and electing Louis XIII. King of the Romans. Wallenstein was supported by the Spaniards, who felt the need of a strong imperial force in Germany to serve as a check upon the aggressiveness of France in the direction of the Upper Rhine and Low Countries. But the French agents at Ratisbon, Father Joseph acting as their secret adviser, adroitly arranged a suspension of hostilities in Italy and Savoy, that was to pave the way for a general European peace. The coalition of French and electoral interests was too strong to be resisted by the emperor. The electors demanded peremptorily the dismissal of Wallenstein from the chief command, and the emperor yielded a reluctant consent. Richelieu subsequently disavowed the negotiations of his agents at Ratisbon and refused to ratify the promised treaty. War was resumed with unabated vigor, and *Ferdinand* saw, only when it was too late, that his sacrifices in behalf of peace had been made in vain. Tradition has put into his mouth the saying, with reference to this Electoral Conference at Ratisbon: that a simple Capuchin monk, namely Father Joseph, had disarmed him with a rosary, and carried off in his cowl no less than six electoral hats. The seventh, that of Bohemia, was of course the emperor's. Whether Richelieu acted throughout in bad faith, or was forced to his disavowal by political complications in France, is a question which Ranke leaves undecided.

The official announcement of his dismissal was brought to Wallenstein, at his headquarters in Memmingen, by two of his most steadfast friends and admirers, Werdenberg and Questenberg. The general, who had been informed already through private channels, received them courteously and with seeming composure. He learned from them that it would be useless for him to expect under the circumstances any support from the emperor in his claims upon Mecklenburg, and he failed also to elicit any promise concerning the future organization of the army. Although the emperor manifested sincere goodwill and the deepest personal interest in the general, it was evident that the triumph of the League, which amounted practically to an assertion of state rights, was complete. Wallenstein's dream of re-establishing by force of arms the supremacy of the emperor, as it had once existed in the Middle Ages, was at an end.

The general dismissed his camp-retinue and retired to his residence at Gitschin. Many of his officers threw up *their commissions* and followed him. The command of

the armies of the emperor and of the League was given to
Tilly.   During the Electoral Conference, and even before
the dismissal of Wallenstein was decided upon, Gustavus
Adolphus had landed in Pomerania.   The conjuncture
was ominous; the champion of Protestantism appears in
Germany at the moment when the ablest supporter of
imperial and Catholic interests is forced to retire.   What
that foreboded, the world was soon to learn.

The measures and movements of the Swedish king
belong rather to the general history of the times.   While
Gustavus was laying cautiously but surely the foundations
for his subsequent victories over the League and his
march to the Rhine and into Bavaria, Wallenstein remained at Gitschin, ostensibly absorbed in administering
and improving his estates.   In reality, his interest in war
and politics was unabated.   He corresponded diligently
with his friends and his former officers, and had his
agents and informers throughout Germany.   He even
entered into negotiations with Gustavus Adolphus with a
view to obtaining Swedish support in attacking the emperor in Bohemia and the Austrian duchies. . The negotiations fell through.   But it will be expedient to defer
the discussion of them to another place, where they can
be treated in connection with other events.

During his period of retirement Wallenstein had full
opportunity of displaying his rare talent in developing
the resources of his estates and in beautifying them.
Much had been already done.   Even while occupied in
prosecuting the war against Christian of Denmark and
Mansfeld, his care for his domestic interests never failed.

Many of his letters to his agent, Gerhard v. Taxis, have been preserved, and have been used by Förster in his work, *Wallenstein als regierender Herzog*. They cover the widest range of subjects, from the institution of a chamber of justice and the revision of municipal regulations to the planting of mulberry trees for the cultivation of the silk-worm and cleaning the streets of Gitschin. Amid the din of battle or the distractions of camp-life, the general still has a watchful eye over the schools and monasteries that he has founded, his breweries, powder-mills, iron-works, his mines and fish-ponds, his hops and garden-flowers and horses. It is worthy of note that in 1625, at a time when Catholic and Protestant, hating each other, were agreed in persecuting the race from which they both derived their religion; Wallenstein writes to Taxis, from Eger: *Dass der Jud zu Gitschin traficiren will, höre ich gern, lasst's ihm nur zu.* Indeed, from beginning to end of his eventful career Wallenstein showed himself to be one who had made tolerance a rule of life a century and a half before the days of Lessing and Mirabeau. His own conversion, if his change from Protestantism to Catholicism may be called such, was purely political in its character and object; the young Bohemian cavalier, like Henry of Navarre, perceived that it was necessary to his success.

In one other particular the general was far ahead of his times. He created an active market for the products of his estates. By purchasing, as general, a large part of the supplies for his army from his own subjects, he kept money at home and made the war, which was ravaging the rest of Germany, a source of profit to those immediately dependent upon him. The cannon-balls fired at Christian of Denmark, the siege-artillery and powder used at Stralsund, weapons, clothing, and even bread for the army came from the duchy of Friedland. Wallenstein himself does not seem to have profited directly by this practice, of which indeed he made no secret; but the supplies had to be obtained somewhere, and he preferred his subjects to strangers.

The enlargement and improvement of the castle at Gitschin was begun in 1627; the fourth story was planned by Pironi in 1629. In 1630, just before the Ratisbon Conference, Wallenstein, in his letters, urges superintendents and workmen to increased dispatch, and suggests changes here and there. From Memmingen he writes to Taxis, June 27, 1630, giving instructions about the erection of two oratories, one for himself and one for his wife, and about the altars in the town-churches. In a postscript he remembers that the plan adopted for the garden made no provision for a fountain in front of the colonnade; he therefore orders one, *eine grossmächtige fontana*. The garden and deer-park at Gitschin were laid out on a generous scale and in the Italian style of the day. The garden was 1,200 feet square, and filled with rare plants and trees. It contained eight artificial water-courses, six fountains, a pond for swans, and a pheasantry. The stables were filled with horses of the choicest breeds, imported from Italy, Turkey, and Mecklenburg. From the garden and park a straight drive, thirty paces broad and three thousand long, lined on each

side by a double row of lindens, led to the Carthusian
monastery at Walditz. This monastery is mentioned by
Schiller in the last scene of the *Tod*. In the year 1813
Gitschin resumed for a brief period its quondam importance. The emperor Francis resided here for five weeks,
during which period the alliance between Russia, Austria,
and Prussia was consummated. The hall in which the
treaty was signed by Nesselrode, Metternich, and Wilhelm v. Humboldt, is to be kept forever, by the terms of
a perpetual trust then created, in the condition in which
it then was. On the 29th of June, 1866, the town of
Gitschin was the scene of the most desperate, and, next
to Sadowa, the most decisive battle of the Austro-Prus-
sian campaign. The fighting lasted until one o'clock at
night, and was for hours a murderous hand-to-hand encounter in the streets. The capture of the town by the
Prussians opened communication between the army of
the Elbe and the army of Silesia, and suggested the combined attack at Sadowa. The churches and monastery,
filled with prisoners and wounded, were visited by King
William on July 2d. On the walls of the churches still
hung the flags captured by Wallenstein in the Thirty
Years' War. The history of Gitschin prior to its acquisition by Wallenstein is a striking passage in the "dark
and bloody" records of Bohemian anarchy (see Fontane,
Der Feldzug in Böhmen u. Mähren, 2te Auflage. Page
206, note).

In connection with Gitschin must be mentioned the
ducal palace in Prague. The frescoes in the grand saloon,
which represented Wallenstein in triumphal procession,

have been painted over, but in other respects the palace is substantially as it was in 1634. For a city residence, the size of the buildings and garden is unusual; everything betokens the large-mindedness and taste of the designer. The most curious room is the bath-room. It is on the ground-floor, opening on the colonnade that encircles the front of the garden. It is a large chamber, resembling a grotto; the ceiling is groined, and both it and the walls are inlaid with shells, stalactites, and crystals. The floor is of stone. The dimensions and the fantastic ornamentation remind the visitor of the semi-oriental public baths at Pesth. According to Garve, Butler's chaplain, the stables contained a hundred blooded horses, and the stalls and mangers were of polished marble.

In his appearance Wallenstein was striking, but not strictly imposing. He was tall and spare, but vigorous, until crippled by the gout. His forehead was high, marked with thought but not with care. His complexion was sallow, his eyes small and piercing. In his later years he was a constant victim to the gout. In temper he was what might be called moody, one day irritable and hard to please, the next amiable and even familiar. He was a sworn enemy to noise and confusion, and enforced absolute quiet in his own quarters; sentries posted in every direction kept off intruding disturbers. In his manners he was accomplished according to the standard of those days; in his youth he had been a favorite with the fair sex. His diet, unless accommodated to the exigencies of a public banquet, was extremely simple; he looked with *disfavor* upon excess in eating and drinking, but

tolerated the uproarious revels of his officers, so long as
they did not interfere with discipline. The essentials of
officer or soldier, in his estimation, were two: bravery,
and obedience. Want of either was punished summarily
and without mercy. After the battle of Lützen Wallenstein held a court-martial at Prague, to inquire into the
conduct of certain officers in the battle. Two lieutenant-
colonels, one captain of infantry, one captain of cavalry,
four lieutenants, one ensign, and two captains of artillery
were beheaded. Seven soldiers were hung, one lieutenant
was declared dishonored and his sword broken under the
gallows, another lieutenant was hung on the gallows side
by side with a cavalryman. The names of forty officers,
who had made their escape, were affixed to the gallows.
Other officers, who had distinguished themselves by their
bravery, were rewarded with princely munificence. The
value of the prizes distributed among the officers and
regiments amounted to 85,000 florins (F. W. B. II. 310).

It is to be regretted that we do not possess a straightforward, perfectly trustworthy description of Wallenstein's character, temper, and mode of life. Gualdo Priorato, who was a contemporary, has written, it is true, a
biographical sketch which has been followed and expanded
by Herchenhahn and others. But Priorato is infected
with the rhetorical mannerism of the century. The substance of his description is so loaded down with flights
would-be eloquence and jejune moralizing, that the read
is tempted to give up every attempt to discriminate
tween the real and the exaggerated, and to reject
whole. We can say of the man Wallenstein little u

than that he was an indefatigable planner and worker,
imperious of will, shrewd and far-sighted, but at the same
time visionary. He was not a genius, like Gustavus
Adolphus or Richelieu. As a strategist, he was unsur-
passed; as a tactician, he was surpassed only by Gustavus.
It has been said, to his disparagement, that he never won
a great battle for himself. This is true, yet it is not less
true that his lieutenants, Schlick, Holck, and the others,
merely executed the plans which he had formed for them.
He committed only one serious blunder, namely in divid-
ing his army in the presence of Gustavus and sending
Pappenheim to Halle. But for Pappenheim's prompt
return, the blunder would have resulted far more disas-
trously at Lützen than it did.

In estimating Wallenstein's personality, we must discriminate between the period before his deposition in
1630 and the period after. It can not be denied that, in
consequence of the dismissal, his disposition underwent a
change for the worse. His good qualities, his consideration for the interests of his manorial subjects, his devotion
to the Austrian dynasty, his large-mindedness, receded to
the background, and irritability, arrogance, ungovernable
spleen, taciturnity, and supreme disregard for views and
judgment other than his own, became so prominent that
his society was scarcely to be endured, even by his best
friends and admirers. The explosions of his temper, to
which his retinue gave the name of *boutades*, were little
more than passing tirades, evincing no set purpose.
But reported at court and exaggerated and distorted by
evil-wishing tongues, they had not infrequently a Catili-

nian ring.   Mention will be made, in a subsequent place, of one of these *boutades*.   See page xxxvii.

Schiller, in his drama, has given to Wallenstein's mind an almost philosophical cast.   This may have been necessary for dramatic effect, as in the case of the celebrated soliloquy in the *Tod*, I. 4.   But the real Wallenstein, schemer though he was, was not given to speculative imaginings.   His mind was rather of the hard, shrewd, positive order; he was no dreamer, but a grasping man of action.   On the other hand, he was undoubtedly bizarre in many of his ways.   The men of the seventeenth century, as a class, exhibit strange freaks of character, engendered probably by the tension of religious controversy and developed by protracted warfare.   Ferdinand II. himself was an odd mixture of bigotry and *bonhomie*.   Wallenstein's predilection for astrology, for instance, has been underdrawn rather than overdrawn by Schiller.   What may appear in the drama a mere caprice, an oddity, a childish pastime, was with Wallenstein himself a sober reality.   Wallenstein really believed in horoscopes and the influences of the planets upon human life.   On receiving Questenberg and Werdenberg at Memmingen, he had before him a paper in Latin, on which were figured the nativities of the emperor and of the duke of Bavaria.   "As you see," he said to the ambassadors, "the stars indicate that the spirit of the duke will predominate over that of the emperor" (R. W. 200).   No less a man than the great Kepler himself, the first to reduce our knowledge of the planetary system to mathematical precision, was still entangled in the superstition *of astrology*.   Kepler cast Wallenstein's horoscope in the year 1609; a copy is extant, with Wallenstein's annotations, and has been published by Helbig. This remarkable document is not only a characterization of the then young man, but in many respects a prognostication (R. W. 2). If Kepler, the most enlightened intellect of his generation, could be a sincere believer in astrology, it need not surprise us that Wallenstein should lend a ready ear to whatever flattered his dreams of greatness. The general was usually accompanied by his court-astrologer, Jean Baptista Seni, or Zenno, a Genoese by birth. Seni was many years in his service, and was in Eger at the time of the assassination.

The circumstances and conditions under which Wallenstein was reinstated generalissimo of the imperial armies differ materially from the account given by Schiller in his drama. In eighteen months Gustavus Adolphus had undone all the work of Wallenstein and Tilly. He had established an almost impregnable base of operations in Pomerania, had cleared Saxony, Brandenburg, Mecklenburg of Catholic invaders, had annihilated Tilly's army at Breitenfeld. Pressing on with feverish haste, he had left to the Elector of Saxony the task of overrunning Bohemia and Silesia, while he himself laid a new base of operations on the Main and Rhine, in Franconia, and among the rich Protestant free cities of South Germany. In a few months more he was to defeat Tilly, at the river Lech, to rout the Bavarian army, chase Maximilian from his duchy, and, on May 17th, 1632, to enter Munich in triumph. The emperor's fortunes seemed hopeless. There was but one man to whom he could turn for help, but one man who could create an Austrian army and lead it against the

Swedish veterans. But would Wallenstein consent to serve an emperor who had abandoned him? The negotiations were protracted and complicated. First, Questenberg was sent to Prague, in November, 1631, soon after the battle of Breitenfeld. But he failed to bring about a satisfactory understanding (F. W. B. II. 185). In December Eggenberg, the emperor's prime minister, betook himself to Znaim, half-way between Prague and Vienna, whither Wallenstein had come to meet him. This conference was decisive. Wallenstein consented to reorganize an Austrian army and to assume command, but only for three months. His ill health, he alleged, would not permit him to remain permanently in active service. We have no official record of the precise terms offered and accepted. Eggenberg's instructions from the emperor were oral. The point upon which everything turned was the Edict of Restitution. In 1629, when Wallenstein's fame and power were at their height in North Germany, the emperor had passed an edict restoring all Catholic Church property which had been converted to Protestant uses since the Passau Convention, in 1552. This arbitrary measure, if strictly enforced, would have worked a revolution in North Germany, and it was justly regarded as the first step toward the forcible conversion of all Protestants. Wallenstein himself had always been averse to the edict, pronouncing it to be a fatal political blunder. It could serve only to embitter the already disaffected and drive them to desperation. Much of Gustavus's success was due to the popular belief in northern and central Germany that in him was the only hope of rescue from the operations of the edict. Wallenstein was well aware of this, and perceived, with a clearness which does him great credit, that an army alone would not suffice him against the Swedes. He must appear with the sword in one hand, and acceptable terms of peace in the other. He must be able to assure his German antagonists that his mission was not to put down Protestantism. In other words, the Edict of Restitution must be abrogated. We have good reason for believing that Wallenstein obtained this concession from the emperor through Eggenberg. For although there is no official record of the conference at Znaim, there is a record of a meeting held soon afterward, in January, 1632, at Aussig, between Trzka, Wallenstein's confidential agent, and Arnim, the commander of the Saxon troops. On this occasion Trzka assured Arnim explicitly that the emperor had consented to abrogate the edict (R. W. 233).

Throughout the winter of 1631–2 the recruiting went on with marvelous results. Wallenstein's prestige attracted, like a magnet, the adventurers of all Germany, in fact, of all Europe. Veteran officers and raw recruits, whoever was in need of money or ambitious of glory, flocked to the recruiting stations in Bohemia. The great general made good his word. In the spring of 1632 an Austrian army was in the field, ready to confront both Swedes and Saxons. Just at this point Wallenstein tendered his resignation. The term of three months had expired; his mission, he said, was accomplished. Whether he acted in sincerity, or took advantage of the situation to obtain *still more* favorable terms, must remain an open question. It was evident that no other man could command the army that he collected. Messenger after messenger was sent to him, urging him to reconsider his resignation. Herchenhahn (II. 127) states that Max v. Wallenstein, the general's favorite cousin, Werdenberg, Questenberg, the abbot of Kremsmünster, and Quiroga were sent. Förster (F. W. B. II. 198–201) mentions Quiroga, Bruneau, and the archbishop of Vienna. The king of Hungary wrote with his own hands a letter, still extant, dated March 25th, in which he assured the general of his earnest desire in the matter. Finally, April 13th, Wallenstein and Eggenberg held a second conference, half-way between Znaim and Vienna. The terms, like those of the first conference, cannot be stated explicitly. Ranke rejects the so-called ' Capitulation,' or formal agreement, which has been cited as authentic by Förster and others, but concedes that the emperor conferred upon the generalissimo the right of confiscation, pardon, amnesty, the supreme military authority, and the right to negotiate peace. Wallenstein was released from the payment of 400,000 thalers, which he still owed as purchase-money on some of his Bohemian estates, and obtained the principality of Glogau in Silesia, as security for the recovery of Mecklenburg or its full equivalent. He was no created, however, generalissimo for life, as some histor ans have asserted. He had already acquired, at the fir conference in December, the right of granting commissio up to and including the rank of colonel. Officers of higher grade were to be confirmed by the emperor (R. V *238, 469).*

Thus furnished with full military and political powers, Wallenstein entered upon the campaign in earnest. The composition and spirit of his army have been so accurately characterized by Schiller, *Picc.* 219—233, that further description would be superfluous. By the end of May the Saxons under Arnim had been driven out of Bohemia, and Wallenstein threw himself with nearly his entire force upon the important city of Nuremberg. Gustavus hastened in person to its relief, also calling in his detached corps under Baner, Oxenstjerna, Bernhard of Weimar, and the Landgrave of Hesse. The number of troops on each side exceeded 60,000. Both armies lay confronting each other, strongly entrenched, for about two months. The losses were heavy, occasioned more by disease and scarcity of provisions than by death in battle. On St. Bartholemew's day,* Sept. 3d, Gustavus made a desperate effort to break through Wallenstein's lines at the Old Fort and the Altenberg. The attempt failed, and the king withdrew his forces to Furth, leaving a strong garrison in Nuremberg. The two great captains of the age had measured each other's strength. Wallenstein found that the Swedes were fully his match, Gustavus encountered for the first time a resistance worthy of his attack. The Swedes made a diversion into Bavaria, Wallenstein boldly marched into electoral Saxony. Gustavus was forced to follow him, fearing lest the Elector might be prevailed upon by threats and tempting offers to break the alliance with Sweden. The shock of

* The Saint's-day is according to old style.

the two armies came at Lützen. Who has not heard of this memorable battle ? It was one of the hardest fought on record, and settled the fate of North Germany. Saxony, and even the territories lying farther north, it is true, were ravaged subsequently by predatory parties, but the ground was not occupied and held in force by the imperial armies. Wallenstein was badly beaten, for, although both sides kept their lines, the temper of the surrounding peasantry was such that he was forced to decamp without his artillery. Bernhard of Weimar had avenged the wrongs of his ancestor, John Frederick.

All that winter Wallenstein's army lay in a crippled condition in Bohemia. The field of Lützen had put an end to Gustavus's career ; it gave to that of Wallenstein a new direction. The imperial general had for the first time a realizing sense of the tenacity of the opposition to Catholic Austria. It became evident to him that Protestant Germany could not be overrun and trampled under foot as it had once been. The most illustrious champion had fallen, but others, of almost equal ability, had taken his place, while the spirit of Gustavus survived. Under his brief but energetic teaching, the Protestants had learned their strength.

Accordingly we find Wallenstein after the battle of Lützen bending his energies chiefly to the restoration of peace. On one occasion alone did he have recourse to battle, at Steinau, in Silesia, where a detachment of the Swedish army, under Thurn, was cut off and captured. Even this move was probably caused by the exigencies of *his situation ;* it became necessary to do something to show his enemies in Vienna that his policy did not arise from cowardice or indifference.

The narrow limits of the present sketch forbid any attempt to enter into the details of Wallenstein's negotiations with the Swedes and the Saxons. Many of those negotiations, indeed, are veiled in obscurity. As in the case of the conditions under which Wallenstein resumed command, we are unable to ascertain with perfect precision what was offered on one side or demanded on the other. To understand the position of such men as Wallenstein, Arnim, the Swedish Chancellor Oxenstjerna, to one another, it is necessary to bear carefully in mind the general drift of European politics. In France, Richelieu was at the head of affairs, crushing sedition at home and fomenting it abroad. Spain and Holland were still involved in hostilities that bade fair to be interminable, and Richelieu was doing all in his power to weaken Spain. On the other hand, Austria was bound to Spain, not only by dynastic ties but by a certain community of religious interests. Behind the Swedes stood Richelieu; the Saxons, although for the time being in alliance with them, claimed the right to act independently. The smaller Protestant powers of Germany gravitated more or less strongly to the Swedes. In the midst of these complications Wallenstein was to represent the interests of the house of Austria. He perceived that all the elements must be taken into account in arranging a peace that should be general and really stable. Some plan must be devised of satisfying the Swedish demands; the Saxons and North Germans must be pacified by the abrogation of the Edict of Restitution; lastly, all measures that ignored the policy of France would be only short-lived. Wallenstein felt assured that Richelieu, although not opposed on principle to the restoration of peace in Germany, would never acquiesce tamely in any arrangement that might leave Austria free to join forces with Spain against the French. He even expressed his willingness to waive a portion of his own personal claims in favor of the public weal (R. W. 275). That he was perfectly sincere in this may be doubted, for we subsequently find him proposing, as compensation for Mecklenburg, his acquisition of the Palatinate, and with it the electoral dignity, after the death of Maximilian of Bavaria (R. W. 297).

Would Wallenstein succeed in making peace upon the basis of religious tolerance? Or rather, would the emperor keep his word, despite the clerical influence at court? How great that influence was, when wielded by such men as Lamormain and Quiroga, can be duly estimated only by one who has made special studies in the history of the Thirty Years' War. Restoration of Catholicism, extirpation of heresy, or at all events reduction of it to the narrowest limits, had been for years the watchword of the clerical party. In their eyes the war was a holy war, the justified means to a righteous end. To abandon the edict of restitution was more than waiving a claim, it was deserting a principle. The opposition to Wallenstein's plans, at first suppressed, became louder and bolder, although no one dared to approach the *emperor directly*. Wallenstein was aware of the intrigues of the clerical party, but he relied upon the assurances already obtained from the emperor, and also upon the perhaps exaggerated sense of his own indispensableness. What he purposed doing and how he expressed himself, may be gathered from the report of the conference with the Saxons, in June, 1633. The general submitted four points as the bases of treaty : 1. That the peace should embrace the entire German realm. 2. That all religions should remain undisturbed. 3. That all who had been dispossessed under the Edict of Restoration should be reinstated. 4. That the Swedes should be recompensed with territorial acquisition. To a remark made by Colonel Burgsdorff, that the Catholics did not consider themselves bound to keep faith with Protestants, Wallenstein replied in a string of assurances and denunciations. To give an idea of his manner, it will be necessary to repeat his words :

Ich wollte, das der Teuffel die Huntsfütter lengest geholet hette. Ich will die Huntsfütter (*i.e.*, the Jesuits) alle aus dem Reich zum teuffel iagen. Item er (here the narrative changes to the third person) bezeuge es mit Gott, so war er wünschen thet, ein kint Gottes zu sein, ia das Gott kein theil an seiner Seele haben sollte, wann er anders in seinen Hertzen meine, als die wort lautteten. Und will der Keyser nicht friede machen, und die Zusage haltten (*i.e.*, fail to ratify W.'s propositions), so will ich ihn darzu zwingen. Der Bayerfürst, der Bayerfürst hat das spiel angefangen. Ich will ihm keine Assistenz leisten. Wollte das die Herren (*i.e.*, the Saxons) *allbereit sein ganzes* lant ruiniret hetten, das weder Henne noch Han noch einiger menſch mehr drinnen zu finden ſey. Unb wollte, baß er (the duke of Bavaria) lengſt tobt wehre. Würt er nicht friede machen wollen, ſo will ich ihn ſelbſt helffen bekriegen, ben ich will einen ehrlichen, aufrichtigen, beſtenbigen frieden im Reich ſtifften, unb nachmals mit beyberley Armeen gegen bem Turden gehen, unb ben Huntsfutt alles nehmen, was er von Europa entzogen. Das anbere mag er behalten. (R. W. 478).

The idea of rallying all the forces of Germany to a combined assault upon the Sultan in his own land had been a favorite one with Wallenstein since 1627. The report from which the above passage is quoted is contained in the archives of Magdeburg. As Ranke has observed, it distinguishes carefully between Wallenstein's propositions, which are definite and sensible, and his mere "expectorations."

The clerical party alone would not have sufficed to thwart the realization of Wallenstein's plan for peace. But they were assisted by the general European policy of Spain. In 1630, at Ratisbon, the Spaniards had sought to retain Wallenstein in command; his dismissal was in direct opposition to their wishes. But now the position was reversed, they were to be the agents of his second downfall. Castañeda, the Spanish ambassador at Vienna, seems to have reached the conclusion, in the summer of 1633, that the spirit of Wallenstein's negotiations was unfavorable to the alliance existing between Spain and Austria. The *general* wished to establish peace, doubtless, but was *unwilling to aid* the Spaniards in their military operations along the Rhine. Castañeda's hopes were revived in a measure by Wallenstein's victory at Steinau, only to be dissipated by the loss of Ratisbon. Bernhard of Weimar, after making a feint in the direction of Saxony, turned abruptly aside from Franconia and appeared before Ratisbon. Taken by surprise, and unprepared for a siege, the Bavarian garrison surrendered on Nov. 5th, 1633. The whole movement was one of the most daring and successful enterprises in the annals of the war. Ratisbon was the key to Bavaria and the region of the upper Danube. The emperor felt himself threatened even in his own duchies. Wallenstein, who had relied upon his victory at Steinau to hold the Swedes in check and induce them to compromise upon the most reasonable terms, was no less disconcerted. Yielding to the clamor of the court, he made an attempt, at the head of a small detachment, to capture Cham, an important town commanding the passes through the Bohemian Forest between Ratisbon and Pilsen. But Bernhard anticipated him, by throwing into Cham a strong garrison. Wallenstein's troops were scattered over Silesia and northern Bohemia, and the detachment under his immediate command was unprovided with siege-artillery. He was obliged, therefore, to fall back upon Pilsen. As may be imagined, the dissatisfaction and distrust at Vienna were greater than ever. The retrograde movement upon Pilsen was regarded as an evidence of his personal dislike to the Duke of Bavaria and his unwillingness to come to the latter's assistance.

Castañeda, Richel (the Bavarian ambassador in Vienna),

and Schlick (President of the Council of War), had come
to an understanding among themselves with reference to
Wallenstein's conduct and the danger which it boded to
the imperial and Catholic interests. Oñate, who was sent
as special envoy to Vienna by the Cardinal-Infant in
Milan, arrived a few days before the capture of Ratisbon.
Coming fresh upon the scene, he was terrified, as he expressed it, to perceive how dependent the emperor was
upon his general, and how little heed the latter paid to
suggestions and remonstrances. Oñate had been instructed to urge upon Wallenstein the desirability of
strengthening the Spanish position in Alsace and the
Breisgau. His request was denied, on the ground that
no troops could be spared from Bohemia. Oñate soon
convinced himself that from Wallenstein the Spaniards
could expect nothing. He even went to the length of
intimating to Eggenberg, in December, 1633, that unless
some change for the better could be effected, the king of
Spain might be obliged to break off his friendly relations
with the emperor (R. W. 368).

It is not to be supposed that Wallenstein was acquainted with all the designs and intrigues of his opponents
in Vienna. But he knew at least enough to be aware
that he was drifting rapidly into a dilemma: either he
must resign, for it was not in the nature of a man like
Wallenstein to co-operate in plans that differed from his
own, or he must carry his point by force, if need be.
That he adopted the latter course is evident from th
official records of his negotiations with the Saxons. Rank
has devoted many pages to the discussion of this

mooted question. It is impossible to repeat his arguments in full in this place. Suffice it to say in a general way that the Saxon general Arnim, the Elector of Saxony, and also the Elector of Brandenburg took part, and that the negotiations assumed a form which menaced directly the sovereign rights of the emperor. Thus Arnim asks the Elector of Saxony for precise instructions on the following points: how he, Arnim, should act in case Wallenstein should manifest the intention of ruining the political integrity of the house of Austria (*ein auf den Verderb des Hauses Oesterreich zielendes Vorhaben verrathe*); how he should act in case Friedland should exceed the powers entrusted to him by the emperor, and make terms with the Protestants, pledging himself to protect them against all attacks; how he should act, in case Wallenstein, fearing that he could not obtain the desired support from the Saxons, might make overtures to France and the Swedes, &c., &c. These records in the Saxon archives are not, it is true, Wallenstein's own documents. But they reveal unmistakably the animus of the negotiations. They prove that Arnim, who was the personal friend of Wallenstein, and who acted throughout with the most deliberate circumspection, submitted to his electoral master terms of agreement which took into account Wallenstein's defection from the emperor, as something to be provided for (R. W. 393–397, 510–523).

These negotiations were carried on during the latter part of January and the early part of February, 1634. They were, therefore, several weeks subsequent to the *notorious officers'-*banquet at Pilsen, and were stimulated.

by the declaration, *Revers*, which that banquet had brought about. Wallenstein persuaded both himself and Arnim that the army was more than ever under his control and would follow him to any length.

The Infanta Donna Isabella, regent of the Netherlands, died at the end of November, 1633. It became highly important that her brother, Don Fernando, Cardinal Infant in Milan, should assume the government of the Netherlands without delay. Inasmuch as the nearest route led through south-western Germany and the Rhine-valley, regions exposed to the attacks of the French, the Cardinal could not venture upon the journey unless protected by a strong force. To this end Oñate was instructed to request assistance from Wallenstein. The general was to detach a force of 6,000 cavalry and send them to Alsace, or to let them serve as the Cardinal's escort through Bohemia and Franconia to Cologne. Father Quiroga, the confessor of the King of Hungary, was sent on this mission to Wallenstein at Pilsen. He arrived on the 5th of January. At the interview held in the evening of the same day, Wallenstein rejected the request, asserting that it was impossible to spare any of his troops. The reason was doubtless a valid one, but Quiroga looked upon the refusal as only a fresh proof of the general's dislike to the Spaniards. Wallenstein even intimated to Quiroga a purpose on his part to resign. The report that he contemplated such a step created an excitement in the camp. The officers, mistrustful of court intrigues and feeling the need of rest after a hard winter's campaign, *looked* upon Quiroga's mission as a covert attempt to force the general to resign. His resignation, they feared, would be their own ruin. The armies of those days were a strange mixture of the volunteer and the contract systems. The captain enlisted his men at his own expense and risk, the colonel organized his regiment in like manner, while over all and responsible for all was the general-in-chief. The officers, accordingly, to borrow the words of Ranke, constituted a corporation of state-creditors. Whether or not they should be reimbursed for their outlay, depended upon the success of the campaign, which depended in turn upon the abilities of the commander. Wallenstein's army was a conglomerate of all creeds and nationalities; its only bond of union was discipline and community of interests. It was in no sense an Austrian national army. Most of the officers had engaged in the enterprise trusting to Wallenstein, and to him alone. His resignation, then, in the face of the victorious Bernhard, foreboded to them financial ruin.

The first meeting of officers was held on the 12th of January. Quiroga's proposition was submitted to them and denounced with unanimity. A committee was appointed to wait upon the general and request him not to resign. Wallenstein, after no little hesitancy,—whether real or feigned would be difficult to decide,—yielded to their request, and promised not to resign without first consulting them, but on condition that the officers, on their part, should pledge themselves to adhere to him. A declaration (*Revers*) was drawn up, in which the officers solemnly covenanted to stand by him under all circumstances, *even to shedding* their last drop of blood. The

Revers was signed first by Henry Julius of Lauenburg, as the officer of highest dignity. At a banquet given by Ilow (not Trzka), the list of signatures was completed.

Schiller has followed popular report in his description of this remarkable banquet. According to that report, the *Revers* contained originally a clause "saving and excepting the allegiance due to the emperor," but Ilow and Trzka prepared a false copy, from which this salvatory clause was omitted, and passed it around for subscription in the excitement and confusion of the banquet. Ranke has shown clearly how the report originated (R. W. 378, 494). In the *Chaos Perduellionis* (see p. lxi.), which is followed by the *Gründlicher Bericht* (see p. lx.), occurs the passage: "But this is to be observed, that the first declaration which had been signed contained the clause: So long as Friedland should remain in the emperor's allegiance. But to them (*i.e.*, the officers) already well in their cups,—for they were conducted almost immediately after the signing to a banquet prepared for the purpose,—other copies were presented for subscription, because there was need of more than one copy. Some officers having noticed the omission of the clause, the talkative Ilow gave as excuse, that it was of no moment, for sufficient mention had been made of his Majesty in the heading (of the declaration)."—Oñate has a slightly different version, and one that probably gives the most exact account, to wit, that the clause stood in the original draught, but was struck out at Wallenstein's request, before the declaration was submitted for subscription. This is confirmed by a subsequent passage in the Gründli

Bericht itself, where mention is made of the second *Revers*, in February. The passage runs: *Weil er* (*i.e.*, Wallenstein) *eben dieselbe clausulam. . . in der vorigen Obligation und Verbündniss* (*habe*) *gar nicht leiden wollen* (M. B. 267). Ranke seems to have overlooked this passage. It is not the only instance of self-contradiction in the *Gründlicher Bericht.*

Whatever view may be taken of this banquet, it is evident that the officers were not tricked into signing in a fit of drunken insubordination. Even according to the *Chaos Perduellionis*, the signing was done before the banquet. Furthermore, we know that Wallenstein, having learned that objections had been raised and scruples expressed on the part of some of the officers, held another conference with them, at which he explained fully his views and position, assuring them that he contemplated nothing adverse to the emperor or the Catholic religion, and guaranteeing the payment of their claims. On the strength of this assurance, the officers corroborated the *Revers* already signed; several copies were prepared, to be signed by those not present in Pilsen (R. W. 380).

Believing that he had thus secured the devotion of the army, Wallenstein urged the negotiations—already described—with Saxony. But side by side with them other negotiations, of a more obscure character, were pending with France and the Swedes. To understand the point in all its bearings, it will be necessary to go back as far as 1631. Not long before the battle of Breitenfeld, overtures were made to Gustavus by Wallenstein. The latter *professed his* willingness to join the party of the Swedish king, and requested to be placed at the head of, ten or twelve thousand troops, wherewith to attack the emperor in Bohemia. This report, which was for a long while doubted or rejected, is now generally accepted. It rests upon the authority of a man who was initiated into all the ramifications of the plot. His name, slightly changed, has been introduced by Schiller in the *Piccolomini*, 2565. Jaroslav Sesyma Raschim of Riesenburg, a Bohemian refugee, acted as messenger between Gustavus and Wallenstein. He saw them repeatedly. In 1635, after Wallenstein's death, he was amnestied and permitted to return to Austria upon condition of preparing a full statement of his negotiations. This he did in Bohemian; a German translation was then made and submitted to the emperor. Khevenhiller used the manuscript, but not with the most scrupulous fidelity. Herchenhahn's biography of Wallenstein, which Schiller used, is also based upon Sesyma's manuscript. Murr published an inaccurate Latin version. The first trustworthy edition was published in 1867, by Dvorsy, from the manuscript originally presented to the emperor. Sesyma's story, although prepared under circumstances that tend to throw discredit upon it, is borne out by other contemporaneous evidence which leaves no room for doubt. See Ranke, 223, 480; also, Droysen, Gustavus Adolphus, II. 411.

We are warranted, therefore, in believing that Wallenstein, while still smarting under what he regarded as the disgrace of his deposition, seriously entertained the project of co-operating with the Swedes in 1631. Upon the *further point*, why the project remained a mere project and was not carried out, we are not so well informed. It is most probable that the two generals could not agree upon the terms, that Wallenstein wished too much independence, that Gustavus did not trust him thoroughly. As Wallenstein subsequently expressed himself, according to Sesyma, with reference to the death of Gustavus: *Es könnten doch zwei Hannen auf einem Müst sich nit vertrugen* (R. W. 283).

After Wallenstein had resumed command of the imperial army, we hear nothing more of intrigues with the Swedes until the summer of 1633. Kinsky, the 'head-centre' of the Bohemian refugees in Dresden, and Feuquières, Richelieu's diplomatic agent, revived the plan of making Bohemia independent (R. W. 305). They drew up jointly a paper in which Wallenstein was urged to enter into an alliance with France and place the crown of Bohemia upon his own head. Wallenstein, absorbed in the Silesian war and negotiations with Saxony, let the time from August to December pass without making a reply; Feuquières regarded the project as having fallen to the ground. It was renewed, however, at the beginning of 1634. On the 10th of January Kinsky approached Feuquières once again with the assurance that the former proposition would now be accepted by Wallenstein. Feuquières, then in Frankfort-on-the-Main, deferred his decision until he might have time to confer with Richelieu. The French court approved, but not with the same readiness as before. Feuquières was instructed to induce Wallenstein to assume the appearance of invoking the *aid of the King of* France in forcing the Spanish to rea-

sonable terms of peace. He was to offer the crown of
Bohemia, if Wallenstein could not be won over on any
other terms (R. W. 398).

It is impossible to ascertain exactly how far Kinsky was
authorized by Wallenstein to negotiate in this manner.
Sesyma, in the third section of his story, speaks of what
he heard from Kinsky and Trzka, but this time he did
not see Wallenstein himself. In the absence of unmis-
takable evidence, we may doubt that Wallenstein ever
entertained seriously the design of assuming the crown or
Bohemia. We know that Thurn's relations with Wallenstein were almost broken off, because the latter would
not commit himself on this point. The designs and
wishes of the Bohemian refugees are not to be confounded
with those of Wallenstein. What the latter really were,
is a matter concerning which we are insufficiently informed. There are certain considerations which render it
difficult to believe that the general could consent to the
scheme elaborated by Kinsky and Feuquières. In the
first place, years before, when the emperor's fortunes
were at their lowest ebb, Wallenstein deliberately shared
them, although in so doing he exposed himself to the
attacks of the Bohemian and Moravian insurgents. He
identified his interests with those of the house of Habsburg. Furthermore, the restoration of the freedom of
election of the Bohemian crown (*Wahlfreiheit*), even
though his own instrumentality, might well appear to
him a step of doubtful expediency. What guarantee
could he have that the Bohemian Estates, once placed
in their former power, might not turn against him and

exact from him the restoration of the confiscated property that he had purchased ten years before? Friedland, Sagan, and Glogau he held solely by virtue of the emperor's authority. And even should he succeed in gaining the crown of Bohemia, of what lasting benefit would it be to him? He had no heir to whom he might bequeath it. He had but one child, a girl of ten years, ineligible to election on account of her youth and disqualified by her sex. He himself was rapidly declining in health. His physicians had predicted that he could not live two years longer, and even at that time he had to be carried from place to place in a litter. We shall probably not err far from the truth if we regard Wallenstein's action concerning the Bohemian crown as a means of bringing a heavier pressure to bear upon the Saxons. He sought to force Saxony and Brandenburg to accept his offer of alliance. That object accomplished, he could, in conjunction with them, compel the Swedes to accept reasonable terms of peace. It would be characteristic of a born intriguer, as Wallenstein undoubtedly was, to pursue such a tortuous policy. The scheme of Feuquières and Kinsky scarcely appeared to him more than a last resort, something to fall back upon if everything else should fail. It certainly never assumed the form of a binding agreement, entered into definitively by both parties.

While Wallenstein was cherishing the delusion that he could rely upon his army, the first step to his overthrow had already been taken. Before the first officers'-conference at Pilsen, he had sent Piccolomini, in whom he *placed the greatest* confidence, to Gallas, his lieutenant-

general, and to Colloredo, then in command of Silesia,
to win them over. The three generals met at Frankfort-
on-the-Oder. They agreed to follow Wallenstein, but
not to the prejudice of their allegiance to the emperor,
and not without some expression, at least on the part of
Colloredo, of mistrust in Wallenstein's ultimate designs.
The emperor and his prime minister, Eggenberg, still
had confidence in Wallenstein's loyalty. They treated
the *Revers* and the other proceedings as a move which
he made in self-defence against the intrigues of his
enemies at court. Oñate, as he has admitted, felt himself to be in the most trying situation. Firmly convinced
of Wallenstein's disloyalty to Austrian and Spanish interests, he could do nothing to shake the emperor's confidence. But before the end of January he received
news which enabled him to act with success. The precise
nature of this news we do not know. In his official
reports to the Cardinal Infant, Oñate lays the principal
stress upon Wallenstein's negotiations with France
Other information came from Bavaria, Bohemia, and
even Savoy. Bearing with him documents of the most
unimpeachable character, he demanded an audience of
the emperor. His statements found at last credence
Even Eggenberg, who had never believed it possible t
the general, with all his bizarrerie, could set himself
opposition to the emperor, declared: on that occasion h
er (Eggenberg) *es mit Händen gegriffen.* Ever since
middle of January the relations with Wallenstein
been entrusted to a special committee of the Pr
Council, composed of Eggenberg, Count Trautmannsd

and the Bishop of Vienna. Oñate was now requested to take part in their conferences. These were numerous and protracted. The emperor, still reluctant, took the matter to heart. He even ordered prayers to be read in church, that he might be guided by heavenly wisdom. The Spanish-Bavarian coalition carried the day. A commission was drawn up, releasing all officers from obedience to Wallenstein and appointing Gallas provisional commander-in-chief. The commission bears the date of January 24th; it was evidently dated back several days. The strictest secrecy was observed. Correspondence was kept up between head-quarters and the War Office, as if nothing had been changed. The emperor himself wrote to Wallenstein in the usual form, as late as February 13th.

The first step was to make sure of the leading officers. To this end a special envoy, Walmerode, was sent to Piccolomini and Aldringer.* It does not appear that he had much difficulty in winning them over. Piccolomini regarded the new commission as releasing him from all his obligations to his former commander. Aldringer and Piccolomini consented even to make a

---

* Aldringer had charge of Wallenstein's forces in Bavaria. Piccolomini was sent by Wallenstein, after the Pilsen *Revers*, to work upon him and bring him into co-operation. They met either in Passau or in Linz. Piccolomini had attended the banquet in Pilsen and signed the *Revers*. Gallas did not come to Pilsen until January 24th. He remained there several weeks, on intimate terms with Wallenstein, even after he had been informed of the patent of deposition.

dash upon Pilsen and carry off Wallenstein as a pri-
soner. They started out on the 7th of February.
Piccolomini reached Pilsen, but finding that the garrison had been changed,—it does not appear that Wallenstein had any suspicion,—and fearing that the new
officers in command might not be approached with
safety, desisted from the attempt. He speedily withdrew from Pilsen, and did not return. Gallas had
come to Pilsen on the 24th of January and remained
there several weeks. His intercourse with Wallenstein
was of the most friendly nature. Soon after Piccolomini
withdrew, he also followed, on the pretense of inducing
Aldringer to come. This latter, feigning ill health, had
not come to Pilsen at all, but remained in Frauenburg,
with Marradas. Here he was joined by Piccolomini,
Gallas, Colloredo, Götz, Hatzfeld, and even Suys. Frauenburg became the centre of a counter-conspiracy.

Wallenstein in the meanwhile had appointed a new
conference, to be held on the 19th of February, at Pilsen.
On that day he met his officers in his private rooms,—
he was ill and unable to leave his bed,—and submitted to
them his propositions. After renewing his promise to
make himself responsible for all their disbursements, he
assured them that his sole object was to establish peace
in the best interests of the emperor. The officers then
met at Ilow's quarters. Ilow reiterated his resolve to
stand by the general to the last extremity. Julius
Heinrich of Saxe-Lauenburg did the same. So also
Trzka, Sparr, Mohr v. Waldt, and the others. There
was scarcely a dissenting voice. A second *Revers* was

drawn up and signed on the following day. In it Wallenstein released the officers from all obligation to him in case he should be found derelict to the emperor or to the Catholic religion, than which nothing could be farther from his intention, but bound them to co-operation against the machinations of his enemies. Orders were given to the officers to conduct their troops to Prague, where the general rendezvous was to be held and where Wallenstein expected to meet Arnim.

The orders came too late. Aldringer had gone from Frauenburg to Vienna to urge the ministry to increased dispatch. On the 18th of February a second commission was issued, declaring Wallenstein to be guilty of a conspiracy against the emperor, and forbidding the officers to receive further orders from him, or from Ilow and Trzka. All orders must come from Gallas, Aldringer, and Piccolomini.

The question was to be decided in Prague itself. Wallenstein ordered Colonel Beck, the officer in charge of the garrison, to come to Pilsen. Beck obeyed, but before leaving, he instructed his lieutenant-colonel, Mohra, to disregard any orders he (Beck) might send from Pilsen. Beck had come to an understanding with Gallas, who also communicated to the garrison the emperor's positive commands. No objections were raised; even preparations were made to resist any attempt on Wallenstein's part to capture the city. Trzka, who set out for Prague to make arrangements for Wallenstein's entry, learned from an officer whom he met what had happened.

The tidings of the loss of Prague was the death-knell

of Wallenstein's hopes. All at once, as by a flash of
lightning, was revealed the abyss over which he hung.
He perceived that his plans had been detected, his
movements foreseen and forestalled, that the men upon
whom he relied most, Gallas and Piccolomini, were acting
against him in concert and with the connivance of the
court, that the army had failed him even while he thought
to hold it more firmly than ever, that instead of dictat-
ing terms he must flee as a culprit. Seldom in the
annals of history has there been such a rude awakening
from illusion, seldom has defeat trod so close upon the
heels of presumptuous confidence. And we may add,
seldom has blindness on one side been contrasted so
sharply with deceit on the other. It seems incredible
that Wallenstein, with all his reputation for astuteness,
should not have fathomed the character and secret im-
pulses of a man like Gallas, or Piccolomini. His enemies
have left on record the clew to their own ignoble motives.
The emperor may be considered as acting in self-defence.
But they, the officers, were actuated by the hope of booty.
In their letters and orders incessant mention is made of
plunder. They were impatient to divide among themselves the gold and silver, the estates of their commander. Wallenstein, on the contrary, bore the news of
his downfall with dignity. To Colonel Beck, whom he
met, he said, "I had peace in my hand." After a moment's
silence he added, "God is just."

The history of Wallenstein's flight from Pilsen and his
death at Eger must be reserved for the introduction to
the Tod. His career ended with the loss of Prague.

Keeping in mind the determining events subsequent to the battle of Lützen, let us endeavor to set an impartial estimate upon the character and actions of the extraordinary man who controlled for a while the destinies of Germany. That Wallenstein's motives were ideally pure, unmixed with selfish considerations and untainted with perfidious vacillations, is a position which no sober-minded historian of the present day would venture to assume. The facts are that he intrigued, not merely with Gustavus Adolphus, but with Arnim and the Electors of Saxony and Brandenburg, with Thurn, Kinsky, Oxenstjerna, and Richelieu. He gave each in turn to understand that an alliance might be effected. But he met no one fully and unequivocally, he satisfied no one as to his perfect sincerity. He was admired and feared, but not respected, in the strict sense of the term, and he was not trusted. Had he confined himself to the projected union with Saxony, keeping aloof from collateral intrigues with Oxenstjerna and Richelieu and throwing himself without reserve into the coalition with Arnim, he might have succeeded. Even had he inspired the Swedes with more confidence, they would have been ready to meet him at Eger, and he would have escaped death. His conduct was not only wrong, morally wrong, but it was injudicious. It was not for a general, even one clothed with plenipotentiary powers, to attempt to coerce his sovereign. A precedent, it is true, was not wanting. Maurice of Saxony had turned against Charles V. But Maurice was himself an independent sovereign, the acknowledged head of a kingdom. Wallenstein was nothing but what the emperor had seen fit to make him. However strong his convictions might have been that the policy urged upon the emperor by the Spaniards was injurious and even fatal, it became his duty, as an officer and a subject, when he perceived that policy about to be adopted, to resign. He was not bound to serve against his own convictions; neither was he justifiable in forcing his convictions upon his superiors.

Yet while thus condemning him, we, who are guided in our judgments by the knowledge of what was then hidden in the future, cannot refrain from expressing our deep regret. Carefully discriminating between Wallenstein's conduct as an officer, and his plan as a thinker and politician, we can give to the latter our cordial assent. After all that has been said, or may still be said upon the subject, there still remains the underlying truth, not to be hid from sight nor argued away, that Wallenstein's plan was justified by subsequent events. It is beyond question that the general fell a sacrifice to the alliance with Spain. There was scarcely a moment up to the middle of January when he could not have made his peace with the Spaniards,—on their terms. Had he evinced a willingness to further their interests, they would have aided in effecting each and all of his schemes for personal aggrandizement. But he not only disliked the Spaniards, he knew and felt that a union with them could bring no good to Germany. He saw clearly, what seems never to have dawned upon the privy-councillors, father-confessors, and ambassadors at Vienna, that Germany and the Austrian *states needed* peace, and that lasting peace could be had

only by pacifying the Lutherans of Saxony and Brandenburg, the Calvinists of the other German states, the
French, and the Swedes. As general in the field, he had
occasion to feel every day the might of the coalition
formed against the emperor, and he knew that its foundations lay in the nature of things, and were not to be
shaken by the loss or gain of a battle. We have on
record one of his sayings which assumes the significance
of a prophecy. To Count Trautmannsdorf, who had come
to Pilsen in November, 1633, to confer with him upon
the necessity of hastening to the relief of Bavaria after
the fall of Ratisbon, he said: And if the emperor should
gain ten victories, what good would it do him? A single
defeat, or even a check (*eine Schlappe*), would undo him
(R. W. 329). The emperor gained his victory. After
Wallenstein's death, the imperial and Spanish forces met
Horn and Bernhard of Weimar at Nördlingen. The battle was the bloodiest of the war, and ended in the total
rout of the Swedes. Furthermore, it paved the way to
the treaty of Prague. The object of the treaty was to establish peace between Austria and Saxony. The Elector
obtained Lausatia, and the emperor's personal guarantee
that Protestantism would be unmolested in Silesia. But
it did not abolish the Edict of Restitution except in sem-
blance. The treaty gave no security to Calvinism as distinguished from Lutheranism, it did not restore the Palatinate, and it did not satisfy the claims of the Swedes.
Wallenstein's words held good. The Swedes and the
minor princes of Germany, after making a show of assent-
ing to the treaty, finally sold themselves outright to the
3*

French. Richelieu and Mazarin resolved the war into a duel between the houses of Bourbon and Spain, with Germany for the battle-field. All that Wallenstein seems to have apprehended came to pass, and in a more hideous form than even he could have imagined. For twelve weary years armies, Swedish only in name, led by Bauer, Torstenson, Wrangel and Königsmarck, paid by French subsidies and aided by French armies under Guébriant, Turenne, and Enghien, ravaged, plundered, burned, and murdered up to the gates of Vienna. Peace came at last, from mere exhaustion; there was nothing left to fight for. Let us examine the terms of the Treaty of Westphalia. Lutheranism and Calvinism were placed on an equality, the year 1624 was fixed upon as the normal-year, thereby annulling the Edict of Restitution, the Imperial Court (*Reichskammergericht*) was made paritetic, the Upper Palatinate was retained by Bavaria, the Lower Palatinate constituted into an eighth electorate, and restored to Frederick's son. But the Swedes were established in Western Pomerania, Switzerland and the Netherlands were formally separated from the empire, and France retained Alsace (excepting Strassburg), Metz, Toul, Verdun, Philippsburg, and the control of the upper Rhine. Spain and Germany were ruined, France emerged triumphant. With such a treaty before him, with an impoverished and humiliated country around him, well might Ferdinand III. have asked the spirit of his bigoted, short-sighted father if the traitor Wallenstein had not indeed held in his hand a better peace.

Two subsidiary points remained to be disposed of. The

first is to account for the popular notion concerning Wallenstein, which was current in the eighteenth century, and is not yet wholly out of vogue, and which Schiller adopted as the controlling motive of his drama.

Fortunately Ranke has worked up this part of the subject almost exhaustively. What is here offered is little more than a condensed statement of his investigations. When the tidings of Wallenstein's death reached Vienna, popular opinion became divided on the question of his guilt. Not a few voices were heard protesting against the assumption of his guilt, and seeking to cast discredit upon the motives of those who had taken part in the assassination. The first reply appeared in March, 1634, under the title: *Apologia, kurtze doch gründliche Ausführung, wie und auss was für Ursachen. . . Albrecht v. Friedland. . . auss dem Mittel geraumet worden.* It is the official declaration, on the part of Leslie, Gordon, and Butler, how and why they came to act as they did. It is a straightforward narrative, and carries conviction with it. It is accepted by Ranke as the best account of the death of Wallenstein; but inasmuch as it deals only with the events at Eger, the discussion of it may be reserved for a subsequent volume. About the same time appeared an anonymous pamphlet, entitled: *Eigentliche Abbildung des Egerischen Pankets,* etc., extolling Wallenstein as a hero, and stigmatizing the officers at Eger as assassins. The pamphlet seems to have little value. Ranke mentions also two or three Italian pamphlets that lean to the side of Wallenstein. In October, 1634, appeared the most important document of all, under the title: *Ausführlicher und gründlicher Bericht.* It purports to be based upon governmental documents and upon evidence obtained subsequent to Wallenstein's death. Inasmuch as it was submitted to the inspection of the King of Hungary before publication, it may be regarded as the official, at least the semi-official, declaration of the Austrian government. A marvellous production! All the official documents of that day are marred by bad spelling, loose grammar, and turgid rhetoric. But the *Gründlicher Bericht* surpasses them all in its lavish use of epithets, and in the hopelessly involved structure of its sentences. At times it is almost impossible to preserve the connection of thought from beginning to end of the period. The style alone is sufficient to expose it to discredit. It accuses the general of having encouraged Gustavus Adolphus to land in Pomerania, and of having facilitated his landing by weakening the garrisons on the coast. The siege of Nuremberg is made to appear a mere farce on Wallenstein's part, and the retreat to Bohemia after the battle of Lützen an act of cowardice. The *Bericht* even charges Wallenstein with proposing terms of peace and suspension of hostilities in 1633 without the emperor's knowledge and consent; yet the author, whoever he was, must have known that the general was authorized to treat for peace, and was in constant correspondence with the emperor on the subject. The *Bericht*, finally, states that the emperor's orders were to the effect that Wallenstein, Trzka, and Ilow should be arrested and conveyed to *some safe* place where they might be properly tried, " or *be secured dead* or alive." The two clauses contradict

one another. We now know that the clause "dead
or alive" was inserted at the suggestion of the King
of Hungary, who observed that it would be advisable
to publish against the traitors *sententiam post mortem*.
The two patents of deposition contain no such order
(F. W. B. III. 177, 200), and the emperor himself solemnly denied ever having given one (R. W. 490). The
impression which the *Bericht* creates, and which it was
intended to create, is that Wallenstein was simply a
traitor to the House of Austria from beginning to
end of his second command.

But the *Bericht*, bad as it is, is not the worst. It
derived much of its malignity from an anonymous
pamphlet, in Latin, entitled: *Alberti Fridlandi perduellionis Chaos*, etc. Although not professing to be of an
official character, it is evidently the work of one moving
in official circles. The third section, under the heading:
Fridlandus, ultimus Machiavelli partus, is the most important. It asserts that Wallenstein and Gustavus had
come to an understanding with each other before the
latter landed in Germany, and that Arnim invaded
Bohemia, in 1631, at Wallenstein's request. Also
that Wallenstein's resuming command was the result
of an agreement between him and Arnim. Nuremberg, Lützen, and even Steinau were mere shams,
pre-arranged to deceive the emperor. Guided by ex-
ternal and internal evidence, Ranke has made it probable that the *Perduellionis Chaos* was instigated by
William Slavata, Wallenstein's uncle and his bitterest
enemy.

Sesyma's report, which has been already discussed, p. xlvi, was prepared in 1635, but not published at that time. Khevenhiller, however, used it, and also the *Gründlicher Bericht* and the *Perduellionis Chaos*, in preparing his *Annales Ferdinandei*. Herchenhahn's *
History of Wallenstein is in the main a reproduction and expansion of Khevenhiller's Annals. In many passages, however, he cites directly from Sesyma's report in manuscript and from the *Gründlicher Bericht*. Murr's *Beyträge* is a curious collection of materials. The first 124 pages are taken up with a diary of the city of Nuremberg, kept by one of Murr's ancestors during the Thirty Years' War. Pages 131–202 contain the *Perduellionis Chaos*. Pages 203–296 contain the *Gründlicher Bericht*, but under an incorrect title; the first half of the title-page should be struck out (R. W. 486). The remainder of the volume consists of odds and ends of information concerning Wallenstein, his student-life at Altdorf, his first wife, his friends, a list of coins which he had made as Duke of Friedland and Duke of Mecklenburg, etc., etc. Not the least interesting portion is the list of epitaphs upon Wallenstein. Schiller has borrowed freely from these allotria.

In preparing his Wallenstein, Schiller used almost exclusively the above mentioned works of Murr and Herchenhahn (B. S. 167, 178). He had already become familiar with Khevenhiller, whom he followed in the

---

* Herchenhahn is tedious, pedantic, and altogether untrustworthy. His work has no value at the present day, save in its *connection with* Schiller's drama.

History of the Thirty Years' War. Düntzer is wrong in
stating (D. W. 163) that Schiller "found all these (traits
of character) in Murr's *Beyträge*, which, together with
his own History of the Thirty Years' War, formed almost
the only source of materials used in the Wallenstein,
as Boxberger has happily observed." The statement
leaves Herchenhahn out of account. But, in the first
place, Boxberger has "happily observed" nothing of the
sort. Boxberger merely shows that Murr was "one of
the principal sources." Furthermore, Herchenhahn
furnished to Schiller what he could not find in Murr, to
wit, a continuous biography of Wallenstein, after which
he modeled his drama. The development of the action
was suggested by Herchenhahn, and not by Murr. Finally,
there are many important "traits of character" which
are taken bodily from Herchenhahn. Thus, *Picc.* 640,
the Duchess cites Wallenstein's pretext for summon-
ing his wife and child to the camp, viz., that he had
decided upon Thekla's fiancé, and wished to make her
acquainted with him. Düntzer (D. W. 188) finds this
without 'motive,' and is at a loss to account for the
allusion. But Herchenhahn, III. 57, mentions among
the visitors in Wallenstein's camp Prince Ulrich of Denmark, "the destined husband of the general's daughter."
The phrase *lutherischer Herr*, in the Duchess' speech in
the *Piccolomini*, assumes significance when connected
with Herchenhahn's statement. Again, Düntzer (D. W.
155) characterizes as a "happy invention" of Schiller's
the trickery with the "count's-title," which plays such an
important part in determining Butler's Conduct, Tod., II.

6. v. 1100–1143. Schiller's inventive genius was undoubtedly great enough, but it was not exercised in this
particular instance. The whole story is narrated by
Herchenhahn, III. 87, only that it is connected with Ilow,
not with Butler. These are but two among many in-
stances that might be cited to show how closely Schiller
has followed Herchenhahn.

From such sources, then, the dramatist borrowed his
materials and took his cue. He wrote under the influence of the *Perduellionis Chaos*, the *Gründlicher
Bericht*, Khevenhiller's Annals, which are themselves
inaccurate, as Ranke has shown, and the quotations that
Herchenhahn has introduced from Sesyma's report. The
poet was not one to make independent investigations for
himself; he took the above mentioned works and fashioned
them into shape for the stage. It need not occasion us
wonderment that he has represented Wallenstein, in the
main, as a mere traitor. There are passages, it is true,
where it appears that his instinct has led him to draw the
great general in a more favorable light. But these aside,
the Wallenstein of the drama is a portraiture distorted
by personal malice, garbled reports, and popular tradition. Indeed, not a little of Herchenhahn's overwrought
rhetoric has crept into the verses of Schiller. The poet
has become slightly infected with the historiographer's
mania for representing not only Wallenstein himself but
everything connected with him as grandiose, extra-
vagant, and awesome.

One more subject of investigation remains : the changes
that Schiller has introduced in the subsidiary persons of

the drama. These changes are numerous, and should be thoroughly understood.

To begin with the most important, Octavio Piccolomini is anything but the Piccolomini of history. Schiller has made the lieutenant-general the embodiment of all the counter-intrigues then afoot between the army and the court. Octavio Piccolomini stands for the real Piccolomini, and for Gallas, Aldringer, Colloredo, and the other officers who met in secrecy at Frauenburg. He is made provisional general-in-chief in place of Wallenstein, whereas history records that the position was given to Gallas. At the conclusion of the *Tod*, Octavio enters Eger. A messenger brings him dispatches announcing his elevation to the rank of prince. The real Piccolomini captured Pilsen after Wallenstein's flight, and the general who entered Eger just after Wallenstein's death was Gallas. The real Piccolomini was not created prince until sixteen years later. He was born about 1600; consequently he was only thirty-four years of age at the time of the events here narrated, and could not have had a son such as Max. He did not marry until 1651, and died in 1656, leaving no children. Schiller was probably induced to make Piccolomini the head of the counter-conspiracy by the circumstance that he displayed more personal animosity towards Wallenstein that did the other officers (R. P. 16, 18).

Max, therefore, is altogether the creation of Schiller's imagination. He is the poet's ideal of a brave, thoroughly noble officer, who preserves his honor untarnished amid searching temptation. The name Max is borrowed from *Wallenstein's* favorite cousin, Max v. Waldstein. Thekla

also, no less than Max, is born of the poet's brain, and
not of flesh and blood. Wallenstein, it is true, had a
daughter. But she was a mere child at the time, in her
tenth year, and her name was Marie Elizabeth. She
became subsequently the wife of Count Rudolph Kaunitz.
Neither she nor her mother came to Pilsen; they were
living at the time at Brück, on the river Leitha, the
boundary between Austria and Hungary. * The duchess,
whose name was Isabella Katharina, and not Elisabeth,
is represented by all the historians as an upright, amiable woman, who lived on the best of terms with her
husband. If we demand by what right the poet deviated
thus intentionally from history, the answer is obvious.
Such characters as Max and Thekla were necessary.
The reader has only to try to imagine the drama without
them. What a blank there would be, had we not this
high-minded, disinterested pair, who intensify, by their
very goodness, the selfish intrigues by which they are
surrounded and involved in the common ruin. Yet
while they are both noble, they are noble in different
ways. Max is guileless, unsuspecting, and easily disconcerted. Thekla, on the other hand, is quick-witted, full
of tact, and endowed with a goodly share of her father's
shrewdness. She is the stronger nature of the two, and
sees through the Countess Trzka's duplicity and Wallenstein's professions.

* So stated by Murr, 338, note 2. See also Herchenhahn, III.
284. But in a confidential report sent to the Elector of Menz
by his secret agent in Vienna, dated February 23d, the duchess
is alluded to as being in Prague (F. W. B. III. 252).

The Countess Trzka, who has been happily named the Lady Macbeth of the drama, is also the poet's creation. Schiller seems to have caught the idea from a passage in Herchenhahn, II. 47, where Wallenstein is represented as saying to Sesyma, who had just returned (1631) with a message from Gustavus Adolphus: " Nobody knows of the matter except myself, the king (Gustavus), Count Thurn, Count Adam Trzka, and the old Countess Trzka. She is to be trusted. I would give a good deal if she were a man, or if her husband, old Trzka, were as sharp-witted as she is." Yet Herchenhahn's statement requires explanation. If by the ' old countess' is meant Count Adam's mother, the statement conflicts with a passage in Richter (R. P. 4), where the mother, Magdalene Trzka, is referred to as having died in 1626. Schiller himself speaks of her as deceased, *Picc.* 2037, 2147. If, on the other hand, the ' old countess' designates Count Adam's wife, Herchenhahn is in direct conflict with Murr (M. B. 338, note 3) and with Caretto, the emperor's secret agent and commissioner-general in 1634, who assert explicitly that Count Trzka's wife knew nothing of Wallenstein's designs (F. W. B. III. 347). In all probability Herchenhahn has misunderstood or misquoted Sesyma's report. The wife of Count Trzka was Maxmiliana v. Harrach, the sister of the Duchess Wallenstein. The historical character that corresponds to Schiller's Countess Trzka is the Countess Kinsky, the sister of Count Trzka. She is mentioned by Caretto as being a worse rebel than her husband, Count Kinsky. Both countesses were in Eger at the time of the assassination of their husbands. The Countess Kinsky (Schiller's

Countess Trzka) did not poison herself, but married subsequently Baron John William Scherffenberg (R. P. 8).
The Count Trzka of the drama, whose name was Adam
Erdmann, had a younger brother, William, and an only
son, who did not long survive his father. The brother,
William, was arrested on the charge of complicity, but
speedily released. Caretto's language implies that the
father of Adam and William was still living at the time
and cognizant of the plot (F. W. B. III. 224, 300, 347).

Schiller's representation of Trzka* and Ilow does not
differ materially from the account of them given by
Herchenhahn, Murr, and other historiographers. It is to
be regretted, however, that no one of the modern historians, not even Ranke, has seen fit to explain thoroughly
the part played by these two officers. We know that
they were regarded as ringleaders, and were expressly ex-
cluded from the general amnesty in the emperor's procla-
mations. But concerning the precise motives that deter-
mined their conduct, and the circumstances that gave
them such influence over Wallenstein, we have still to be
informed.

Seni, the astrologer, was with Wallenstein in Pilsen
and Eger. He was arrested and taken to Vienna, but
speedily released. Concerning Isolani, it may be observed

---

* With regard to the pronunciation of this name, the spelling
of which has been restored to its Bohemian form, it may be
observed that the *r* has the force of a vowel, but is scarcely
audible; the *z* is pronounced as in 'azure,' the stress of the voice
lies upon the vowel *a*. Schiller, in the *Lager*, has spelled the
word in several places Tertschka.

that he does not play quite such an important part in the historical record as he does in the drama. The other officers do not require especial examination. A full analysis of Butler's character, however, must be reserved for the volume which is to treat of *Wallenstein's Tod*. Rittmeister Neumann was not Trzka's adjutant, but Wallenstein's secretary, and he was not shot at Pilsen, as stated in *Tod*, III. 20, v. 2251, but was killed with Ilow, Kinsky, and Trzka at Eger.

The character of Questenberg in the drama, like that of the Countess Trzka, differs signally from the facts of history. It is a skilful blending of the real Questenberg, and of three other persons: Quiroga, Walmerode, and Gebhard. The real Questenberg was sent to Wallenstein to induce him to resume command, in November, 1631 (F. W. B. II. 186). He was sent, however, to Prague, and not to Znaim, as stated in *Picc.* 106. In this passage Schiller has anticipated the march of events. He represents Tilly as having been already defeated by Gustavus at the passage of the Lech, whereas the battle did not take place until April, 1632. The real Questenberg, as all authorities concur in stating, was the warm friend of Wallenstein, and believed in him to the last. He could not, by any possibility, have played the part assigned to him by Schiller. He was sent to Wallenstein, at Pilsen, in December, 1633, to urge the general to remove his army from Bohemia into other winter-quarters in Franconia and Thuringia. This plan was submitted by Wallenstein to a council of his officers, and was rejected by *them as impossible*, in fact, as tantamount to the ruin of the

army. The officers' report is dated Dec. 17th. In s
then, Schiller's lines, *Picc.* 1185–1195, rest upon hi
cal basis. The allusion to Colonel Suys will be expl
in another place. But the subsequent demand,
1226–1231, that Wallenstein should detach a force t
as escort for the Cardinal Infant, was not made by (
tenberg, but by Quiroga, who came to Pilsen on Jar
5th. It is not probable that Questenberg was in F
at the time of the first *Revers*, since we find him wr
to the emperor, Dec. 30th, announcing his intentic
being in Prague in four or five days (F. W. B. III.
The officers' council of December, which was bre
about by Questenberg's mission, should not be confou
with the more memorable banquet and *Revers* which
the result of Quiroga's mission and which have
already discussed, page xliii. Quiroga was not in F
at the time of the banquet (Jan. 12), for he states, i
report to Oñate, that he reached the town on Thur
January 5th, and left on the following Sunday mor
(R. W. 524, 527). He was in Vienna and had an
ence with the emperor before Jan. 18th (F. W. B.
160). Walmerode was sent by the court, in the l
part of January or beginning of February, not to
lenstein, but to Piccolomini, Gallas, Aldringer, and
generals, to confer with them secretly, and conduc
counter-conspiracy, see p. li. It does not appear
Walmerode came to Pilsen. Gebhard, one of the
peror's councillors, was sent to Pilsen,—after the
Revers and before Oñate had held his memorable i
view with the emperor, see p. l,—to take part in

lenstein's negotiations for peace, which were still regarded as lawful and feasible. He remained with Wallenstein, and the two were actually in conference when the tidings of the loss of Prague reached Wallenstein (R. W. 383, 427). Both he and the real Questenberg were friends of Wallenstein; Quiroga and Walmerode were enemies. As the Octavio Piccolomini of the drama is the embodiment of all the officers who carried on the counter-conspiracy against the general, so Questenberg, as Schiller has depicted him, symbolizes the conduct and views of the court and the war office in Vienna.

The action of the *Lager*, *Piccolomini*, and *Tod* I–III, covers three days. Into this brief space of time the dramatist has compressed events extending over many weeks, from the middle of December, 1633, to February 22d, 1634. Indeed, in IV. 112 of the *Lager*, the capture of Ratisbon by Bernhard of Weimar is announced as a recent event, whereas the town had surrendered early in November. The two officers'-conferences and the two *Reverse* are merged into one, and in general the action proceeds with feverish haste. In consequence of this extreme condensation, Schiller has committed several anachronisms, which will be explained in the Commentary.

An account of the composition of the Wallenstein-trilogy will be given in the introduction to the *Lager*.

Die Piccolomini

in

Fünf Aufzügen.

Personen.

Wallenstein, Herzog zu Friedland, kaiserlicher Generalissimus im dreißigjährigen Kriege.

Octavio Piccolomini, Generallieutenant.

Max Piccolomini, sein Sohn, Oberst bei einem Kürassierregiment.

Graf Terzky, Wallensteins Schwager, Chef mehrerer Regimenter.

Illo, Feldmarschall, Wallensteins Vertrauter.

Isolani, General der Kroaten.

Buttler, Chef eines Dragonerregiments.

Tiefenbach,
Don Maradas,
Götz,   } Generale unter Wallenstein.
Colalto,

Rittmeister Neumann, Terzkys Adjutant.

Kriegsrath von Questenberg, vom Kaiser gesendet.

Baptista Seni, Astrolog.

Herzogin von Friedland, Wallensteins Gemahlin.

Thekla, Prinzessin von Friedland, ihre Tochter.

Gräfin Terzky, der Herzogin Schwester.

Ein Cornet.

Kellermeister des Grafen Terzky.

Friedländische Pagen und Bediente.

Terzkysche Bediente und Hoboisten.

Mehrere Obersten und Generale.

Erster Aufzug.

Ein alter gothischer Saal auf dem Rathhause
zu Pilsen, mit Fahnen und anderm Kriegs-
geräthe decorirt.

Erster Auftritt.

Illo mit Buttler und Isolani.

Illo.

Spät kommt ihr — doch ihr kommt! Der weite Weg,
Graf Isolan, entschuldigt euer Säumen.

Isolani.

Wir kommen auch mit leeren Händen nicht!
Es ward uns angesagt bei Donauwörth,
5 Ein schwedischer Transport sei unterwegs
Mit Proviant, an die sechshundert Wagen.
Den griffen die Kroaten mir noch auf;
Wir bringen ihn.

Illo.

       Er kommt uns g'rad zu Paß,
Die stattliche Versammlung hier zu speisen.

Buttler.

10 Es ist schon lebhaft hier, ich seh's.

Isolani.

       Ja, ja,

Die Kirchen selber liegen voll Soldaten;
(sich umschauend)
Auch auf dem Rathhaus, seh' ich, habt ihr euch
Schon ziemlich eingerichtet. Nun, nun! der Soldat
Behilft und schickt sich, wie er kann.

Illo.

15 Von dreißig Regimentern haben sich
Die Obersten zusammen schon gefunden;
Den Terzky trefft ihr hier, den Tiefenbach,
Colalto, Götz, Maradas, Hinnersam,
Auch Sohn und Vater Piccolomini, —
20 Ihr werdet manchen alten Freund begrüßen.
Nur Gallas fehlt uns noch und Altringer.

Buttler.

Auf Gallas wartet nicht.

Illo (stutzt).
Wie so? Wißt ihr —

Isolani (unterbricht ihn).

Max Piccolomini hier? O führt mich zu ihm!
Ich seh' ihn noch — es sind jetzt zehen Jahr —
25 Als wir bei Dessau mit dem Mansfeld schlugen,
Den Rappen sprengen von der Brück' herab
Und zu dem Vater, der in Nöthen war,
Sich durch der Elbe reißend Wasser schlagen.
Da sproßt' ihm kaum der erste Flaum ums Kinn;
30 Jetzt, hör' ich, soll der Kriegsheld fertig sein.

Illo.

Ihr sollt ihn heut' noch sehn. Er führt aus Kärnthen
Die Fürstin Friedland her und die Prinzessin;
Sie treffen diesen Vormittag noch ein.

Buttler.

Auch Frau und Tochter ruft der Fürst hieher?
35 Er ruft hier viel zusammen.

Isolani.

Desto besser.
Erwartet' ich doch schon von nichts als Märschen
Und Batterien zu hören und Attaken;
Und siehe da! der Herzog sorgt dafür,
Daß auch was Holdes uns das Aug' ergetze.

Illo.

(der nachdenkend gestanden, zu Buttlern, den er ein wenig auf die Seite führt)
40 Wie wißt ihr, daß Graf Gallas außen bleibt?

Buttler (mit Bedeutung).

Weil er auch m i ch gesucht zurückzuhalten.

Illo (warm).

Und ihr seid fest geblieben?
(drückt ihm die Hand)
Wackrer Buttler!

Buttler.

Nach der Verbindlichkeit, die mir der Fürst
Noch kürzlich aufgelegt —

Illo.

45 Ja, Generalmajor! Ich gratuliere!

Isolani.

Zum Regiment, nicht wahr, das Ihm der Fürst
Geschenkt? Und noch dazu dasselbe, hör' ich,
Wo Er vom Reiter hat heraufgedient?
Nun, das ist wahr! dem ganzen Corps gereicht's
50 Zum Sporn, zum Beispiel, macht einmal ein alter
Verdienter Kriegsmann seinen Weg.

Buttler.

Ich bin verlegen,
Ob ich den Glückwunsch schon empfangen darf;
Noch fehlt vom Kaiser die Bestätigung.

Isolani.

Greif zu, greif zu! Die Hand, die Ihn dahin
55 Gestellt, ist stark genug, Ihn zu erhalten,
Trotz Kaiser und Ministern.

Illo.

Wenn wir alle
So gar bedenklich wollten sein!
Der Kaiser gibt uns nichts, vom Herzog
Kommt alles, was wir hoffen, was wir haben.

Isolani (zu Illo).

60 Herr Bruder, hab' ich's schon erzählt? Der Fürst
Will meine Creditoren contentieren,
Will selber mein Kassier sein künftighin,
Zu einem ordentlichen Mann mich machen.
Und das ist nun das drittemal, bedenk' Er!
65 Daß mich der Königlichgesinnte vom
Verderben rettet und zu Ehren bringt.

Illo.

Könnt' er nur immer, wie er gerne wollte!
Er schenkte Land und Leut' an die Soldaten.
Doch wie verkürzen sie in Wien ihm nicht den Arm,
70 Beschneiden, wo sie können, ihm die Flügel!
Da! diese neuen, saubern Forderungen,
Die dieser Questenberger bringt!

Buttler.

Ich habe mir

Von diesen kaiserlichen Forderungen auch
Erzählen lassen; doch ich hoffe,
75 Der Herzog wird in keinem Stücke weichen.

Illo.

Von seinem Recht gewißlich nicht, wenn nur nicht
— Vom Platze!

Buttler (betroffen).
            Wißt ihr etwas? Ihr erschreckt mich.

Isolani (zugleich).
Wir wären alle ruiniert!

Illo.
                    Brecht ab!
Ich sehe unsern Mann dort eben kommen
80 Mit Gen'rallieutnant Piccolomini.

Buttler (den Kopf bedenklich schüttelnd).
                        Ich fürchte,
Wir gehn nicht von hier, wie wir kamen.

Zweiter Auftritt.

Vorige. Octavio Piccolomini. Questenberg.

Octavio (noch in der Entfernung).
Wie? Noch der Gäste mehr? Gestehn Sie, Freund!
Es brauchte diesen thränenvollen Krieg,
So vieler Helden ruhmgekrönte Häupter
85 In e i n e s Lagers Umkreis zu versammeln.

Questenberg.
In kein Friedländisch Heereslager komme,
Wer von dem Kriege Böses denken will.

Beinah' vergessen hätt' ich seine Plagen,
Da mir der Ordnung hoher Geist erschienen,
90 Durch die er, weltzerstörend, selbst besteht,
Das Große mir erschienen, das er bildet.

Octavio.

Und siehe da! ein tapfres Paar, das würdig
Den Heldenreihen schließt. Graf Isolan
Und Obrist Buttler. — Nun, da haben wir
95 Vor Augen gleich das ganze Kriegeshandwerk.
(Buttlern und Isolani präsentierend)
Es ist die Stärke, Freund, und Schnelligkeit.

Questenberg (zu Octavio).

Und zwischen beiden der erfahrne Rath.

Octavio (Questenbergen an jene vorstellend).

Den Kammerherrn und Kriegsrath Questenberg,
Den Ueberbringer kaiserlicher Befehle,
100 Der Soldaten großen Gönner und Patron
Verehren wir in diesem würdigen Gaste.
(Allgemeines Stillschweigen).

Illo (nähert sich Questenbergen).

Es ist das erstemal nicht, Herr Minister,
Daß Sie im Lager uns die Ehr' erweisen.

Questenberg.

Schon einmal sah ich mich vor diesen Fahnen.

Illo.

105 Und wissen Sie, wo das gewesen ist?
Zu Znaim war's, in Mähren, wo Sie sich
Von Kaisers wegen eingestellt, den Herzog
Um Uebernahm' des Regiments zu flehen.

Questenberg.

Zu fle h n, Herr General? So weit ging weder
110 Mein Auftrag, daß ich wüßte, noch mein Eifer.

Illo.

Nun, ihn zu zwingen, wenn Sie wollen. Ich
Erinn're mich's recht gut. Graf Tilly war
Am Lech aufs Haupt geschlagen, offen stand
Das Baierland dem Feind, nichts hielt ihn auf,
115 Bis in das Herz von Oestreich vorzudringen.
Damals erschienen S i e und Werdenberg
Vor unserm Herrn, mit Bitten in ihn stürmend
Und mit der kaiserlichen Ungnad' drohend,
Wenn sich der Fürst des Jammers nicht erbarme.

Isolani (tritt dazu).

120 Ja, ja! 's ist zu begreifen, Herr Minister,
Warum Sie sich bei Ihrem heut'gen Auftrag
An jenen alten just nicht gern erinnern.

Questenberg.

Wie sollt' ich nicht! Ist zwischen beiden doch
Kein Widerspruch! D a m a l e n galt es, Böhmen
125 Aus Feindes Hand zu reißen; h e u t e soll ich's
Befrei'n von seinen Freunden und Beschützern.

Illo.

Ein schönes Amt! Nachdem wir dieses Böhmen
Mit unserm Blut dem Sachsen abgefochten,
Will man zum Dank uns aus dem Lande werfen!

Questenberg.

130 Wenn es nicht bloß ein Elend mit dem andern
Vertauscht soll haben, muß das arme Land
Von Freund und Feindes Geißel gleich befreit sein.

Illo.

Ei was! Es war ein gutes Jahr, der Bauer kann
Schon wieder geben.   ·

Questenberg.

Ja, wenn Sie von Heerden
135 Und Weideplätzen reden, Herr Feldmarschall —

Isolani.

Der Krieg ernährt den Krieg.   Gehn Bauern drauf,
Ei, so gewinnt der Kaiser mehr Soldaten.

Questenberg.

Und wird um so viel Unterthanen ärmer!

Isolani.

Pah, seine Unterthanen sind wir alle!

Questenberg.

140 Mit Unterschied, Herr Graf!   Die einen füllen
Mit nützlicher Geschäftigkeit den Beutel,
Und andre wissen nur ihn brav zu leeren.
Der Degen hat den Kaiser arm gemacht;
Der Pflug ist's, der ihn wieder stärken muß.

Buttler.

145 Der Kaiser wär' nicht arm, wenn nicht so viel
— Blutigel saugten an dem Mark des Landes.

Isolani.

So arg kann's auch nicht sein.   Ich sehe ja,
(indem er sich vor ihn hinstellt und seinen Anzug mustert)
Es ist noch lang' nicht alles Gold gemünzt.

Questenberg.

Gottlob!   Noch etwas weniges hat man
150 Geflüchtet — vor den Fingern der Kroaten.

Illo.

Da! Der Slawata und der Martiniz,
Auf die der Kaiser, allen guten Böhmen
Zum Aergernisse, Gnadengaben häuft,
Die sich vom Raube der vertriebnen Bürger mästen,
155 Die von der allgemeinen Fäulniß wachsen,
Allein im öffentlichen Unglück ernten,
Mit königlichem Prunk dem Schmerz des Landes
Hohn sprechen, — d i e und ihresgleichen laßt
Den Krieg bezahlen, den verderblichen,
160 Den sie allein doch angezündet haben.

Buttler.

Und diese Landschmaruzer, die die Füße
Beständig unter'm Tisch des Kaisers haben,
Nach allen Benefizen hungrig schnappen,
Die wollen dem Soldaten, der vor'm Feind liegt,
165 Das Brot vorschneiden und die Rechnung streichen.

Isolani.

Mein Lebtag denk' ich dran, wie ich nach Wien
Vor sieben Jahren kam, um die Remonte
Für unsre Regimenter zu betreiben,
Wie sie von einer Antecamera
170 Zur andern mich herumgeschleppt, mich unter
Den Schranzen stehen lassen, stundenlang,
Als wär' ich da, ums Gnadenbrot zu betteln.
Zuletzt —da schickten sie mir einen Kapuziner,
Ich dacht', es wär' um meiner Sünden willen!
175 Nein doch, das war der Mann, mit dem
Ich um die Reiterpferde sollte handeln!

Ich mußt' auch abziehn unverrichteter Ding'.
Der Fürst nachher verschaffte mir in drei Tagen,
Was ich zu Wien in dreißig nicht erlangte.

Questenberg.

180 Ja, ja! Der Posten fand sich in der Rechnung;
Ich weiß, wir haben noch daran zu zahlen.

Illo.

Es ist der Krieg ein roh, gewaltsam Handwerk.
Man kommt nicht aus mit sanften Mitteln, alles
Läßt sich nicht schonen. Wollte man's erpassen,
185 Bis sie zu Wien aus vier und zwanzig Uebeln
Das kleinste ausgewählt, man paßte lange! ·
Frisch mitten durchgegriffen, das ist besser!
Reiß' dann, was mag! Die Menschen, in der Regel,
Verstehen sich aufs Flicken und aufs Stückeln,
190 Und finden sich in ein verhaßtes Müssen.
Weit besser, als in eine bittre Wahl.

Questenberg.

Ja, das ist wahr! die Wahl spart uns der Fürst.

Illo.

Der Fürst trägt Vatersorge für die Truppen;✓
Wir sehen, wie's der Kaiser mit uns meint.

Questenberg.

195 Für jeden Stand hat er ein gleiches Herz,
Und kann den einen nicht dem andern opfern. ·

Isolani.

Drum stößt er uns zum Raubthier in die Wüste,
Um seine theuren Schafe zu behüten.

Questenberg (mit Hohn).

Herr Graf! dies Gleichniß machen Sie, nicht ich.

Illo.

200 Doch wären wir, wofür der Hof uns nimmt,
Gefährlich war's, die Freiheit uns zu geben.

Queſtenberg (mit Ernſt).

Genommen iſt die Freiheit, nicht gegeben;
Drum thut es noth, den Zaum ihr anzulegen. -

Illo.

Ein wildes Pferd erwarte man zu finden.

Queſtenberg.

205 Ein beßrer Reiter wird's beſänftigen.

Illo.

Es trägt den e i n e n nur, der es gezähmt.

Queſtenberg.

Iſt es gezähmt, ſo folgt es einem Kinde.

Illo.

Das Kind, ich weiß, hat man ihm ſchon gefunden.

Queſtenberg.

Sie kümmre nur die Pflicht und nicht der Name.

Buttler.

(der ſich bisher mit Piccolomini ſeitwärts gehalten, doch mit ſichtbarem
Antheil an dem Geſpräche, tritt näher)

210 Herr Präſident! Dem Kaiſer ſteht in Deutſchland
Ein ſtattlich Kriegsvolk da, es cantonnieren
In dieſem Königreich wohl dreißigtauſend,
Wohl ſechzehntauſend Mann in Schleſien;
Zehn Regimenter ſtehn am Weſerſtrom,
215 Am Rhein und Main; in Schwaben bieten ſechs,
In Baiern zwölf den Schwediſchen die Spitze;
Nicht zu gedenken der Beſatzungen,
Die an der Grenz' die feſten Plätze ſchirmen. -
All dieſes Volk gehorcht Friedländiſchen

220 Hauptleuten.   Die's befehligen, sind alle
In eine Schul' gegangen, eine Milch
Hat sie ernährt, ein Herz belebt sie alle.
Fremdlinge stehn sie da auf diesem Boden;
Der Dienst allein ist ihnen Haus und Heimat.

225 Sie treibt der Eifer nicht fürs Vaterland,
Denn Tausende, wie mich, gebar die Fremde;
Nicht für den Kaiser, wohl die Hälfte kam
Aus fremdem Dienst selbstflüchtig uns herüber,
Gleichgültig, unter'm Doppeladler fechtend,

230 Wie unter'm Löwen und den Lilien.   ·   .
Doch alle führt an gleich gewalt'gem Zügel
Ein einziger, durch gleiche Lieb' und Furcht
Zu einem Volke sie zusammenbindend.
Und wie des Blitzes Funke sicher, schnell,

235 Geleitet an der Wetterstange, läuft,
Herrscht sein Befehl vom letzten fernen Posten,
Der an die Dünen branden hört den Belt,
Der in der Etsch fruchtbare Thäler sieht,
Bis zu der Wache, die ihr Schilderhaus

240 Hat aufgerichtet an der Kaiserburg.

Questenberg.
Was ist der langen Rede kurzer Sinn?

Buttler.
Daß der Respect, die Neigung, das Vertraun,
Das uns dem Friedland unterwürfig macht,
Nicht auf den ersten besten sich verpflanzt,

245 Den uns der Hof aus Wien herübersendet.
Uns ist im treuen Angedenken noch,
Wie das Commando kam in Friedlands Hände.

War's etwa kaiserliche Majestät,
Die ein gemachtes Heer ihm übergab,
250 Den Führer nur gesucht zu ihren Truppen?
Noch gar nicht war das Heer. Erschaffen erst
Mußt' es der Friedland, er empfing es nicht,
Er gab's dem Kaiser! Von dem Kaiser nicht
Erhielten wir den Wallenstein zum Feldherrn.
255 So ist es nicht, so nicht! Vom Wallenstein
Erhielten wir den Kaiser erst zum Herrn,
Er knüpft uns, er allein, an diese Fahnen.

      Octavio (tritt dazwischen).

Es ist nur zur Erinnerung, Herr Kriegsrath,
Daß Sie im Lager sind und unter Kriegern.
260 Die Kühnheit macht, die Freiheit den Soldaten.
Vermöcht' er keck zu handeln, dürft' er nicht
Keck reden auch? Eins geht ins andre drein.
Die Kühnheit dieses würd'gen Officiers,
         (auf Buttlern zeigend)
Die jetzt in ihrem Ziel sich nur vergriff,
265 Erhielt, wo nichts als Kühnheit retten konnte,
Bei einem furchtbarn Aufstand der Besatzung
Dem Kaiser seine Hauptstadt Prag.
      (Man hört von fern eine Kriegsmusik.)

      Illo.
              Das sind sie!
Die Wachen salutieren. Dies Signal
Bedeutet uns, die Fürstin sei herein.

      Octavio (zu Questenberg).

270 So ist auch mein Sohn Max zurück. Er hat sie
Aus Kärnthen abgeholt und hergeleitet.

Isolani (zu Illo).

Gehn wir zusammen hin, sie zu begrüßen?

Illo.

Wohl! Laßt uns gehen.   Oberst Buttler, kommt!

(zum Octavio)

Erinnert euch, daß wir vor Mittag noch

275 Mit diesem Herrn beim Fürsten uns begegnen.

Dritter Auftritt.

Octavio und Questenberg, die zurückbleiben.

Questenberg.

(mit Zeichen des Erstaunens)

Was hab' ich hören müssen, Gen'rallieutenant!
Welch zügelloser Trotz! Was für Begriffe!
Wenn dieser Geist der allgemeine ist —

Octavio.

Drei Viertel der Armee vernahmen Sie.

Questenberg.

280 Weh uns! Wo dann ein zweites Heer gleich finden,
Um dieses zu bewachen! Dieser Illo, fürcht' ich,
Denkt noch viel schlimmer, als er spricht. Auch dieser
        Buttler
Kann seine böse Meinung nicht verbergen.

Octavio.

Empfindlichkeit, gereizter Stolz, nichts weiter!
285 Diesen Buttler geb' ich noch nicht auf; ich weiß,
Wie dieser böse Geist zu bannen ist.

Questenberg.

(voll Unruh auf und ab gehend)

Nein! das ist schlimmer, o viel schlimmer, Freund,
Als wir's in Wien uns hatten träumen lassen!
Wir sahen's nur mit Höflingsaugen an,
290 Die von dem Glanz des Throns geblendet waren;
Den Feldherrn hatten wir noch nicht gesehn,
Den allvermögenden, in seinem Lager.
Hier ist's ganz anders!
Hier ist kein Kaiser mehr.   Der Fürst ist Kaiser!
295 Der Gang, den ich an Ihrer Seite jetzt
Durchs Lager that, schlägt meine Hoffnung nieder.

Octavio.

Sie sehn nun selbst, welch ein gefährlich Amt
Es ist, das Sie vom Hof mir überbrachten,
Wie mißlich die Person, die ich hier spiele.
300 Der leiseste Verdacht des Generals,
Er würde Freiheit mir und Leben kosten,
Und sein verwegenes Beginnen nur
Beschleunigen.

Questenberg.

Wo war die Ueberlegung,
Als wir dem Rasenden das Schwert vertraut
305 Und solche Macht gelegt in solche Hand!
Zu stark für dieses schlimmverwahrte Herz
War die Versuchung! Hätte sie doch selbst
Dem bessern Mann gefährlich werden müssen!
Er wird sich weigern, sag' ich Ihnen,
310 Der kaiserlichen Ordre zu gehorchen.

Er kann's und wird's.   Sein unbestrafter Trotz
Wird unsre Ohnmacht schimpflich offenbaren.

Octavio.

Und glauben Sie, daß er Gemahlin, Tochter
Umsonst hieher ins Lager kommen ließ,
315 Gerade jetzt, da wir zum Krieg uns rüsten?
Daß er die letzten Pfänder seiner Treu'
Aus Kaisers Landen führt, das deutet uns
Auf einen nahen Ausbruch der Empörung.

Questenberg.

Weh uns! und wie dem Ungewitter stehn,
320 Das drohend uns umzieht von allen Enden?
Der Reichsfeind an den Grenzen, Meister schon
Vom Donaustrom, stets weiter um sich greifend;
Im innern Land des Aufruhrs Feuerglocke,
Der Bauer in Waffen, alle Stände schwierig;
325 Und die Armee, von der wir Hilf' erwarten,
Verführt, verwildert, aller Zucht entwohnt,
Vom Staat, von ihrem Kaiser losgerissen,
Vom Schwindelnden die Schwindelnde geführt,
Ein furchtbar Werkzeug, dem verwegensten
330 Der Menschen blind gehorchend hingegeben.

Octavio.

Verzagen wir auch nicht zu früh, mein Freund!
Stets ist die Sprache kecker als die That,
Und mancher, der in blindem Eifer jetzt
Zu jedem Aeußersten entschlossen scheint,
335 Find't unerwartet in der Brust ein Herz,
Spricht man des Frevels wahren Namen aus.
Zudem — ganz unvertheidigt sind wir nicht.

Graf Altringer und Gallas, wissen Sie,
Erhalten in der Pflicht ihr kleines Heer,
340 Verstärken es noch täglich. Ueberraschen
Kann er uns nicht; Sie wissen, daß ich ihn
Mit meinen Horchern rings umgeben habe;
Vom kleinsten Schritt erhalt' ich Wissenschaft
Sogleich — ja, mir entdeckt's sein eigner Mund.

Questenberg.

345 Ganz unbegreiflich ist's, daß er den Feind nicht merkt
An seiner Seite.

Octavio.

Denken Sie nicht etwa,
Daß ich durch Lügenkünste, gleißnerische
Gefälligkeit in seine Gunst mich stahl,
Durch Heuchelworte sein Vertrauen nähre.
350 Befiehlt mir gleich die Klugheit und die Pflicht,
Die ich dem Reich, dem Kaiser schuldig bin,
Daß ich mein wahres Herz vor ihm verberge,
Ein falsches hab' ich niemals ihm geheuchelt!

Questenberg.

Es ist des Himmels sichtbarliche Fügung.

Octavio.

355 Ich weiß nicht, was es ist, was ihn an mich
Und meinen Sohn so mächtig zieht und kettet.
Wir waren immer Freunde, Waffenbrüder;
Gewohnheit, gleichgetheilte Abenteuer
Verbanden uns schon frühe; doch ich weiß
360 Den Tag zu nennen, wo mit einemmal
Sein Herz mir aufging, sein Vertrauen wuchs.
Es war der Morgen vor der Lützner Schlacht.

Mich trieb ein böser Traum, ihn aufzusuchen,
Ein ander Pferd zur Schlacht ihm anzubieten.
365 Fern von den Zelten, unter einem Baum,
Fand ich ihn eingeschlafen. Als ich ihn
Erweckte, mein Bedenken ihm erzählte,
Sah er mich lange staunend an; drauf fiel er
Mir um den Hals und zeigte eine Rührung,
370 Wie jener kleine Dienst sie gar nicht werth war.
Seit jenem Tag verfolgt mich sein Vertrauen
In gleichem Maß, als ihn das meine flieht.

Questenberg.

Sie ziehen Ihren Sohn doch ins Geheimniß?

Octavio.

Nein!

Questenberg.

Wie? auch warnen wollen Sie ihn nicht,
375 In welcher schlimmen Hand er sich befinde?

Octavio.

Ich muß ihn seiner Unschuld anvertrauen.
Verstellung ist der offnen Seele fremd;
Unwissenheit allein kann ihm die Geistesfreiheit
Bewahren, die den Herzog sicher macht.

Questenberg (besorglich).

380 Mein würd'ger Freund! Ich hab' die beste Meinung
Vom Oberst Piccolomini — doch — wenn —
Bedenken Sie —

Octavio.

Ich muß es darauf wagen. Still! da kommt er.

Vierter Auftritt.

Max Piccolomini. Octavio Piccolomini. Questenberg.

Max.

Da ist er ja gleich selbst.   Willkommen, Vater!
(er umarmt ihn ; wie er sich umwendet, bemerkt er Questenberg und tritt
kalt zurück)
385 Beschäftigt, wie ich seh'?   Ich will nicht stören.

Octavio.

Wie, Max? Sieh diesen Gast doch näher an.
Aufmerksamkeit verdient ein alter Freund;
Ehrfurcht gebührt dem Boten deines Kaisers.

Max (trocken).

Von Questenberg! Willkommen, wenn was gutes
390 Ins Hauptquartier Sie herführt.

Questenberg (hat seine Hand gefaßt).

Ziehen Sie
Die Hand nicht weg, Graf Piccolomini!
Ich fasse sie nicht bloß von meinetwegen,
Und nichts gemeines will ich damit sagen.
(beide Hände fassend)
Octavio — Max Piccolomini!
395 Heilbringend vorbedeutungsvolle Namen!
Nie wird das Glück von Oesterreich sich wenden,
So lang' zwei solche Sterne, segenreich
Und schützend, leuchten über seinen Heeren.

Max.

Sie fallen aus der Rolle, Herr Minister!
400 Nicht Lobens wegen sind Sie hier; ich weiß,

Sie sind geschickt, zu tadeln und zu schelten.
Ich will voraus nichts haben vor den andern.

Octavio (zu Max).

Er kommt vom Hofe, wo man mit dem Herzog
Nicht ganz so wohl zufrieden ist, als hier.

Max.

405 Was gibt's aufs nen denn an ihm auszustellen?
Daß er für sich allein beschließt, was er
Allein versteht? Wohl! daran thut er recht,
Und wird's dabei auch sein Verbleiben haben.
Er ist nun einmal nicht gemacht, nach andern
410 Geschmeidig sich zu fügen und zu wenden,
Es geht ihm wider die Natur, er kann's nicht.
Geworden ist ihm eine Herrscherseele,
Und ist gestellt auf einen Herrscherplatz.
Wohl uns, daß es so ist! Es können sich
415 Nur wenige regieren, den Verstand
Verständig brauchen. Wohl dem Ganzen, findet
Sich einmal einer, der ein Mittelpunkt
Für viele Tausend wird, ein Halt; sich hinstellt,
Wie eine feste Säul', an die man sich
420 Mit Lust mag schließen und mit Zuversicht.
So einer ist der Wallenstein, und taugte
Dem Hof ein andrer besser, — der Armee
Frommt nur ein solcher.

Questenberg.

　　　　Der Armee! Ja wohl!

Max.

Und eine Lust ist's, wie er alles weckt
425 Und stärkt und neu belebt um sich herum,

Wie jede Kraft sich ausspricht, jede Gabe
Gleich deutlicher sich wird in seiner Nähe!
Jedwedem zieht er seine Kraft hervor,
Die eigenthümliche, und zieht sie groß,
430 Läßt jeden ganz das bleiben, was er ist;
Er wacht nur drüber, das er's immer sei
Am rechten Ort; so weiß er aller Menschen
Vermögen zu dem seinigen zu machen.

Questenberg.

Wer spricht ihm ab, daß er die Menschen kenne,
435 Sie zu gebrauchen wisse! Ueber'm Herrscher
Vergißt er nur den Diener ganz und gar,
Als wär' mit seiner Würd' er schon geboren.

Max.

Ist er's denn nicht? Mit jeder Kraft dazu
Ist er's, und mit der Kraft noch obendrein,
440 Buchstäblich zu vollstrecken die Natur,
Dem Herrschtalent den Herrschplatz zu erobern.

Questenberg.

So kommt's zuletzt auf seine Großmuth an,
Wie viel wir überall noch gelten sollen!

Max.

Der selt'ne Mann will seltenes Vertrauen.
445 Gebt ihm den Raum, das Ziel wird er sich setzen.

Questenberg.

Die Proben geben's.

Max.

     Ja, so sind sie! Schreckt
Sie alles gleich, was eine Tiefe hat;
Ist ihnen nirgends wohl, als wo's recht flach ist.

Octavio (zu Questenberg).

Ergeben Sie sich nur in gutem, Freund!
450 Mit dem da werden Sie nicht fertig.

Max.

Da rufen sie den Geist an in der Noth,
Und grauet ihnen gleich, wenn er sich zeigt.
Das Ungemeine soll, das Höchste selbst
Geschehn, wie das Alltägliche. │ Im Felde
455 Da bringt die Gegenwart, Persönliches
Muß herrschen, eignes Auge sehn. Es braucht
Der Feldherr jedes Große der Natur,
So gönne man ihm auch, in ihren großen
Verhältnissen zu leben. Das Orakel
460 In seinem Innern, das lebendige,
Nicht todte Bücher, alte Ordnungen,
Nicht modrigte Papiere soll er fragen.

Octavio.

Mein Sohn, laß uns die alten, engen Ordnungen
Gering nicht achten! Köstlich unschätzbare
465 Gewichte sind's, die der bedrängte Mensch
An seiner Dränger raschen Willen band;
Denn immer war die Willkür fürchterlich.
Der Weg der Ordnung, ging er auch durch Krümmen,
Er ist kein Umweg. G'rad aus geht des Blitzes,
470 Geht des Kanonballs fürchterlicher Pfad,
Schnell auf dem nächsten Wege langt er an,
Macht sich zermalmend Platz, um zu zermalmen.
Mein Sohn! die Straße, die der Mensch befährt,
Worauf der Segen wandelt, diese folgt
475 Der Flüsse Lauf, der Thäler freien Krümmen,

Umgeht das Weizenfeld, den Rebenhügel,
Des Eigenthums gemeßne Grenzen ehrend.
So führt sie später, sicher doch zum Ziel.

Questenberg.

O! hören Sie den Vater, hören Sie
480 Ihn, der ein Held ist und ein Mensch zugleich!

Octavio.

Das Kind des Lagers spricht aus dir, mein Sohn.
Ein fünfzehnjähr'ger Krieg hat dich erzogen,
Du hast den Frieden nie gesehn! Es gibt
Noch höhern Werth, mein Sohn, als kriegerischen;
485 Im Kriege selber ist das Letzte nicht der Krieg.
Die großen, schnellen Thaten der Gewalt,
Des Augenblicks erstaunenswerthe Wunder,
Die sind es nicht, die das Beglückende,
Das ruhig, mächtig Dauernde erzeugen.
490 In Hast und Eile bauet der Soldat
Von Leinwand seine leichte Stadt; da wird
Ein augenblicklich Brausen und Bewegen,
Der Markt bewegt sich, Straßen, Flüsse sind
Bedeckt mit Fracht, es rührt sich das Gewerbe.
495 Doch eines Morgens plötzlich siehet man
Die Zelte fallen, weiter rückt die Horde,
Und ausgestorben, wie ein Kirchhof, bleibt
Der Acker, das zerstampfte Saatfeld liegen,
Und um des Jahres Ernte ist's gethan.

Max.

500 O! laß den Kaiser Friede machen, Vater!
Den blut'gen Lorbeer geb' ich hin mit Freuden

Fürs erste Veilchen, das der März uns bringt,
Das duftige Pfand der neuverjüngten Erde.

Octavio.

Wie wird dir? Was bewegt dich so auf einmal?

Max.

505 Ich hab' den Frieden nie gesehen? Ich hab' ihn
Gesehen, alter Vater. Eben komm' ich,
Jetzt eben davon her. Es führte mich
Der Weg durch Länder, wo der Krieg nicht hin
Gekommen. O! das Leben, Vater,

510 Hat Reize, die wir nie gekannt. Wir haben
Des schönen Lebens öde Küste nur
Wie ein umirrend Räubervolk befahren,
Das, in sein dumpfig enges Schiff gepreßt,
Im wüsten Meer mit wüsten Sitten haust,

515 Vom großen Land nichts als die Buchten kennt,
Wo es die Diebeslandung wagen darf.
Was in den innern Thälern köstliches
Das Land verbirgt, o! davon, davon ist
Auf unsrer wilden Fahrt uns nichts erschienen.

Octavio (wird aufmerksam).

520 Und hätt' es diese Reise dir gezeigt?

Max.

Es war die erste Muße meines Lebens.
Sag' mir, was ist der Arbeit Ziel und Preis,
Der peinlichen, die mir die Jugend stahl,
Das Herz mir öde ließ und unerquickt

525 Den Geist, den keine Bildung noch geschmücket?
Denn dieses Lagers lärmendes Gewühl,
Der Pferde Wiehern, der Trompete Schmettern,

Des Dienstes immer gleichgestellte Uhr,
Die Waffenübung, das Commandowort, —
530 Dem Herzen gibt es nichts, dem lechzenden.
Die Seele fehlt dem nichtigen Geschäft,
Es gibt ein andres Glück und andre Freuden.

Octavio.
Viel lerntest du auf diesem kurzen Weg, mein Sohn!

Max.
O schöner Tag! wenn endlich der Soldat
535 Ins Leben heimkehrt, in die Menschlichkeit,
Zum frohen Zug die Fahnen sich entfalten,
Und heimwärts schlägt der sanfte Friedensmarsch.
Wenn alle Hüte sich und Helme schmücken
Mit grünen Maien, dem letzten Raub der Felder!
540 Der Städte Thore gehen auf, von selbst,
Nicht die Petarde braucht sie mehr zu sprengen;
Von Menschen sind die Wälle rings erfüllt,
Von friedlichen, die in die Lüfte grüßen;
Hell klingt von allen Thürmen das Geläut,
545 Des blut'gen Tages frohe Vesper schlagend.
Aus Dörfern und aus Städten wimmelnd strömt
Ein jauchzend Volk, mit liebend emsiger
Zudringlichkeit des Heeres Fortzug hindernd.
Da schüttelt, froh des noch erlebten Tags,
550 Dem heimgekehrten Sohn der Greis die Hände.
Ein Fremdling tritt er in sein Eigenthum,
Das längst verlaßne, ein; mit breiten Aesten
Deckt ihn der Baum bei seiner Wiederkehr,
Der sich zur Gerte bog, als er gegangen,
555 Und schamhaft tritt als Jungfrau ihm entgegen,

Die er einst an der Amme Brust verließ.
O! glücklich, wem dann auch sich eine Thür,
Sich zarte Arme sanft umschlingend öffnen —

Questenberg (gerührt).

O, daß Sie von so ferner, ferner Zeit,
560 Und nicht von morgen, nicht von heute sprechen!

Max.
(mit Heftigkeit sich zu ihm wendend)

Wer sonst ist schuld daran, als ihr in Wien?
Ich will's nur frei gestehen, Questenberg!
Als ich vorhin Sie stehen sah, es preßte
Der Unmuth mir das Innerste zusammen.
565 Ihr seid es, die den Frieden hindern, ihr!
Der Krieger ist's, der ihn erzwingen muß.
Dem Fürsten macht ihr's Leben sauer, macht
Ihm alle Schritte schwer, ihr schwärzt ihn an —
Warum? Weil an Europas großem Besten
570 Ihm mehr liegt als an ein paar Hufen Landes,
Die Oestreich mehr hat oder weniger.
Ihr macht ihn zum Empörer und Gott weiß
Zu was noch mehr, weil er die Sachsen schont,
Beim Feind Vertrauen zu erwecken sucht,
575 Das doch der einz'ge Weg zum Frieden ist;
Denn hört der Krieg im Kriege nicht schon auf,
Woher soll Friede kommen? Geht nur, geht!
Wie ich das Gute liebe, haß' ich euch;
Und hier gelob' ich's an, verspritzen will ich
580 Für ihn, für diesen Wallenstein, mein Blut,
Das letzte meines Herzens, tropfenweis', eh' daß
Ihr über seinen Fall frohlocken sollt! (Er geht ab.)

Act: 6.

Fünfter Auftritt.

Questenberg. Octavio Piccolomini.

Questenberg.

O weh uns! Steht es so?

(dringend und ungeduldig)

Freund, und wir lassen ihn in diesem Wahn

585 Dahingehn, rufen ihn nicht gleich

Zurück, daß wir die Augen auf der Stelle

Ihm öffnen?

Octavio.

(aus einem tiefen Nachdenken zu sich kommend)

Mir hat er sie jetzt geöffnet,

Und mehr erblick' ich, als mich freut.

Questenberg.

Was ist es, Freund?

Octavio.

Fluch über diese Reise!

Questenberg.

590 Wie so? Was ist es?

Octavio.

Kommen Sie! Ich muß

Sogleich die unglückselige Spur verfolgen,

Mit meinen Augen sehen. Kommen Sie!

(Will ihn fortführen.)

Questenberg.

Was denn? Wohin?

Octavio (pressiert).

Zu ihr!

Questenberg.

Zu —

Octavio (corrigiert sich).

Zum Herzog! Gehn wir! O! ich fürchte alles:
595 Ich seh' das Netz geworfen über ihn,
Er kommt mir nicht zurück, wie er gegangen.

Questenberg.

Erklären Sie mir nur —

Octavio.

Und konnt' ich's nicht
Vorhersehn? nicht die Reise hintertreiben?
Warum verschwieg ich's ihm? Sie hatten Recht.
600 Ich mußt' ihn warnen. Jetzo ist's zu spät.

Questenberg.

Was ist zu spät? Besinnen Sie sich, Freund,
Daß Sie in lauter Räthseln zu mir reden.

Octavio (gefaßter).

Wir gehn zum Herzog. Kommen Sie! Die Stunde
Rückt auch heran, die er zur Audienz
605 Bestimmt hat. Kommen Sie!
Verwünscht, dreimal verwünscht sei diese Reise!
(Er führt ihn weg, der Vorhang fällt.)

Zweiter Aufzug.

Saal beim Herzog von Friedland.

Erster Auftritt.

Bediente setzen Stühle und breiten Fußteppiche aus. Gleich darauf **Seni,** der Astrolog, wie ein italienischer Doctor schwarz und etwas phantastisch gekleidet. Er tritt in die Mitte des Saals, ein weißes Stäbchen in der Hand, womit er die Himmelsgegenden bezeichnet.

Bedienter.
(mit einem Rauchfaß herumgehend)

Greift an! Macht, daß ein Ende wird! Die Wache
Ruft ins Gewehr. Sie werden gleich erscheinen.

Zweiter Bedienter.

Warum denn aber ward die Erkerstube,
610 Die rothe, abbestellt, die doch so leuchtet?

Erster Bedienter.

Das frag' den Mathematicus. Der sagt,
Es sei ein Unglückszimmer.

Zweiter Bedienter.
Narrenspossen!

Das heißt die Leute scheren. Saal ist Saal.
Was kann der Ort viel zu bedeuten haben?

Seni (mit Gravität).
615 Mein Sohn, nichts in der Welt ist unbedeutend.

Das Erste aber und Hauptſächlichſte
Bei allem irb'ſchen Ding iſt Ort und Stunde.

Dritter Bedienter.

Laß dich mit dem nicht ein, Nathanael.
Muß ihm der Herr doch ſelbſt den Willen thun.

Seni (zählt die Stühle).

620 Elf! Eine böſe Zahl.   Zwölf Stühle ſetzt!
Zwölf Zeichen hat der Thierkreis, fünf und ſieben;
Die heil'gen Zahlen liegen in der Zwölfe.

Zweiter Bedienter.

Was habt ihr gegen Elf? Das laßt mich wiſſen.

Seni.

Elf iſt die Sünde.   Elfe überſchreitet
625 Die zehn Gebote.

Zweiter Bedienter.

                    So! Und warum nennt ihr
Die Fünfe eine heil'ge Zahl?

Seni.

                              Fünf iſt
Des Menſchen Seele.   Wie der Menſch aus Gutem
Und Böſem iſt gemiſcht, ſo iſt die Fünfe
Die erſte Zahl aus Grad' und Ungerade.

Erſter Bedienter.

630 Der Narr!

Dritter Bedienter.

            Ei, laß ihn doch! Ich hör' ihm gerne zu,
Denn mancherlei doch denkt ſich bei den Worten.

Zweiter Bedienter.

Hinweg! Sie kommen! Da, zur Seitenthür' hinaus!
(Sie eilen fort ; Seni folgt langſam.)

Zweiter Auftritt.

Wallenstein. Die Herzogin.

Wallenstein.

Nun, Herzogin, Sie haben Wien berührt,
Sich vorgestellt der Königin von Ungarn?

Herzogin.

635 Der Kaiserin auch. Bei beiden Majestäten
Sind wir zum Handkuß zugelassen worden.

Wallenstein.

Wie nahm man's auf, daß ich Gemahlin, Tochter
Zu dieser Winterszeit ins Feld beschieden?

Herzogin.

Ich that nach Ihrer Vorschrift, führte an,
640 Sie hätten über unser Kind bestimmt,
Und möchten gern dem künftigen Gemahl
Noch vor dem Feldzug die Verlobte zeigen.

Wallenstein.

Muthmaßte man die Wahl, die ich getroffen?

Herzogin.

Man wünschte wohl, sie möcht' auf keinen fremden,
645 Noch lutherischen Herrn gefallen sein.

Wallenstein.

Was wünschen Sie, Elisabeth?

Herzogin.

Ihr Wille, wissen Sie, war stets der meine.

Wallenstein (nach einer Pause).

Nun — Und wie war die Aufnahm' sonst am Hofe?
(Herzogin schlägt die Augen nieder und schweigt)
Verbergen Sie mir nichts! Wie war's damit?

Herzogin.

650 O mein Gemahl! Es ist nicht alles mehr
Wie sonst.   Es ist ein Wandel vorgegangen.

Wallenstein.

Wie? Ließ man's an der alten Achtung fehlen?

Herzogin.

Nicht an der Achtung.   Würdig und voll Anstand
War das Benehmen.   Aber an die Stelle
655 Huldreich vertraulicher Herablassung
War feierliche Förmlichkeit getreten.
Ach! und die zarte Schonung, die man zeigte,
Sie hatte mehr vom Mitleid als der Gunst.
Nein! Herzog Albrechts fürstliche Gemahlin,
660 Graf Harrachs edle Tochter, hätte so —
Nicht eben so empfangen werden sollen!

Wallenstein.

Man schalt gewiß mein neuestes Betragen.

Herzogin.

O hätte man's gethan! Ich bin's von lang her
Gewohnt, Sie zu entschuldigen, zufrieden
665 Zu sprechen die entrüsteten Gemüther.
Nein, niemand schalt Sie.   Man verhüllte sich
In ein so lastend feierliches Schweigen.
Ach! hier ist kein gewöhnlich Mißverständniß, keine
Vorübergehende Empfindlichkeit.
670 Etwas unglücklich unersetzliches ist
Geschehn! Sonst pflegte mich die Königin
Von Ungarn immer ihre liebe Muhme
Zu nennen, mich beim Abschied zu umarmen.

Wallenstein.

Jetzt unterließ sie's?

Herzogin.

(ihre Thränen trocknend, nach einer Pause)

Sie umarmte mich,

675 Doch erst, als ich den Urlaub schon genommen, schon
Der Thüre zuging, kam sie auf mich zu,
Schnell, als besänne sie sich erst, und drückte
Mich an den Busen, mehr mit schmerzlicher
Als zärtlicher Bewegung.

Wallenstein (ergreift ihre Hand).

Fassen Sie sich!

680 Wie war's mit Eggenberg, mit Liechtenstein
Und mit den andern Freunden?

Herzogin (den Kopf schüttelnd).

Keinen sah ich.

Wallenstein.

Und der hispanische Conte Ambassador,
Der sonst so warm für mich zu sprechen pflegte?

Herzogin.

Er hatte keine Zunge mehr für Sie.

Wallenstein.

685 Die Sonnen also scheinen uns nicht mehr,
Fortan muß eignes Feuer uns erleuchten.

Herzogin.

Und wär' es, theurer Herzog, wär's an dem,
Was man am Hofe leise flistert, sich
Im Lande laut erzählt, was Pater Lamormain

690 Durch einige Winke —

Wallenstein (schnell).

Lamormain! Was sagt der?

Herzogin.

Man zeihe Sie verwegner Ueberschreitung
Der anvertrauten Vollmacht, freventlicher
Verhöhnung höchster, kaiserlicher Befehle.
Die Spanier, der Baiern stolzer Herzog
695 Stehn auf als Kläger wider Sie,
Ein Ungewitter zieh' sich über Ihnen
Zusammen, noch weit drohender als jenes,
Das Sie vordem zu Regensburg gestürzt.
Man spreche, sagt er — ach! ich kann's nicht sagen —

Wallenstein (gespannt).

Nun?

Herzogin.

700 Von einer zweiten — (sie stockt)

Wallenstein.

Zweiten —

Herzogin.

Schimpflichern

— Absetzung.

Wallenstein.

Spricht man?
(heftig bewegt durch das Zimmer gehend)

O sie zwingen mich, sie stoßen
Gewaltsam, wider meinen Willen, mich hinein!

Herzogin.
(sich bittend an ihn schmiegend)

O wenn's noch Zeit ist, mein Gemahl, wenn es
Mit Unterwerfung, mit Nachgiebigkeit
705 Kann abgewendet werden, — geben Sie nach!
Gewinnen Sie's dem stolzen Herzen ab!
Es ist ihr Herr und Kaiser, dem Sie weichen.

O laſſen Sie es länger nicht geſchehn,
Daß hämiſche Bosheit Ihre gute Abſicht
710 Durch giftige, verhaßte Deutung ſchwärze!
Mit Siegeskraft der Wahrheit ſtehn Sie auf,
Die Lügner, die Verläumder zu beſchämen!
Wir haben ſo der guten Freunde wenig.
Sie wiſſen's! Unſer ſchnelles Glück hat uns
715 Dem Haß der Menſchen bloßgeſtellt. Was ſind wir,
Wenn kaiſerliche Huld ſich von uns wendet!

Dritter Auftritt.

Gräfin Terzky, welche die **Prinzeſſin Thekla** an der Hand führt, zu den
Vorigen.

Gräfin.

Wie, Schweſter? Von Geſchäften ſchon die Rede,
Und, wie ich ſeh', nicht von erfreulichen,
Eh' er noch ſeines Kindes froh geworden?
720 Der Freude gehört der erſte Augenblick.
Hier, Vater Friedland, das iſt deine Tochter!
(Thekla nähert ſich ihm ſchüchtern und will ſich auf ſeine Hand beugen; er
empfängt ſie in ſeinen Armen und bleibt einige Zeit in ihrem Anſchauen
verloren ſtehen.

Wallenstein.

Ja! Schön iſt mir die Hoffnung aufgegangen.
Ich nehme ſie zum Pfande größern Glücks.

Herzogin.

Ein zartes Kind noch war ſie, als Sie gingen,
725 Das große Heer dem Kaiſer aufzurichten.

Hernach, als Sie vom Feldzug heimgekehrt
Aus Pommern, war die Tochter schon im Stifte,
Wo sie geblieben ist bis jetzt.

Wallenstein.

         Indeß

Wir hier im Feld gesorgt, sie groß zu machen,
730 Das höchste Irdische ihr zu erfechten,
Hat Mutter Natur in stillen Klostermauren
Das ihrige gethan, dem lieben Kind
Aus freier Gunst das Göttliche gegeben,
Und führt sie ihrem glänzenden Geschick
735 Und meiner Hoffnung schön geschmückt entgegen.

Herzogin (zur Prinzessin).

Du hättest deinen Vater wohl nicht wieder
Erkannt, mein Kind? Kaum zähltest du acht Jahre,
Als du sein Angesicht zuletzt gesehn.

Thekla.

Doch, Mutter, auf den ersten Blick! Mein Vater
740 Hat nicht gealtert. Wie sein Bild in mir gelebt,
So steht er blühend jetzt vor meinen Augen.

Wallenstein (zur Herzogin).

Das holde Kind! Wie fein bemerkt und wie
Verständig! Sieh, ich zürnte mit dem Schicksal,
Daß mir's den Sohn versagt, der meines Namens
745 Und meines Glückes Erbe könnte sein,
In einer stolzen Linie von Fürsten
Mein schnell verlöschtes Dasein weiter leiten.
Ich that dem Schicksal Unrecht. Hier auf dieses
Jungfräulich blühende Haupt will ich den Kranz

750 Des kriegerischen Lebens niederlegen;
Nicht für verloren acht' ich's, wenn ich's einst,
In einen königlichen Schmuck verwandelt,
Um diese schöne Stirne flechten kann.

(Er hält sie in seinen Armen, wie Piccolomini hereintritt.)

Vierter Auftritt.

Max Piccolomini und bald darauf Graf Terzky zu den Vorigen.

Gräfin.

Da kommt der Paladin, der uns beschützte.

Wallenstein.

755 Sei mir willkommen, Max! Stets warst du mir
Der Bringer irgend einer schönen Freude,
Und, wie das glückliche Gestirn des Morgens,
Führst du die Lebenssonne mir herauf.

Max.

Mein General —

Wallenstein.

Bis jetzt war es der Kaiser,
760 Der dich durch meine Hand belohnt. Heut' hast du
Den Vater dir, den glücklichen, verpflichtet,
Und diese Schuld muß Friedland selbst bezahlen.

Max.

Mein Fürst! Du eiltest sehr, sie abzutragen.
Ich komme mit Beschämung, ja, mit Schmerz;
765 Denn kaum bin ich hier angelangt, hab' Mutter
Und Tochter deinen Armen überliefert,
So wird aus deinem Marstall, reich geschirrt,

Ein prächt'ger Jagdzug mir von dir gebracht,
Für die gehabte Müh' mich abzulohnen.

770 Ja, ja, mich abzulohnen! Eine Müh',
Ein Amt bloß war's! Nicht eine Gunst, für die
Ich's vorschnell nahm und dir schon volles Herzens
Zu danken kam. Nein, so war's nicht gemeint,
Daß mein Geschäft mein schönstes Glück sein sollte!

(Terzky tritt herein und übergibt dem Herzog Briefe, welche dieser schnell erbricht.)

Gräfin (zu Max).

775 Belohnt er Ihre Mühe? Seine Freude
Vergilt er Ihnen. Ihnen steht es an,
So zart zu denken; meinem Schwager ziemt's,
Sich immer groß und fürstlich zu beweisen.

Thekla.

So müßt' auch ich an seiner Liebe zweifeln,

780 Denn seine gütigen Hände schmückten mich,
Noch eh' das Herz des Vaters mir gesprochen.

Max.

Ja, er muß immer geben und beglücken!

(er ergreift der Herzogin Hand; mit steigender Wärme)

Was dank' ich ihm nicht alles! O was sprech' ich
Nicht alles aus in diesem theuren Namen Friedland!

785 Zeitlebens soll ich ein Gefangner sein
Von diesem Namen, darin blühen soll
Mir jedes Glück und jede schöne Hoffnung,
Fest, wie in einem Zauberringe, hält
Das Schicksal mich gebannt in diesem Namen!

Gräfin.

(welche unterdessen den Herzog sorgfältig beobachtet, bemerkt, daß er bei den Briefen nachdenkend geworden)

790 Der Bruder will allein sein. Laßt uns gehen.

Wallenstein.
(wendet sich schnell um, faßt sich und spricht heiter zur Herzogin)

Noch einmal, Fürstin, heiß' ich Sie im Feld willkommen.
Sie sind die Wirthin dieses Hofs.   Du, Max,
Wirst diesmal noch dein altes Amt verwalten,
Indeß wir hier des Herrn Geschäfte treiben.
(Max Piccolomini bietet der Herzogin den Arm, Gräfin führt die Prinzessin ab.)

Terzky (ihm nachrufend).
795 Versäumt nicht, der Versammlung beizuwohnen.

Fünfter Auftritt.

Wallenstein. Terzky.

Wallenstein.
(in tiefem Nachdenken zu sich selbst)

Sie hat ganz recht gesehn.   So ist's, und stimmt
Vollkommen zu den übrigen Berichten.
Sie haben ihren letzten Schluß gefaßt
In Wien, mir den Nachfolger schon gegeben.
800 Der Ungarn König ist's, der Ferdinand,
Des Kaisers Söhnlein, der ist jetzt ihr Heiland,
Das neu aufgehende Gestirn! Mit uns
Gedenkt man fertig schon zu sein, und wie
Ein Abgeschiedner sind wir schon beerbet.
805 Drum keine Zeit verloren!
(indem er sich umwendet, bemerkt er den Terzky und gibt ihm einen Brief)
Graf Altringer läßt sich entschuldigen,
Auch Gallas; das gefällt mir nicht.

Terzky.

        Und wenn du
Noch länger säumst, bricht einer nach dem andern.

Wallenstein.

Der Altringer hat die Tiroler Pässe;
810 Ich muß ihm einen schicken, daß er mir
Die Spanier aus Mailand nicht herein läßt.
Nun, der Sesin, der alte Unterhändler,
Hat sich ja kürzlich wieder blicken lassen.
Was bringt er uns vom Grafen Thurn?

Terzky.

       Der Graf entbietet dir,
815 Er hab' den schweb'schen Kanzler aufgesucht
Zu Halberstadt, wo jetzo der Convent ist;
Der aber sagt, er sei es müd', und wolle
Nichts weiter mehr mit dir zu schaffen haben.

Wallenstein.

Wie so?

Terzky.

    Es sei dir nimmer Ernst mit deinen Reden,
820 Du wollst die Schweden nur zum Narren haben,
Dich mit den Sachsen gegen sie verbinden,
Am Ende sie mit einem elenden Stück Geldes
Abfertigen.

Wallenstein.

    So! Meint er wohl, ich soll ihm
Ein schönes deutsches Land zum Raube geben,
825 Daß wir zuletzt auf eignem Grund und Boden
Selbst nicht mehr Herren sind? Sie müssen fort,
Fort, fort! Wir brauchen keine solche Nachbarn.

Terzky.

Gönn' ihnen doch das Fleckchen Land! Geht's ja
Nicht von dem deinen! Was bekümmert's dich,
30 Wenn du das Spiel gewinnest, wer es zahlt?

Wallenstein.

Fort, fort mit ihnen!   Das verstehst du nicht.
Es soll nicht von mir heißen, daß ich Deutschland
Zerstücket hab', verrathen an den Fremdling,
Um meine Portion mir zu erschleichen.
35 Mich soll das Reich als seinen Schirmer ehren,
Reichsfürstlich mich erweisend, will ich würdig
Mich bei des Reiches Fürsten niedersetzen.
Es soll im Reiche keine fremde Macht
Mir Wurzel fassen, und am wenigsten
40 Die Gothen sollen's, diese Hungerleider,
Die nach dem Segen unsers deutschen Landes
Mit Neidesblicken raubbegierig schauen.
Beistehen sollen sie mir in meinen Planen,
Und dennoch nichts dabei zu fischen haben.

Terzky.

45 Doch mit den Sachsen willst du ehrlicher
Verfahren? Sie verlieren die Geduld,
Weil du so krumme Wege machst.
Was sollen alle diese Masken? Sprich!
Die Freunde zweifeln, werden irr' an dir;
50 Der Oxenstirn, der Arnheim, keiner weiß,
Was er von deinem Zögern halten soll.
Am End' bin ich der Lügner; alles geht
Durch mich.   Ich hab' nicht einmal deine Handschrift.

Wallenstein.

Ich geb' nichts schriftliches von mir, du weißt's.

Terzky.

853 Woran erkennt man aber deinen Ernst,
Wenn auf das Wort die That nicht folgt? Sag' selbst,
Was du bisher verhandelt mit dem Feind,
Hätt' alles auch recht gut geschehn sein können,
Wenn du nichts mehr damit gewollt, als ihn
860 Zum besten haben.

Wallenstein.
(nach einer Pause, indem er ihn scharf ansieht:)

Und woher weißt du, daß ich ihn nicht wirklich
Zum besten habe? daß ich nicht euch alle
Zum besten habe? Kennst du mich so gut?
Ich wüßte nicht, daß ich mein Innerstes
865 Dir aufgethan!   Der Kaiser, es ist wahr,
Hat übel mich behandelt.   W e n n ich wollte,
Ich könnt' ihm recht viel Böses dafür thun.
Es macht mir Freude, meine Macht zu kennen;
Ob ich sie wirklich brauchen werde, d a v o n, denk' ich,
870 Weißt d u nicht mehr zu sagen, als ein andrer.

Terzky.

So hast du stets dein Spiel mit uns getrieben!

Sechster Auftritt.

Illo zu den Vorigen.

Wallenstein.

Wie steht es draußen? Sind sie vorbereitet?

Illo.

Du findest sie in der Stimmung, wie du wünschest.
Sie wissen um des Kaisers Forderungen
875 Und toben.

Wallenstein.

Wie erklärt sich Isolan?

Illo.

Der ist mit Leib und Seele dein, seitdem du
Die Pharobank ihm wieder aufgerichtet.

Wallenstein.

Wie nimmt sich der Colalto? Hast du dich
Des Deodat und Tiefenbach versichert?

Illo.

880 Was Piccolomini thut, das thun sie auch.

Wallenstein.

So, meinst du, kann ich was mit ihnen wagen?

Illo.

Wenn du der Piccolomini gewiß bist.

Wallenstein.

Wie meiner selbst.   D i e lassen nie von mir.

Terzky.

Doch wollt' ich, daß du dem Octavio,
885 Dem Fuchs, nicht so viel trautest.

Wallenftein.

Lehre du
Mich meine Leute kennen! Sechzehnmal
Bin ich zu Feld gezogen mit dem Alten,
Zudem ich hab' sein Horoſkop geſtellt,
Wir ſind geboren unter gleichen Sternen,
890 Und kurz —

(geheimnißvoll)

Es hat damit ſein eigenes Bewenden.
Wenn du mir alſo gut ſagſt für die andern —

Illo.

Es iſt nur e i n e Stimme unter allen:
Du dürfſt das Regiment nicht niederlegen.
Sie werden an dich deputieren, hör' ich. |

Wallenftein.

895 Wenn ich mich gegen ſ i e verpflichten ſoll,
So müſſen ſie's auch gegen mich.

Illo.

Verſteht ſich.

Wallenftein.

Parole müſſen ſie mir geben, eidlich, ſchriftlich,
Sich meinem Dienſt zu weihen, u n b e d i n g t.

Illo.

Warum nicht?

Terzky.

Unbedingt? Des Kaiſers Dienſt,
900 Die Pflichten gegen Oeſtreich werden ſie
Sich immer vorbehalten.

Wallenftein (den Kopf ſchüttelnd).

Unbedingt
Muß ich ſie haben. Nichts von Vorbehalt!

Illo.

Ich habe einen Einfall. Gibt uns nicht
Graf Terzky ein Bankett heut' Abend?

Terzky.

Ja,

905 Und alle Generale sind geladen.

Illo (zum Wallenstein).

Sag'! Willst du völlig freie Hand mir lassen?
Ich schaffe dir das Wort der Generale,
So wie du's wünschest.

Wallenstein.

Schaff' mir ihre Handschrift.
Wie du dazu gelangen magst, ist deine Sache.

Illo.

910 Und wenn ich dir's nun bringe, schwarz auf weiß,
Daß alle Chefs, die hier zugegen sind,
Dir blind sich überliefern, willst du dann
Ernst machen endlich, mit beherzter That
Das Glück versuchen?

Wallenstein.

Schaff' mir die Verschreibung!

Illo.

915 Bedenke, was du thust! Du kannst des Kaisers
Begehren nicht erfüllen, kannst das Heer
Nicht schwächen lassen, nicht die Regimenter
Zum Spanier stoßen lassen, willst du nicht
Die Macht auf ewig aus den Händen geben.

920 Bedenk' das andre auch! Du kannst des Kaisers
Befehl und ernste Ordre nicht verhöhnen,
Nicht länger Ausflucht suchen, temporisieren,

Willst du nicht förmlich brechen mit dem Hof.
Entschließ dich! Willst du mit entschloßner That
925 Zuvor ihm kommen? Willst du, ferner zögernd,
Das Aeußerste erwarten?

Wallenstein.

Das geziemt sich,
Eh' man das Aeußerste beschließt!

Illo.

O nimm der Stunde wahr, eh' sie entschlüpft!
So selten kommt der Augenblick im Leben,
930 Der wahrhaft wichtig ist und groß. Wo eine
Entscheidung soll geschehen, da muß vieles
Sich glücklich treffen und zusammenfinden;
Und einzeln nur, zerstreuet zeigen sich
Des Glückes Fäden, die Gelegenheiten,
935 Die, nur in einen Lebenspunkt zusammen
Gedrängt, den schweren Früchteknoten bilden.
Sieh, wie entscheidend, wie verhängnißvoll
Sich's jetzt um dich zusammenzieht! Die Häupter
Des Heers, die besten, trefflichsten, um dich,
940 Den königlichen Führer, her versammelt!
Nur deinen Wink erwarten sie! O laß
Sie so nicht wieder auseinander gehen!
So einig führst du sie im ganzen Lauf
Des Krieges nicht zum zweitenmal zusammen.
945 Die hohe Flut ist's, die das schwere Schiff
Vom Strande hebt, und jedem einzelnen
Wächst das Gemüth im großen Strom der Menge.
Jetzt hast du sie, jetzt noch! Bald sprengt der Krieg
Sie wieder auseinander, dahin, dorthin;

950 In eignen kleinen Sorgen und Int'ressen
Zerstreut sich der gemeine Geist.   Wer heute,
Vom Strome fortgerissen, sich vergißt,
Wird nüchtern werden, sieht er sich allein,
Nur seine Ohnmacht fühlen und geschwind
955 Umlenken in die alte, breitgetret'ne
Fahrstraße der gemeinen Pflicht, nur wohl-
Behalten unter Dach zu kommen suchen.

Wallenstein.

Die Zeit ist noch nicht da.

Terzky.

So sagst du immer.
Wann aber wird es Zeit sein?

Wallenstein.

Wenn ich's sage.

Illo.

960 O! du wirst auf die Sternenstunde warten,
Bis dir die irdische entflieht! Glaub' mir,
In deiner Brust sind deines Schicksals Sterne!
Vertrauen zu dir selbst, Entschlossenheit
Ist deine Venus! Der Maleficus,
965 Der einz'ge, der dir schadet, ist der Zweifel.

Wallenstein.

Du red'st, wie du's verstehst.   Wie oft und vielmals
Erklärt' ich dir's! Dir stieg der Jupiter
Hinab bei der Geburt, der helle Gott;
Du kannst in die Geheimnisse nicht schauen.
970 Nur in der Erde magst du finster wühlen,
Blind, wie der Unterirdische, der mit dem bleichen

Bleifarb'nen Schein ins Leben dir geleuchtet.
Das Irdische, Gemeine magst du sehn,
Das Nächste mit dem Nächsten klug verknüpfen;
975 Darin vertrau' ich dir und glaube dir.
Doch was geheimnißvoll bedeutend webt
Und bildet in den Tiefen der Natur,
Die Geisterleiter, die aus dieser Welt des Staubes
Bis in die Sternenwelt mit tausend Sprossen
980 Hinauf sich baut, an der die himmlischen
Gewalten wirkend auf und nieder wandeln,
Die Kreise in den Kreisen, die sich eng'
Und enger ziehn um die centralische Sonne, —
Die sieht das Aug' nur, das entsiegelte,
985 Der hellgebornen, heitern Joviskinder.

(nachdem er einen Gang durch den Saal gemacht, bleibt er stehen und fährt fort)

Die himmlischen Gestirne machen nicht
Bloß Tag und Nacht, Frühling und Sommer, nicht
Dem Sä'mann bloß bezeichnen sie die Zeiten
Der Aussaat und der Ernte. Auch des Menschen Thun
990 Ist eine Aussaat von Verhängnissen,
Gestreuet in der Zukunft dunkles Land,
Den Schicksalsmächten hoffend übergeben.
Da thut es noth, die Saatzeit zu erkunden,
Die rechte Sternenstunde auszulesen,
995 Des Himmels Häuser forschend zu durchspüren,
Ob nicht der Feind des Wachsens und Gedeihens
In seinen Ecken schadend sich verberge.
Drum laßt mir Zeit. Thut ihr indeß das eure.
Ich kann jetzt noch nicht sagen, was ich thun will.
1000 Nachgeben aber werd' ich nicht. Ich nicht!

Absetzen sollen sie mich auch nicht.   Darauf
Verlaßt euch.

Kammerdiener (kommt).
Die Herr'n Generale.

Wallenstein.
Laß sie kommen.

Terzky.
Willst du, daß alle Chefs zugegen seien?

Wallenstein.
Das braucht's nicht.   Beide Piccolomini,
1005 Maradas, Buttler, Forgatsch, Deodat,
Caraffa, Isolani mögen kommen.
(Terzky geht hinaus mit dem Kammerdiener.)

Wallenstein (zu Illo).
Hast du den Questenberg bewachen lassen?
Sprach er nicht ein'ge in geheim?

Illo.
Ich hab' ihn scharf bewacht.   Er war mit niemand
1010 Als dem Octavio.

Siebenter Auftritt.

**Vorige, Questenberg, beide Piccolomini, Buttler, Isolani, Maradas und
noch drei andere Generale treten herein.   Auf den Wink des Generals nimmt
Questenberg ihm gerad' gegenüber Platz, die andern folgen nach ihrem Range.
Es herrscht eine augenblickliche Stille.**

Wallenstein.
Ich hab' den Inhalt Ihrer Sendung zwar
Vernommen, Questenberg, und wohl erwogen,
Auch meinen Schluß gefaßt, den nichts mehr ändert.

Doch es gebührt sich, daß die Commandeurs
1015 Aus Ihrem Mund des Kaisers Willen hören.
Gefall' es Ihnen denn, sich Ihres Auftrags
Vor diesen edeln Häuptern zu entledigen.

Questenberg.

Ich bin bereit, doch bitt' ich zu bedenken,
Daß kaiserliche Herrschgewalt und Würde
1020 Aus meinem Munde spricht, nicht eigne Kühnheit.

Wallenstein.

Den Eingang spart.

Questenberg.

            Als Seine Majestät,
Der Kaiser, Ihren muthigen Armeen
Ein ruhmgekröntes, kriegserfahrnes Haupt
Geschenkt in der Person des Herzogs Friedland,
1025 Geschah's in froher Zuversicht, das Glück
Des Krieges schnell und günstig umzuwenden.
Auch war der Anfang Ihren Wünschen hold,
Gereiniget ward Böheim von den Sachsen,
Der Schweden Siegeslauf gehemmt; es schöpften
1030 Auf's neue leichten Athem diese Länder,
Als Herzog Friedland die zerstreuten Feindesheere
Herbei von allen Strömen Deutschlands zog,
Herbei auf e i n e n Sammelplatz beschwor
Den Rheingraf, Bernhard, Banner, Oxenstirn,
1035 Und jenen nie besiegten König selbst,
Um endlich hier im Angesichte Nürnbergs
Das blutig große Kampfspiel zu entscheiden.

Wallenstein.

Zur Sache, wenn's beliebt.

Questenberg.

Ein neuer Geist
Verkündigte sogleich den neuen Feldherrn.
1040 Nicht blinde Wuth mehr rang mit blinder Wuth,
In hellgeschiednem Kampfe sah man jetzt
Die Festigkeit der Kühnheit widerstehn,
Und weise Kunst die Tapferkeit ermüden.
Vergebens lockt man ihn zur Schlacht; er gräbt
1045 Sich tief und tiefer nur im Lager ein,
Als gält' es, hier ein ewig Haus zu gründen.
Verzweifelnd endlich will der König stürmen,
Zur Schlachtbank reißt er seine Völker hin,
Die ihm des Hungers und der Seuchen Wuth
1050 Im leichenvollen Lager langsam tödtet.
Durch den Verhack des Lagers, hinter welchem
Der Tod aus tausend Röhren lauert, will
Der Niegehemmte stürmend Bahn sich brechen.
Da ward ein Angriff und ein Widerstand,
1055 Wie ihn kein glücklich Auge noch gesehn.
Zerrissen endlich führt sein Volk der König
Vom Kampfplatz heim, und nicht ein Fußbreit Erde
Gewann es ihm, das grause Menschenopfer.

Wallenstein.

Ersparen Sie's, uns aus dem Zeitungsblatt
1060 Zu melden, was wir schaudernd selbst erlebt.

Questenberg.

Anklagen ist mein Amt und meine Sendung,
Es ist mein Herz, was gern beim Lob verweilt.
In Nürnbergs Lager ließ der schwedische König
Den Ruhm, in Lützens Ebenen das Leben.

1065 Doch wer erstaunte nicht, als Herzog Friedland
Nach diesem großen Tag, wie ein Besiegter,
Nach Böheim floh, vom Kriegesschauplatz schwand,
Indeß der junge Weimarische Held
Ins Frankenland unaufgehalten drang,

1070 Bis an die Donau reißend Bahn sich machte,
Und stand mit einemmal vor Regensburg,
Zum Schrecken aller gut kathol'schen Christen.
Da rief der Baiern wohlverdienter Fürst
Um schnelle Hilf' in seiner höchsten Noth,

1075 Es schickt der Kaiser sieben Reitende
An Herzog Friedland ab mit dieser Bitte,
Und fleht, wo er als Herr befehlen kann.
Umsonst! Es hört in diesem Augenblick
Der Herzog nur den alten Haß und Groll,

1080 Gibt das gemeine Beste preis, die Rachgier
An einem alten Feinde zu vergnügen.
Und so fällt Regensburg!

Wallenstein.

Von welcher Zeit ist denn die Rede, Max?
Ich hab' gar kein Gedächtniß mehr.

Max.

Er meint,

1085 Wie wir in Schlesien waren.

Wallenstein.

So! So! So!
Was aber hatten wir denn dort zu thun?

Max.

Die Schweden d'raus zu schlagen und die Sachsen.

Wallenstein.

Recht! Ueber der Beschreibung da vergeß' ich
Den ganzen Krieg — (zu Questenberg)
                        Nur weiter fortgefahren!

Questenberg.

1090 Am Oderstrom vielleicht gewann man wieder,
Was an der Donau schimpflich ward verloren.
Erstaunenswerthe Dinge hoffte man
Auf dieser Kriegesbühne zu erleben,
Wo Friedland in Person zu Felde zog,
1095 Der Nebenbuhler Gustavs einen — Thurn
Und einen Arnheim vor sich fand. Und wirklich
Gerieth man nahe g'nug hier aneinander,
Doch um als Freund, als Gast sich zu bewirthe...
Ganz Deutschland seufzte unter Kriegeslast,
1100 Doch Friede war's im Wallensteinischen Lager.

Wallenstein.

Manch blutig Treffen wird um nichts gefochten,
Weil einen Sieg der junge Feldherr braucht.
Ein Vortheil des bewährten Feldherrn ist's,
Daß er nicht nöthig hat zu schlagen, um
1105 Der Welt zu zeigen, er versteh' zu siegen.
Mir konnt' es wenig helfen, meines Glücks
Mich über einen Arnheim zu bedienen;
Viel nützte Deutschland meine Mäßigung,
Wär' mir's geglückt, das Bündniß zwischen Sachsen
1110 Und Schweden, das verderbliche, zu lösen.

Questenberg.

Es glückte aber nicht, und so begann
Aufs neu das blut'ge Kriegesspiel. Hier endlich

Rechtfertigte der Fürst den alten Ruhm.
Auf Steinaus Feldern streckt das schwedische Heer
1115 Die Waffen, ohne Schwertstreich überwunden,
Und hier, mit andern, lieferte des Himmels
Gerechtigkeit den alten Aufruhrstifter,
Die fluchbeladne Fackel dieses Kriegs,
Matthias Thurn, des Rächers Händen aus.
1120 Doch in großmüth'ge Hand wär er gefallen,
Statt Strafe fand er Lohn, und reich beschenkt
Entließ der Fürst den Erzfeind seines Kaisers.

Wallenstein (lacht).

Ich weiß, ich weiß.   Sie hatten schon in Wien
Die Fenster, die Balcons voraus gemiethet,
1125 Ihn auf dem Armensünderkarrn zu sehn.
Die Schlacht hätt' ich mit Schimpf verlieren mögen,
Doch das vergeben mir die Wiener nicht,
Daß ich um ein Spektakel sie betrog!

Questenberg.

Befreit war Schlesien, und alles rief
1130 Den Herzog nun ins hartbedrängte Baiern.
Er setzt auch wirklich sich in Marsch, gemächlich
Durchzieht er Böheim auf dem längsten Wege;
Doch eh' er noch den Feind gesehen, wendet
Er schleunig um, bezieht sein Winterlager, drückt
1135 Des Kaisers Länder mit des Kaisers Heer.

Wallenstein.

Das Heer war zum Erbarmen, jede Nothdurft, jede
Bequemlichkeit gebrach, der Winter kam.
Was denkt die Majestät von Ihren Truppen?
Sind wir nicht Menschen? nicht der Kält' und Nässe,

1140 Nicht jeder Nothdurft sterblich unterworfen?
Fluchwürdig Schicksal des Soldaten! Wo
Er hinkommt, flieht man vor ihm; wo er weggeht,
Verwünscht man ihn! Er muß sich alles nehmen;
Man gibt ihm nichts, und, jeglichem gezwungen
1145 Zu nehmen, ist er jeglichem ein Gräuel.
Hier stehen meine Generals. Caraffa!
Graf Deodati! Buttler! Sagt es ihm,
Wie lang' der Sold den Truppen ausgeblieben?

Buttler.

Ein Jahr schon fehlt die Löhnung.

Wallenstein.

Und sein Sold
1150 Muß dem Soldaten werden; darnach heißt er!

Questenberg.

Das klingt ganz anders, als der Fürst von Friedland
Vor acht, neun Jahren sich vernehmen ließ.

Wallenstein.

Ja, meine Schuld ist es, weiß wohl, ich selbst
Hab' mir den Kaiser so verwöhnt. Da! Vor neun Jahren,
1155 Beim Dänenkriege, stellt' ich eine Macht ihm auf
Von vierzigtausend Köpfen oder fünfzig,
Die aus dem eignen Säckel keinen Deut
Ihm kostete. Durch Sachsens Kreise zog
Die Kriegesfurie, bis an die Scheren
1160 Des Belts den Schrecken seines Namens tragend.
Da war noch eine Zeit! Im ganzen Kaiserstaate
Kein Nam' geehrt, gefeiert, wie der meine,
Und Albrecht Wallenstein, so hieß
Der dritte Edelstein, in seiner Krone!

1165 Doch auf dem Regensburger Fürstentag,
Da brach es auf! Da lag es kund und offen,
Aus welchem Beutel ich gewirthschaft't hatte.
Und was war nun mein Dank dafür, daß ich,
Ein treuer Fürstenknecht, der Völker Fluch.
1170 Auf mich gebürdet, diesen Krieg, der nur
Ihn groß gemacht, die Fürsten zahlen lassen?
Was? Aufgeopfert wurd' ich ihren Klagen,
— Abgesetzt wurd' ich!

Questenberg.

Eure Gnaden weiß,
Wie sehr auf jenem unglücksvollen Reichstag
1175 Die Freiheit ihm gemangelt.

Wallenstein.

Tod und Teufel!
Ich hatte, was ihm Freiheit schaffen konnte.
Nein, Herr! Seitdem es mir so schlecht bekam,
Dem Thron zu dienen auf des Reiches Kosten,
Hab' ich vom Reich ganz anders denken lernen.
1180 Vom Kaiser freilich hab' ich diesen Stab,
Doch führ' ich jetzt ihn als des Reiches Feldherr,
Zur Wohlfahrt aller, zu des Ganzen Heil,
Und nicht mehr zur Vergrößerung des Einen!
Zur Sache doch.   Was ist's, das man von mir begehrt?

Questenberg.

1185 Fürs erste wollen Seine Majestät,
Daß die Armee ohn' Aufschub Böhmen räume.

Wallenstein.

In dieser Jahreszeit? Und wohin will man,
Daß wir uns wenden?

II. Aufzug, 7. Auftritt.

Questenberg.

Dahin, wo der Feind ist.
Denn Seine Majestät will Regensburg
1190 Vor Ostern noch vom Feind gesäubert sehn,
Daß länger nicht im Dome lutherisch
Gepredigt werde, ketzerischer Gräu'l
Des Festes reine Feier nicht besudle.

Wallenstein.

Kann das geschehen, meine Generals?

Illo.

1195 Es ist nicht möglich.

Buttler.

Es kann nicht geschehn.

Questenberg.

Der Kaiser hat auch schon dem Oberst Suys
Befehl geschickt, nach Baiern vorzurücken.

Wallenstein.

Was that der Suys?

Questenberg.

Was er schuldig war.
Er rückte vor.

Wallenstein.

Er rückte vor! Und ich,
1200 Sein Chef, gab ihm Befehl, ausdrücklichen,
Nicht von dem Platz zu weichen! Steht es so
Um mein Commando? Das ist der Gehorsam,
Den man mir schuldig, ohne den kein Kriegsstand
Zu denken ist? Sie, meine Generale,
1205 Seien Richter! Was verdient der Officier,
Der eidvergessen seine Ordre bricht?

131

Illo.

Den Tod!

Wallenstein.

(da die Uebrigen bedenklich schweigen, mit erhöhter Stimme)

Graf Piccolomini, was hat er
Verdient?

Max (nach einer langen Pause).

Nach des Gesetzes Wort — der Tod!

Isolani.

Den Tod!

Buttler.

Den Tod nach Kriegesrecht!

(Questenberg steht auf. Wallenstein folgt, es erheben sich alle.)

Wallenstein.

1210 Dazu verdammt ihn das Gesetz, nicht ich!
Und wenn ich ihn begnadige, geschieht's
Aus schuld'ger Achtung gegen meinen Kaiser.

Questenberg.

Wenn's so steht, hab' ich hier nichts mehr zu sagen.

Wallenstein.

Nur auf Bedingung nahm ich dies Commando;
1215 Und gleich die erste war, daß mir zum Nachtheil
Kein Menschenkind, auch selbst der Kaiser nicht,
Bei der Armee zu sagen haben sollte.
Wenn für den Ausgang ich mit meiner Ehre
Und meinem Kopf soll haften, muß ich Herr
1220 Darüber sein. Was machte diesen Gustav
Unwiderstehlich, unbesiegt auf Erden?
Dies: daß er König war in seinem Heer!
Ein König aber, einer, der es ist,
Ward nie besiegt noch, als durch seinesgleichen.
1225 Jedoch zur Sach'! Das Beste soll noch kommen.

Questenberg.

Der Cardinal-Infant wird mit dem Frühjahr
Aus Mailand rücken und ein spanisch Heer
Durch Deutschland nach den Niederlanden führen.
Damit er sicher seinen Weg verfolge,
130 Will der Monarch, daß hier aus der Armee
Acht Regimenter ihn zu Pferd begleiten.

Wallenstein.

Ich merk', ich merk'.   Acht Regimenter! Wohl,
Wohl ausgesonnen, Pater Lamormain!
Wär' der Gedank' nicht so verwünscht gescheid,
135 Man wär' versucht, ihn herzlich dumm zu nennen.
Achttausend Pferde! Ja, ja! es ist richtig,
Ich seh' es kommen.

Questenberg.

Es ist nichts dahinter
Zu sehn.   Die Klugheit räth's, die Noth gebeut's.

Wallenstein.

Wie, mein Herr Abgesandter? Ich soll's wohl
140 Nicht merken, daß man's müde ist, die Macht,
Des Schwertes Griff in meiner Hand zu sehn?
Daß man begierig diesen Vorwand hascht,
Den span'schen Namen braucht, mein Volk zu mindern,
Ins Reich zu führen eine neue Macht,
145 Die mir nicht untergeben sei.   Mich so
Gerad' bei Seit' zu werfen, dazu bin ich
Euch noch zu mächtig.   Mein Vertrag erheischt's,
Daß alle Kaiserheere mir gehorchen,
So weit die deutsche Sprach' geredet wird.

1250 Von span'schen Truppen aber und Infanten,
　　　Die durch das Reich als Gäste wandernd ziehn,
　　　Steht im Vertrage nichts.　Da kommt man denn
　　　So in der Stille hinter ihm herum,
　　　Macht mich erst schwächer, dann entbehrlich, bis
1255 Man kürzeren Prozeß kann mit mir machen.
　　　Wozu die krummen Wege, Herr Minister?
　　　Gerad' heraus! Den Kaiser drückt das Pactum
　　　Mit mir.　Er möchte gerne, daß ich ginge.
　　　Ich will ihm den Gefallen thun; das war
1260 Beschloßne Sache, Herr, noch eh' Sie kamen.
　　　(es entsteht eine Bewegung unter den Generalen, welche immer zunimmt)
　　　Es thut mir leid um meine Obersten;
　　　Noch seh' ich nicht, wie sie zu ihren vorgeschoßnen Geldern,
　　　Zum wohlverdienten Lohne kommen werden.
　　　Neu Regiment bringt neue Menschen auf,
1265 Und früheres Verdienst veraltet schnell.
　　　Es dienen viel Ausländische im Heer,
　　　Und war der Mann nur sonsten brav und tüchtig,
　　　Ich pflegte eben nicht nach seinem Stammbaum,
　　　Noch seinem Katechismus viel zu fragen.
1270 Das wird auch anders werden künftighin!
　　　Nun — mich geht's nichts mehr an.

　　　　　　　　　　　　　　　　　(Er setzt sich.)

Max.

　　　　　　　　　　　　　Da sei Gott für,
　　　Daß es bis dahin kommen soll!　Die ganze
　　　Armee wird furchtbar gährend sich erheben!
　　　Der Kaiser wird mißbraucht, es kann nicht sein.

Isolani.

1275 Es kann nicht sein, denn alles ging' zu Trümmern.

Wallenstein.

Das wird es, treuer Isolan. Zu Trümmern
Wird alles gehn, was wir bedächtig bauten.
Deßwegen aber find't sich doch ein Feldherr,
Und auch ein Kriegsheer läuft noch wohl dem Kaiser
180 Zusammen, wenn die Trommel wird geschlagen.

Max.
(geschäftig, leidenschaftlich von einem zum andern gehend und sie besänftigend)

Hör' mich, mein Feldherr! Hört mich, Obersten!
Laß dich beschwören, Fürst! Beschließe nichts,
Bis wir zusammen Rath gehalten, dir
Vorstellungen gethan. Kommt, meine Freunde!
185 Ich hoff', es ist noch alles herzustellen.

Terzky.

Kommt, kommt! im Vorsaal treffen wir die andern.
(Gehen.)

Buttler (zu Questenberg).

Wenn guter Rath Gehör bei Ihnen findet,
Vermeiden Sie's, in diesen ersten Stunden
Sich öffentlich zu zeigen, schwerlich möchte Sie
190 Der goldne Schlüssel vor Mißhandlung schützen.
(Laute Bewegungen draußen.)

Wallenstein.

Der Rath ist gut. Octavio, du wirst
Für unsers Gastes Sicherheit mir haften.
Gehaben Sie sich wohl, von Questenberg!
(als dieser reden will)

Nichts, nichts von dem verhaßten Gegenstand,
195 Sie thaten Ihre Schuldigkeit. Ich weiß
Den Mann von seinem Amt zu unterscheiden.
(Indem Questenberg mit dem Octavio abgehen will, dringen Götz, Tiefenbach, Colalto herein, denen noch mehrere Commandeurs folgen.)

Göt.

Wo ist er, der uns unsern General —

Tiefenbach (zugleich).

Was müssen wir erfahren, du willst uns —

Colalto (zugleich).

Wir wollen mit dir leben, mit dir sterben.

Wallenstein (mit Ansehen, indem er auf Illo zeigt).

1300 Hier der Feldmarschall weiß um meinen Willen.

(Geht ab.)

Dritter Aufzug.

Ein Zimmer.

Erster Auftritt.

Illo und Terzky.

Terzky.

Nun sagt mir! Wie gedenkt ihr's diesen Abend
Beim Gastmahl mit den Obristen zu machen?

Illo.

Gebt Acht! Wir setzen eine Formel auf,
Worin wir uns dem Herzog insgesammt
1305 Verschreiben, sein zu sein mit Leib und Leben,
Nicht unser letztes Blut für ihn zu sparen;
Jedoch der Eidespflichten unbeschadet,
Die wir dem Kaiser schuldig sind.   Merkt wohl!
Die nehmen wir in einer eignen Clausel
1310 Ausdrücklich aus und retten das Gewissen.
Nun hört! Die also abgefaßte Schrift
Wird ihnen vorgelegt vor Tische, keiner
Wird daran Anstoß nehmen.   Hört nun weiter!
Nach Tafel, wenn der trübe Geist des Weins
1315 Das Herz nun öffnet und die Augen schließt,

Läßt man ein unterschobnes Blatt, worin
Die Clausel fehlt, zur Unterschrift herumgehn.

Terzky.

Wie? Denkt ihr, daß sie sich durch einen Eid
Gebunden glauben werden, den wir ihnen
1320 Durch Gaukelkunst betrüglich abgelistet?

Illo.

Gefangen haben wir sie immer. Laßt sie
Dann über Arglist schrei'n, so viel sie mögen.
Am Hofe glaubt man ihrer Unterschrift
Doch mehr, als ihrem heiligsten Betheuern.
1325 Verräther sind sie einmal, müssen's sein;
So machen sie aus der Noth wohl eine Tugend.

Terzky.

Nun, mir ist alles lieb, geschieht nur was,
Und rücken wir nur einmal von der Stelle. /

Illo.

Und dann liegt auch so viel nicht dran, wie weit
1330 Wir damit langen bei den Generalen.
Genug, wenn wir's dem Herrn nur überreden,
Sie seien sein; denn handelt er nur erst
Mit seinem Ernst, als ob er sie schon hätte,
So hat er sie und reißt sie mit sich fort.

Terzky.

1335 Ich kann mich manchmal gar nicht in ihn finden.
Er leiht dem Feind sein Ohr, läßt mich dem Thurn,
Dem Arnheim schreiben, gegen den Sesina
Geht er mit kühnen Worten frei heraus,
Spricht stundenlang mit uns von seinen Planen,

40 Und mein' ich nun, ich hab' ihn — weg auf einmal
Entschlüpft er, und es scheint, als wär' es ihm
Um nichts zu thun, als nur am Platz zu bleiben.

Illo.

Er seine alten Plane aufgegeben!
Ich sag euch, daß er wachend, schlafend mit
45 Nichts anderm umgeht, daß er Tag für Tag
Deßwegen die Planeten fragt —

Terzky.

　　　　　　Ja, wißt ihr,
Daß er sich in der Nacht, die jetzo kommt,
Im astrologischen Thurme mit dem Doctor
Einschließen wird und mit ihm observieren?
50 Denn es soll eine wicht'ge Nacht sein, hör' ich,
Und etwas großes, langerwartetes
Am Himmel vorgehn.

Illo.

　　　　Wenn's hier unten nur geschieht.
Die Generale sind voll Eifer jetzt
Und werden sich zu allem bringen lassen,
55 Nur um den Chef nicht zu verlieren.   Seht!
So haben wir den Anlaß vor der Hand
Zu einem engen Bündniß wieder'n Hof.
Unschuldig ist der Name zwar, es heißt:
Man will ihn beim Commando bloß erhalten.
60 Doch, wißt ihr, in der Hitze des Verfolgens
Verliert man bald den Anfang aus den Augen.
Ich denk' es schon zu karten, daß der Fürst
Sie willig finden, willig g l a u b e n soll
Zu jedem Wagstück.   Die Gelegenheit

1365 Soll ihn verführen.   Ist der große Schritt
Nur erst gethan, den sie zu Wien ihm nicht verzeihn,
So wird der Nothzwang der Begebenheiten
Ihn weiter schon und weiter führen; nur
Die Wahl ist's, was ihm schwer wird; drängt die Noth,
1370 Dann kommt ihm seine Stärke, seine Klarheit.

Terzky.

Das ist es auch, worauf der Feind nur wartet,
Das Heer uns zuzuführen.

Illo.

Kommt! wir müssen
Das Werk in diesen nächsten Tagen weiter fördern,
Als es in Jahren nicht gedieh.   Und steht's
1375 Nur erst hier unten glücklich, gebet Acht,
So werden auch die rechten Sterne scheinen!
Kommt zu den Obersten!   Das Eisen muß
Geschmiedet werden, weil es glüht.

Terzky.

Geht ihr hin, Illo.
Ich muß die Gräfin Terzky hier erwarten.
1380 Wißt, daß wir auch nicht müßig sind; wenn e i n
Strick reißt, ist schon ein andrer in Bereitschaft.

Illo.

Ja, eure Hausfrau lächelte so listig.
Was habt ihr?

Terzky.

Ein Geheimniß!   Still, sie kommt!
(Illo geht ab.)

Zweiter Auftritt.

Graf und Gräfin Terzky, die aus einem Cabinet heraustritt. Hernach ein
Bedienter, darauf **Jllo.**

Terzky.

Kommt sie? Ich halt' ihn länger nicht zurück.

Gräfin.

85 Gleich wird sie da sein. Schick' ihn nur.

Terzky.

Zwar weiß ich nicht, ob wir uns Dank damit
Beim Herrn verdienen werden. Ueber diesen Punkt,
Du weißt's, hat er sich nie herausgelassen.
Du hast mich überredet und. mußt wissen,
90 Wie weit du gehen kannst.

Gräfin.

   Ich nehm's auf mich.
(für sich)
Es braucht hier keiner Vollmacht. Ohne Worte, Schwager,
Verstehn wir uns. Errath' ich etwa nicht,
Warum die Tochter hergefordert worden,
Warum just e r gewählt, sie abzuholen?
95 Denn dieses vorgespiegelte Verlöbniß
Mit einem Bräutigam, den Niemand kennt,
Mag andre blenden! Ich durchschaue dich.
Doch dir geziemt es nicht, in solchem Spiel
Die Hand zu haben. Nicht doch! Meiner Feinheit
00 Bleibt alles überlassen. Wohl! Du sollst
Dich in der Schwester nicht betrogen haben.

Bedienter (kommt).

Die Generale!   (Ab.)

Terzky (zur Gräfin).

Sorg' nur, daß du ihm
Den Kopf recht warm machst, was zu denken gibst
Wenn er zu Tisch kommt, daß er sich nicht lange
1405 Bedenke bei der Unterschrift.

Gräfin.

Sorg' du für deine Gäste! Geh und schick' ihn.

Terzky.

Denn alles liegt dran, daß er unterschreibt.

Gräfin.

Zu deinen Gästen.   Geh!

Illo (kommt zurück).

Wo bleibt ihr, Terzky?
Das Haus ist voll, und alles wartet euer.

Terzky.

1410 Gleich, gleich!

(zur Gräfin)

Und daß er nicht zu lang' verweilt.
Es möchte bei dem Alten sonst Verdacht —

Gräfin.

Unnöth'ge Sorgfalt!

(Terzky und Illo gehen.)

Dritter Auftritt.

Gräfin Terzky. Max Piccolomini.

Max (blickt schüchtern herein).

Base Terzky! Darf ich?
(tritt bis in die Mitte des Zimmers, wo er sich unruhig umsieht)
Sie ist nicht da! Wo ist sie?

Gräfin.

Sehen Sie nur recht

In jene Ecke, ob sie hinter'm Schirm

1415 Vielleicht versteckt —

Max.

Da liegen ihre Handschuh'!

(will haftig darnach greifen, Gräfin nimmt sie zu sich)

Ungüt'ge Tante! Sie verleugnen mir —

Sie haben Ihre Luft dran, mich zu quälen.

Gräfin.

Der Dank für meine Müh'!

Max.

O, fühlten Sie,

Wie mir zu Muthe ist! Seitdem wir hier sind,

1420 So an mich halten, Wort' und Blicke wägen!

Das bin ich nicht gewohnt!

Gräfin.

Sie werden sich

An manches noch gewöhnen, schöner Freund!

Auf dieser Probe Ihrer Folgsamkeit

Muß ich durchaus bestehen, nur unter d e r Bedingung

1425 Kann ich mich überall damit befassen.

Max.

Wo aber ist sie? Warum kommt sie nicht?

Gräfin.

Sie müssen's ganz in meine Hände legen.

Wer kann es besser auch mit Ihnen meinen!

Kein Mensch darf wissen, auch Ihr Vater nicht,

1430 Der gar nicht!

Max.

Damit hat's nicht Noth. Es ist

Hier kein Gesicht, an das ich's richten möchte,

Was die entzückte Seele mir bewegt.
O Tante Terzky! Ist denn alles hier
Verändert, oder bin nur ich's! Ich sehe mich
1435 Wie unter fremden Menschen. Keine Spur
Von meinen vor'gen Wünschen mehr und Freuden.
Wo ist das alles hin? Ich war doch sonst
In eben dieser Welt nicht unzufrieden.
Wie schal ist alles nun und wie gemein!
1440 Die Kameraden sind mir unerträglich,
Der Vater selbst, ich weiß ihm nichts zu sagen,
Der Dienst, die Waffen sind mir eitler Tand.
So müßt' es einem sel'gen Geiste sein,
Der aus den Wohnungen der ew'gen Freude
1445 Zu seinen Kinderspielen und Geschäften,
Zu seinen Neigungen und Brüderschaften,
Zur ganzen armen Menschheit wiederkehrte.

Gräfin.

Doch muß ich bitten, ein'ge Blicke noch
Auf diese ganz gemeine Welt zu werfen,
1450 Wo eben jetzt viel wichtiges geschieht.

Max.

Es geht hier etwas vor um mich, ich seh's
An ungewöhnlich treibender Bewegung;
Wenn's fertig ist, kommt's wohl auch bis zu mir.
Wo denken Sie, daß ich gewesen, Tante?
1455 Doch keinen Spott! Mich ängstigte des Lagers
Gewühl, die Flut zudringlicher Bekannten,
Der fade Scherz, das nichtige Gespräch,
Es wurde mir zu eng, ich mußte fort,
Stillschweigen suchen diesem vollen Herzen

160 Und eine reine Stelle für mein Glück.

Kein Lächeln, Gräfin! In der Kirche war ich.

Es ist ein Kloster hier, zur Himmelspforte,

Da ging ich hin, da fand ich mich allein.

Ob dem Altar hing eine Mutter Gottes,

165 Ein schlecht Gemälde war's, doch war's der Freund,

Den ich in diesem Augenblicke suchte.

Wie oft hab' ich die Herrliche gesehn

In ihrem Glanz, die Inbrunst der Verehrer —

Es hat mich nicht gerührt, und jetzt auf einmal

170 Ward mir die Andacht klar, so wie die Liebe.

Gräfin.

Genießen Sie Ihr Glück. Vergessen Sie

Die Welt um sich herum. Es soll die Freundschaft

Indessen wachsam für Sie sorgen, handeln.

Nur sei'n Sie dann auch lenksam, wenn man Ihnen

175 Den Weg zu Ihrem Glücke zeigen wird.

Max.

Wo aber bleibt sie denn! O goldne Zeit

Der Reise, wo uns jede neue Sonne

Vereinigte, die späte Nacht nur trennte!

Da rann kein Sand, und keine Glocke schlug.

180 Es schien die Zeit dem Ueberseligen

In ihrem ew'gen Laufe stillzustehen.

O! der ist aus dem Himmel schon gefallen,

Der an der Stunden Wechsel denken muß!

Die Uhr schlägt keinem Glücklichen.

Gräfin.

185 Wie lang' ist es, daß Sie Ihr Herz entdeckten?

145

Max.

Heut' früh wagt' ich das erste Wort.

Gräfin.

Wie? Heute erst in diesen zwanzig Tagen?

Max.

Auf jenem Jagdschloß war es, zwischen hier
Und Nepomuk, wo Sie uns eingeholt,
1490 Der letzten Station des ganzen Wegs.
In einem Erker standen wir, den Blick
Stumm in das öde Feld hinausgerichtet,
Und vor uns ritten die Dragoner auf,
Die uns der Herzog zum Geleit gesendet.
1495 Schwer lag auf mir des Scheidens Bangigkeit,
Und zitternd endlich wagt' ich dieses Wort:
Dies alles mahnt mich, Fräulein, daß ich heut
Von meinem Glücke scheiden muß. Sie werden
In wenig Stunden einen Vater finden,
1500 Von neuen Freunden sich umgeben sehn;
Ich werde nun ein Fremder für Sie sein,
Verloren in der Menge ✝ „Sprechen Sie
„Mit meiner Base Terzky!" fiel sie schnell
Mir ein, die Stimme zitterte, ich sah
1505 Ein glühend Roth die schönen Wangen färben,
Und von der Erde langsam sich erhebend
Trifft mich ihr Auge — ich beherrsche mich
Nicht länger —

(die Prinzessin erscheint an der Thüre und bleibt stehen, von der Gräfin, aber
nicht von Piccolomini bemerkt)

Fasse kühn sie in die Arme,
Mein Mund berührt den ihrigen — da rauscht' es

1510 Im nahen Saal und trennte uns — S i e waren's.
Was nun geschehen, wissen Sie.

Gräfin.
(nach einer Pause, mit einem verstohlenen Blick auf Thekla)
Und sind Sie so bescheiden oder haben
So wenig Neugier, daß Sie mich nicht auch
Um m e i n Geheimniß fragen?

Max.
Ihr Geheimniß?

Gräfin.
1515 Nun ja! Wie ich unmittelbar nach Ihnen
Ins Zimmer trat, wie ich die Nichte fand,
Was sie in diesem ersten Augenblick
Des überraschten Herzens —

Max (lebhaft).
Nun?

———————————

Vierter Auftritt.

Vorige. Thekla, welche schnell hervortritt.

Thekla.
Spart euch die Mühe, Tante!
Das hört er besser von mir selbst.

Max (tritt zurück.)
Mein Fräulein!
1520 Was ließen Sie mich sagen, Tante Terzky!

Thekla (zur Gräfin).
Ist er schon lange hier?

Gräfin.

Ja wohl, und seine Zeit ist bald vorüber.
Wo bleibt ihr auch so lang'?

Thekla.

Die Mutter weinte wieder so.   Ich seh' sie leiden,
1525 — Und kann's nicht ändern, daß ich glücklich bin.

Max (in ihren Anblick verloren).

Jetzt hab' ich wieder Muth, Sie anzusehn.
Heut' konnt' ich's nicht.   Der Glanz der Edelsteine,
Der Sie umgab, verbarg mir die Geliebte.

Thekla.

So sah mich nur Ihr Auge, nicht Ihr Herz.

Max.

1530 O! diesen Morgen, als ich Sie im Kreise
Der Ihrigen, in Vaters Armen fand,
Mich einen Fremdling sah in diesem Kreise,
Wie drängte mich's in diesem Augenblick,
Ihm um den Hals zu fallen, V a t e r ihn
1535 Zu nennen! Doch sein strenges Auge hieß
Die heftig wallende Empfindung schweigen,
Und jene Diamanten schreckten mich,
Die, wie ein Kranz von Sternen, Sie umgaben.
Warum auch mußt' er beim Empfange gleich
1540 Den Bann um Sie verbreiten, gleich zum Opfer
Den Engel schmücken, auf das heitre Herz
Die traur'ge Bürde seines Standes werfen!
Wohl darf die Liebe werben um die Liebe,
Doch solchem Glanz darf nur ein König nah'n.

Thekla.

1545 O! still von dieser Mummerei! Sie sehn,

Wie schnell die Bürde abgeworfen ward.

(zur Gräfin)

Er ist nicht heiter.   Warum ist er's nicht?

Ihr, Tante, habt ihn mir so schwer gemacht!

War er doch ein ganz andrer auf der Reise!

1550 So ruhig hell! so froh beredt! Ich wünschte

Sie immer so zu sehn und niemals anders.

Max.

Sie fanden sich in Ihres Vaters Armen,

In einer neuen Welt, die Ihnen huldigt,

Wär's auch durch Neuheit nur, Ihr Auge reizt.

Thekla.

1555 Ja! Vieles reizt mich hier, ich will's nicht leugnen,

Mich reizt die bunte, kriegerische Bühne,

Die vielfach mir ein liebes Bild erneuert,

Mir an das Leben, an die Wahrheit knüpft,

Was mir ein schöner Traum nur hat geschienen.

Max.

1560 Mir machte sie mein wirklich Glück zum Traum.

Auf einer Insel in des Aethers Höh'n

Hab' ich gelebt in diesen letzten Tagen;

Sie hat sich auf die Erd' herabgelassen,

Und diese Brücke, die zum alten Leben

1565 Zurück mich bringt, trennt mich von meinem Himmel.

Thekla.

Das Spiel des Lebens sieht sich heiter an,

Wenn man den sichern Schatz im Herzen trägt,

Und froher kehr' ich, wenn ich es gemustert,

Zu meinem schönern Eigenthum zurück —

(abbrechend, und in einem scherzhaften Ton)

1570 Was hab' ich neues nicht und unerhörtes

In dieser kurzen Gegenwart gesehn!
Und doch muß alles dies dem Wunder weichen,
Das dieses Schloß geheimnißvoll verwahrt.

Gräfin (nachsinnend).

Was wäre das? Ich bin doch auch bekannt
1375 In allen dunkeln Ecken dieses Hauses.

Thekla (lächelnd).

Von Geistern wird der Weg dazu beschützt,
Zwei Greife halten Wache an der Pforte.

Gräfin (lacht).

Ach so! der astrologische Thurm! Wie hat sich
Dies Heiligthum, das sonst so streng verwahrt wird,
1380 Gleich in den ersten Stunden euch geöffnet?

Thekla.

Ein kleiner alter Mann mit weißen Haaren
Und freundlichem Gesicht, der seine Gunst
Mir gleich geschenkt, schloß mir die Pforten auf.

Max.

Das ist des Herzogs Astrolog, der Seni.

Thekla.

1385 Er fragte mich nach vielen Dingen, wann ich
Geboren sei, in welchem Tag und Monat,
Ob eine Tages- oder Nachtgeburt —

Gräfin.

Weil er das Horoskop euch stellen wollte.

Thekla.

Auch meine Hand besah er, schüttelte
1390 Das Haupt bedenklich, und es schienen ihm
Die Linien nicht eben zu gefallen.

Gräfin.

Wie fandet ihr es denn in diesem Saal?
Ich hab' mich stets nur flüchtig umgesehn.

Thekla.

Es ward mir wunderbar zu Muth, als ich
1395 Aus vollem Tageslichte schnell hineintrat,
Denn eine düstre Nacht umgab mich plötzlich,
Von seltsamer Beleuchtung schwach erhellt.
In einem Halbkreis standen um mich her
Sechs oder sieben große Königsbilder,
1600 Den Scepter in der Hand, und auf dem Haupt
Trug jedes einen Stern, und alles Licht
Im Thurm schien von den Sternen nur zu kommen.
Das wären die Planeten, sagte mir
Mein Führer, sie regierten das Geschick,
1605 Drum seien sie als Könige gebildet.
Der äußerste, ein grämlich finstrer Greis
Mit dem trübgelben Stern, sei der S a t u r n u s ;
Der mit dem rothen Schein, grad' von ihm über,
In kriegerischer Rüstung, sei der M a r s ,
1610 Und beide bringen wenig Glück den Menschen.
Doch eine schöne Frau stand ihm zur Seite,
Sanft schimmerte der Stern auf ihrem Haupt,
Das sei die B e n u s , das Gestirn der Freude.
Zur linken Hand erschien M e r c u r geflügelt.
1615 Ganz in der Mitte glänzte silberhell
Ein heitrer Mann, mit einer Königsstirn,
Das sei der J u p i t e r , des Vaters Stern,
Und M o n d und S o n n e standen ihm zur Seite.

Max.

O, nimmer will ich seinen Glauben schelten

1620 An der Gestirne, an der Geister Macht.

Nicht bloß der S t o l z des Menschen füllt den Raum

Mit Geistern, mit geheimnißvollen Kräften,

Auch für ein liebend Herz ist die gemeine

Natur zu eng, und tiefere Bedeutung

1625 Liegt in dem Märchen meiner Kinderjahre,

Als in der Wahrheit, die das Leben lehrt.

Die heitre Welt der Wunder ist's allein,

Die dem entzückten Herzen Antwort gibt,

Die ihre ew'gen Räume mir eröffnet,

1630 Mir tausend Zweige reich entgegenstreckt,

Worauf der trunkne Geist sich selig wiegt.

Die Fabel ist der Liebe Heimatwelt,

Gern wohnt sie unter Feen, Talismanen,

Glaubt gern an Götter, weil sie göttlich ist.

1635 Die alten Fabelwesen sind nicht mehr,

Das reizende Geschlecht ist ausgewandert;

Doch eine Sprache braucht das Herz, es bringt

Der alte Trieb die alten Namen wieder,

Und an dem Sternenhimmel gehn sie jetzt,

1640 Die sonst im Leben freundlich mit gewandelt;

Dort winken sie dem Liebenden herab,

Und jedes Große bringt uns J u p i t e r

Noch diesen Tag, und V e n u s jedes Schöne.

Thekla.

Wenn d a s die Sternenkunst ist, will ich froh

1645 Zu diesem heitern Glauben mich bekennen.

Es ist ein holder, freundlicher Gedanke,

1735 Aus Himmelshöhen fiel es uns herab,
Und nur dem Himmel wollen wir's verdanken.
Er kann ein Wunder für uns thun.

Sechster Auftritt.

Gräfin Terzky zu den Vorigen.

Gräfin (pressiert).

Mein Mann schickt her. Es sei die höchste Zeit.
Er soll zur Tafel —
(da jene nicht darauf achten, tritt sie zwischen sie)
Trennt euch!

Thekla.

O, nicht doch!

1740 Es ist ja kaum ein Augenblick.

Gräfin.

Die Zeit vergeht euch schnell, Prinzessin Nichte.

Max.

Es eilt nicht, Base.

Gräfin.

Fort, fort! Man vermißt Sie.
Der Vater hat sich zweimal schon erkundigt.

Thekla.

Ei nun! der Vater!

Gräfin.

Das versteht ihr, Nichte.

Thekla.

1745 Was soll er überall bei der Gesellschaft?
Es ist sein Umgang nicht; es mögen würd'ge,

Verdiente Männer sein; er aber ist
Für sie zu jung, taugt nicht in die Gesellschaft.

Gräfin.

Ihr möchtet ihn wohl lieber ganz behalten?

Thekla (lebhaft).

1750 Ihr habt's getroffen.   Das ist meine Meinung.
Ja, laßt ihn ganz hier, laßt den Herren sagen —

Gräfin.

Habt ihr den Kopf verloren, Nichte?   Graf!
Sie wissen die Bedingungen.

Max.

Ich muß gehorchen, Fräulein.   Leben Sie wohl.
(da Thekla sich schnell von ihm wendet)
1755 Was sagen Sie?

Thekla (ohne ihn anzusehen).

Nichts.   Gehen Sie.

Max.

Kann ich's,
Wenn Sie mir zürnen?

(Er nähert sich ihr, ihre Augen begegnen sich; sie steht einen Augenblick schweigend, dann wirft sie sich ihm an die Brust, er drückt sie fest an sich.)

Gräfin.

Weg!   Wenn jemand käme!
Ich höre Lärmen — fremde Stimmen nahen.

(Max reißt sich aus ihren Armen und geht, die Gräfin begleitet ihn.   Thekla
folgt ihm anfangs mit den Augen, geht unruhig durch das Zimmer und bleibt
dann in Gedanken versenkt stehen.   Eine Guitarre liegt auf dem Tische, sie
ergreift sie, und nachdem sie eine Weile schwermüthig präludirt hat, fällt sie
in den Gesang.)

Siebenter Auftritt.

Thekla (spielt und fingt).

Der Eichwald brauset, die Wolken ziehn,
Das Mägdlein wandelt an Ufers Grün,
1760 Es bricht sich die Welle mit Macht, mit Macht,
Und sie singt hinaus in die finstre Nacht,
Das Auge von Weinen getrübet.

Das Herz ist gestorben, die Welt ist leer,
Und weiter gibt sie dem Wunsche nichts mehr.
1765 Du Heilige, rufe dein Kind zurück!
Ich habe genossen das irdische Glück,
Ich habe gelebt und geliebet.

Achter Auftritt.

Gräfin kommt zurück. **Thekla.**

Gräfin.

Was war das, Fräulein Nichte? Fi! Ihr werft euch
Ihm an den Kopf. Ihr solltet euch doch, dächt' ich,
1770 Mit eurer Person ein wenig theurer machen.

Thekla (indem sie aufsteht).

Was meint ihr, Tante?

Gräfin.

Ihr sollt nicht vergessen,
Wer ihr seid, und wer er ist. Ja, das ist euch
Noch gar nicht eingefallen, glaub' ich.

Thekla.

Was denn?

Gräfin.

Daß ihr des Fürsten Friedland Tochter seid.

Thekla.

1775 Nun? und was mehr?

Gräfin.

Was? Eine schöne Frage!

Thekla.

Was wir geworden sind, ist e r geboren.
Er ist von altlombardischem Geschlecht,
Ist einer Fürstin Sohn!

Gräfin.

Sprecht ihr im Traum?
Fürwahr! Man wird ihn höflich noch drum bitten,
1780 Die reichste Erbin in Europa zu beglücken
Mit seiner Hand.

Thekla.

Das wird nicht nöthig sein.

Gräfin.

Ja, man wird wohl thun, sich nicht auszusetzen.

Thekla.

Sein Vater liebt ihn, Graf Octavio
Wird nichts dagegen haben —

Gräfin.

1785 Sein Vater! Seiner! Und der eure, Nichte?

Thekla.

Nun ja! Ich denk', ihr fürchtet s e i n e n Vater,
Weil ihr's vor dem, vor seinem Vater, mein' ich,
So sehr verheimlicht.

Gräfin (sieht sie forschend an).

Nichte, ihr seid falsch!

Thekla.

Seid ihr empfindlich, Tante? O seid gut!

Gräfin.

1790 Ihr haltet euer Spiel schon für gewonnen —
Jauchzt nicht zu frühe!

Thekla.

Seid nur gut!

Gräfin.

Es ist noch nicht so weit.

Thekla.

Ich glaub' es wohl.

Gräfin.

Denkt ihr, er habe sein bedeutend Leben
In kriegerischer Arbeit aufgewendet,
1795 Jedwedem stillen Erdenglück entsagt,
Den Schlaf von seinem Lager weggebannt,
Sein edles Haupt der Sorge hingegeben,
Nur um ein glücklich Paar aus euch zu machen?
Um dich zuletzt aus diesem Stift zu ziehn,
1800 Den Mann dir im Triumphe zuzuführen,
Der deinen Augen wohlgefällt? Das hätt' er
Wohlfeiler haben können! Diese Saat
Ward nicht gepflanzt, daß du mit kind'scher Hand
Die Blume brächest und zur leichten Zier
1805 An deinen Busen stecktest!

Thekla.

Was er mir nicht gepflanzt, das könnte doch
Freiwillig mir die schönen Früchte tragen.
Und wenn mein gütig freundliches Geschick

Aus seinem furchtbar ungeheuren Dasein
1810 Des Lebens Freude mir bereiten will —

Gräfin.

Du siehst's wie ein verliebtes Mädchen an.
Blick' um dich her.   Besinn dich, wo du bist.
Nicht in ein Freudenhaus bist du getreten,
Zu keiner Hochzeit findest du die Wände
1815 Geschmückt, der Gäste Haupt bekränzt.   Hier ist
Kein Glanz, als der von Waffen.   Oder denkst du,
Man führte diese Tausende zusammen,   •
Beim Brautfest dir den Reihen aufzuführen?
Du siehst des Vaters Stirn gedankenvoll,
1820 Der Mutter Aug' in Thränen, auf der Wage liegt
Das große Schicksal unsers Hauses!
Laß jetzt des Mädchens kindische Gefühle,
Die kleinen Wünsche hinter dir! Beweise,
Daß du des Außerordentlichen Tochter bist!
1825 Das Weib soll sich nicht selber angehören,
An fremdes Schicksal ist sie fest gebunden.
Die aber ist die beste, die sich Fremdes
Aneignen kann mit Wahl, an ihrem Herzen
Es trägt und pflegt mit Innigkeit und Liebe.

Thekla.

1830 So wurde mir's im Kloster vorgesagt.
Ich hatte keine Wünsche, kannte mich
Als seine Tochter nur, des Mächtigen,
Und seines Lebens Schall, der auch zu mir drang,
Gab mir kein anderes Gefühl, als dies:
1835 Ich sei bestimmt, mich leidend ihm zu opfern.

Gräfin.

Das ist dein Schicksal. Füge dich ihm willig.
Ich und die Mutter geben dir das Beispiel.

Thekla.

Das Schicksal hat mir den gezeigt, dem ich
Mich opfern soll; ich will ihm freudig folgen.

Gräfin.

1840 Dein Herz, mein liebes Kind, und nicht das Schicksal.

Thekla.

Der Zug des Herzens ist des Schicksals Stimme.
Ich bin die Seine. Sein Geschenk allein
Ist dieses neue Leben, das ich lebe.
Er hat ein Recht an sein Geschöpf. Was war ich,
1845 Eh' seine schöne Liebe mich beseelte?
Ich will auch von mir selbst nicht kleiner denken,
Als der Geliebte. Der kann nicht gering sein,
Der das Unschätzbare besitzt. Ich fühle
Die Kraft mit meinem Glücke mir verliehn.
1850 Ernst liegt das Leben vor der ernsten Seele.
Daß ich mir selbst gehöre, weiß ich nun.
Den festen Willen hab' ich kennen lernen,
Den unbezwinglichen, in meiner Brust,
Und an das Höchste kann ich alles setzen.

Gräfin.

1855 Du wolltest dich dem Vater widersetzen,
Wenn er es anders nun mit dir beschlossen?
Ihm denkst du's abzuzwingen? Wisse, Kind,
Sein Nam' ist Friedland!

Thekla.

                    Auch der meinige.
Er soll in mir die echte Tochter finden.

Gräfin.

1860 Wie? Sein Monarch, sein Kaiser zwingt ihn nicht,
Und du, sein Mädchen, wolltest mit ihm kämpfen?

Thekla.

Was niemand wagt, kann seine Tochter wagen.

Gräfin.

Nun wahrlich! Darauf ist er nicht bereitet.
Er hätte jedes Hinderniß besiegt,
1865 Und in dem eignen Willen seiner Tochter
Sollt' ihm der neue Streit entstehn? Kind! Kind!
Noch hast du nur das Lächeln deines Vaters,
Hast seines Zornes Auge nicht gesehen.
Wird sich die Stimme deines Widerspruchs,
1870 Die zitternde, in seine Nähe wagen?
Wohl magst du dir, wenn du allein bist, große Dinge
Vorsetzen, schöne Rednerblumen flechten,
Mit Löwenmuth den Taubensinn bewaffnen.
Jedoch versuch's! Tritt vor sein Auge hin,
1875 Das fest auf dich gespannt ist, und sag': Nein!
Vergehen wirst du vor ihm, wie das zarte Blatt
Der Blume vor dem Feuerblick der Sonne.
Ich will dich nicht erschrecken, liebes Kind!
Zum Aeußersten soll's ja nicht kommen, hoff' ich.
1880 Auch weiß ich seinen Willen nicht.   Kann sein,
Daß seine Zwecke deinem Wunsch begegnen.
Doch das kann nimmermehr sein Wille sein,
Daß du, die stolze Tochter seines Glücks,
Wie ein verliebtes Mädchen dich geberdest,
1885 Wegwerfest an den Mann, der, wenn ihm je

Daß über uns, in unermeßnen Höh'n,
Der Liebe Kranz aus funkelnden Gestirnen,
Da wir erst wurden, schon geflochten ward.

Gräfin.

1650 Nicht Rosen bloß, auch Dornen hat der Himmel.
Wohl dir, wenn sie den Kranz dir nicht verletzen!
Was Venus band, die Bringerin des Glücks,
Kann Mars, der Stern des Unglücks, schnell zerreißen.

Max.

Bald wird sein düstres Reich zu Ende sein!

1655 Gesegnet sei des Fürsten ernster Eifer,
Er wird den Oelzweig in den Lorbeer flechten
Und der erfreuten Welt den Frieden schenken.
Dann hat sein großes Herz nichts mehr zu wünschen,
Er hat genug für seinen Ruhm gethan,

1660 Kann jetzt sich selber leben und den Seinen.
Auf seine Güter wird er sich zurückziehn,
Er hat zu Gitschin einen schönen Sitz,
Auch Reichenberg, Schloß Friedland liegen heiter,
Bis an den Fuß der Riesenberge hin

1665 Streckt sich das Jagdgehege seiner Wälder.
Dem großen Trieb, dem prächtig schaffenden,
Kann er dann ungebunden, frei willfahren.
Da kann er fürstlich jede Kunst ermuntern
Und alles würdig Herrliche beschützen,

1670 Kann bauen, pflanzen, nach den Sternen sehn,
Ja, wenn die kühne Kraft nicht ruhen kann,
So mag er kämpfen mit dem Element,
Den Fluß ableiten und den Felsen sprengen,
Und dem Gewerb die leichte Straße bahnen.

1075 Aus unfern Kriegsgeschichten werden dann
Erzählungen in langen Winternächten —

Gräfin.

Ich will denn doch gerathen haben, Vetter,
Den Degen nicht zu frühe wegzulegen.
Denn eine Braut, wie die, ist es wohl werth,
1080 Daß mit dem Schwert um sie geworben werde.

Max.

O! wäre sie mit Waffen zu gewinnen!

Gräfin.

Was war das? Hört ihr nichts? Mir war's, als hört' ich
Im Tafelzimmer heft'gen Streit und Lärmen.

(Sie geht hinaus.)

Fünfter Auftritt.

Thekla und **Max Piccolomini.**

Thekla.

(sobald die Gräfin sich entfernt hat, schnell und heimlich zu Piccolomini)

1085 Trau' ihnen nicht.   Sie meinen's falsch.

Max.

Sie könnten —

Thekla.

...h hier als mir.   Ich sah es gleich,
Zweck.

Max.

Zweck! Aber welchen?
...von, uns Hoffnungen —

Thekla.

Das weiß ich nicht.   Doch glaub' mir, es ist nicht
1690 Ihr Ernst, uns zu beglücken, zu verbinden.

Max.

Wozu auch diese Terzkys? Haben wir
Nicht deine Mutter? Ja, die Gütige
Verdient's, daß wir uns kindlich ihr vertrauen.

Thekla.

Sie liebt dich, schätzt dich hoch vor allen andern;
1695 Doch nimmer hätte sie den Muth, ein solch
Geheimniß vor dem Vater zu bewahren.
Um ihrer Ruhe willen muß es ihr
Verschwiegen bleiben.

Max.

Warum überall
Auch das Geheimniß? Weißt du, was ich thun will?
1700 Ich werfe mich zu deines Vaters Füßen,
Er soll mein Glück entscheiden, er ist wahrhaft,
Ist unverstellt und haßt die krummen Wege,
Er ist so gut, so edel —

Thekla.
Das bist du!

Max.

Du kennst ihn erst seit heut'.   Ich aber lebe
1705 Schon zehen Jahre unter seinen Augen.
Ist's denn das erstemal, daß er das Seltne,
Das Ungehoffte thut? Es sieht ihm gleich,
Zu überraschen wie ein Gott; er muß
Entzücken stets und in Erstaunen setzen.

Verdiente Männer sein; er aber ist
Für sie zu jung, taugt nicht in die Gesellschaft.

Gräfin.

Ihr möchtet ihn wohl lieber ganz behalten?

Thekla (lebhaft).

1750 Ihr habt's getroffen. Das ist meine Meinung.
Ja, laßt ihn ganz hier, laßt den Herren sagen —

Gräfin.

Habt ihr den Kopf verloren, Nichte? Graf!
Sie wissen die Bedingungen.

Max.

Ich muß gehorchen, Fräulein. Leben Sie wohl.

(da Thekla sich schnell von ihm wendet)

1755 Was sagen Sie?

Thekla (ohne ihn anzusehen).

Nichts. Gehen Sie.

Max.

Kann ich's,

Wenn Sie mir zürnen?

(Er nähert sich ihr, ihre Augen begegnen sich; sie steht einen Augenblick schweigend, dann wirft sie sich ihm an die Brust, er drückt sie fest an sich.)

Gräfin.

Weg! Wenn jemand käme!
Ich höre Lärmen — fremde Stimmen nahen.

(Max reißt sich aus ihren Armen und geht, die Gräfin begleitet ihn. Thekla
folgt ihm anfangs mit den Augen, geht unruhig durch das Zimmer und bleibt
dann in Gedanken versenkt stehen. Eine Guitarre liegt auf dem Tische, sie
ergreift sie, und nachdem sie eine Weile schwermüthig präludirt hat, fällt sie
in den Gesang.)

Siebenter Auftritt.

Thekla (spielt und singt).

Der Eichwald brauset, die Wolken ziehn,
Das Mägdlein wandelt an Ufers Grün,
1760 Es bricht sich die Welle mit Macht, mit Macht,
Und sie singt hinaus in die finstre Nacht,
Das Auge von Weinen getrübet.

Das Herz ist gestorben, die Welt ist leer,
Und weiter gibt sie dem Wunsche nichts mehr.
1765 Du Heilige, rufe dein Kind zurück!
Ich habe genossen das irdische Glück,
Ich habe gelebt und geliebet.

Achter Auftritt.

Gräfin kommt zurück. **Thekla.**

Gräfin.

Was war das, Fräulein Nichte? Fi! Ihr werft euch
Ihm an den Kopf. Ihr solltet euch doch, dächt' ich,
1770 Mit eurer Person ein wenig theurer machen.

Thekla (indem sie aufsteht).

Was meint ihr, Tante?

Gräfin.

Ihr sollt nicht vergessen,
Wer ihr seid, und wer er ist. Ja, das ist euch
Noch gar nicht eingefallen, glaub' ich.

Thekla.

Was denn?

1910 Es schießt der Blitz herab aus heitern Höh'n,
    Aus unterird'schen Schlünden fahren Flammen,
    Blindwüthend schleudert selbst der Gott der Freude
    Den Pechkranz in das brennende Gebäude!

                              (Sie geht ab.)

166

Vierter Aufzug.

Scene: Ein großer, festlich erleuchteter Saal, in der Mitte desselben und nach der Tiefe des Theaters eine reich ausgeschmückte Tafel, an welcher acht Generale, worunter **Octavio Piccolomini, Terzky** und **Maradas**, sitzen. Rechts und links davon, mehr nach hinten zu, noch zwei andere Tafeln, welche jede mit sechs Gästen besetzt sind. Vorwärts steht der Credenztisch, die ganze vordere Bühne bleibt für die aufwartenden Pagen und Bedienten frei. Alles ist in Bewegung, Spielleute von Terzkys Regiment ziehen über den Schauplatz um die Tafel herum. Noch ehe sie sich ganz entfernt haben, erscheint **Max Piccolomini**; ihm kommt **Terzky** mit einer Schrift, **Isolani** mit einem Pocal entgegen.

Erster Auftritt.

Terzky. Isolani. Max Piccolomini.

Isolani.

Herr Bruder, was wir lieben! Nun, wo steckt Er?
1915 Geschwind an Seinen Platz! Der Terzky hat
Der Mutter Ehrenweine preisgegeben;
Es geht hier zu, wie auf dem Heidelberger Schloß.
Das Beste hat Er schon versäumt. Sie theilen
Dort an der Tafel Fürstenhüte aus,
1920 Des Eggenberg, Slawata, Lichtenstein,
Des Sternbergs Güter werden ausgeboten,
Sammt allen großen böhm'schen Lehen; wenn
Er hurtig macht, fällt auch für Ihn was ab.
Marsch! Setz' Er sich!

Colalto und **Göt.**
(rufen an der zweiten Tafel)
Graf Piccolomini!

Terzky.

1925 Ihr sollt ihn haben! Gleich! Lies diese Eidesformel,
Ob dir's gefällt, so wie wir's aufgesetzt.
Es haben's alle nach der Reih' gelesen,
Und jeder wird den Namen drunter setzen.

Max (liest).

" Ingratis servire nefas."

Isolani.

1930 Das klingt wie ein latein'scher Spruch. Herr Bruder,
Wie heißt's auf deutsch?

Terzky.

Dem Undankbaren dient kein rechter Mann!

Max.

„Nachdem unser hochgebietender Feldherr, der durch-
„lauchtige Fürst von Friedland, wegen vielfältig empfang-
„ener Kränkungen des Kaisers Dienst zu verlassen gemeint
„gewesen, auf unser einstimmiges Bitten aber sich bewegen
„lassen, noch länger bei der Armee zu verbleiben und ohne
„unser Genehmhalten sich nicht von uns zu trennen: als
„verpflichten wir uns wieder insgesammt, und jeder für sich
„insbesondere, anstatt eines körperlichen Eides, auch bei
„ihm ehrlich und getreu zu halten, uns auf keinerlei Weise
„von ihm zu trennen und für denselben alles das Unsrige,
„bis auf den letzten Blutstropfen, aufzusetzen, s o w e i t
„n ä m l i c h u n s e r d e m K a i s e r g e l e i s t e t e r E i d
„e s e r l a u b e n w i r d. (Die letzten Worte werden von Isolani
nachgesprochen.) „Wie wir denn auch, wenn einer oder der

„andere von uns, diesem Verbündniß zuwider, sich von der
„gemeinen Sache absondern sollte, denselben als einen
„bundesflüchtigen Verräther erklären, und an seinem Hab
„und Gut, Leib und Leben Rache dafür zu nehmen ver-
„bunden sein wollen. Solches bezeugen wir mit Unter-
„schrift unsers Namens."

Terzky.

Bist du gewillt, dies Blatt zu unterschreiben?

Isolani.

Was sollt' er nicht! Jedweder Officier
1935 Von Ehre kann das, muß das. Dint' und Feder!

Terzky.

Laß gut sein bis nach Tafel.

Isolani (Max fortziehend).

Komm' Er, komm' Er!

(Beide gehen an die Tafel.)

_____

Zweiter Auftritt.

Terzky. Neumann.

Terzky.

(winkt dem Neumann, der am Credenztisch gewartet, und tritt mit ihm vorwärts)

Bringst du die Abschrift, Neumann? Gib! Sie ist
Doch so verfaßt, daß man sie leicht verwechselt?

Neumann.

Ich hab' sie Zeil' um Zeile nachgemalt,
1940 Nichts als die Stelle von dem Eid blieb weg,
Wie deine Excellenz es mir geheißen.

Terzky.

Gut! Leg' sie dorthin, und mit dieser gleich
Ins Feuer! Was sie soll, hat sie geleistet.

(Neumann legt die Copie auf den Tisch und tritt wieder zum Schenktisch.)

Dritter Auftritt.

Illo kommt aus dem zweiten Zimmer. Terzky.

Illo.

Wie ist es mit dem Piccolomini?

Terzky.

1945 Ich denke, gut. Er hat nichts eingewendet.

Illo.

Er ist der einz'ge, dem ich nicht recht traue,
Er und der Vater. Habt ein Aug' auf beide!

Terzky.

Wie sieht's an eurer Tafel aus? Ich hoffe,
Ihr haltet eure Gäste warm?

Illo.

Sie sind

1950 Ganz cordial. Ich denk', wir haben sie.
Und wie ich's euch vorausgesagt, schon ist
Die Red' nicht mehr davon, den Herzog bloß
Bei Ehren zu erhalten. Da man einmal
Beisammen sei, meint Montecuculi,

1955 So müsse man in seinem eignen Wien
Dem Kaiser die Bedingung machen. Glaubt mir,
Wär's nicht um diese Piccolomini,
Wir hätten den Betrug uns können sparen.

Terzky.

Was will der Buttler? Still!

Vierter Auftritt.

Buttler zu den Vorigen.

Buttler.
(von der zweiten Tafel kommend)
                    Laßt euch nicht stören.

1960 Ich hab' euch wohlverstanden, Feldmarschall.
Glück zum Geschäfte! Und was mich betrifft,—
(geheimnißvoll)
So könnt ihr auf mich rechnen.

Illo (lebhaft).
                    Können wir's?

Buttler.
Mit oder ohne Clausel! gilt mir gleich.
Versteht ihr mich? Der Fürst kann meine Treu'
1965 Auf jede Probe setzen, sagt ihm das.
Ich bin des Kaisers Officier, so lang ihm
Beliebt, des Kaisers General zu bleiben,
Und bin des Friedlands Knecht, sobald es ihm
Gefallen wird, sein eigner Herr zu sein.

Terzky.
1970 Ihr treffet einen guten Tausch. Kein Karger,
Kein Ferdinand ist's, dem ihr euch verpflichtet.

Buttler (ernst).
Ich biete meine Treu' nicht feil, Graf Terzky,
Und wollt' euch nicht gerathen haben, mir
Vor einem halben Jahr noch abzudingen,
1975 Wozu ich jetzt freiwillig mich erbiete.
Ja, mich sammt meinem Regiment bring' ich
Dem Herzog, und nicht ohne Folgen soll
Das Beispiel bleiben, denk' ich, das ich gebe.

Illo.

Wem ist es nicht bekannt, daß Oberst Buttler
1980 Dem ganzen Heer voran als Muster leuchtet!

Buttler.

Meint ihr, Feldmarschall? Nun, so reut mich nicht
Die Treue, vierzig Jahre lang bewahrt,
Wenn mir der wohlgesparte gute Name
So volle Rache kauft im sechzigsten!
1985 Stoßt euch an meine Rede nicht, ihr Herrn.
Euch mag es gleichviel sein, w i e ihr mich habt,
Und werdet, hoff' ich, selber nicht erwarten,
Daß euer Spiel mein g'rades Urtheil krümmt,
Daß Wankelsinn und schnellbewegtes Blut,
1990 Noch leichte Ursach' sonst den alten Mann
Vom langgewohnten Ehrenpfade treibt.
Kommt! Ich bin darum minder nicht entschlossen,
Weil ich es deutlich weiß, wovon ich scheide.

Illo.

Sagt's rund heraus, wofür wir euch zu halten!

Buttler.

1995 Für einen Freund! Nehmt meine Hand darauf.
Mit allem, was ich hab', bin ich der Eure.
Nicht Männer bloß, auch Geld bedarf der Fürst.
Ich hab' in seinem Dienst mir was erworben,
Ich leih' es ihm, und überlebt er mich,
2000 Ist's ihm vermacht schon längst, er ist mein Erbe.
Ich steh' allein da in der Welt und kenne
Nicht das Gefühl, das an ein theures Weib
Den Mann und an geliebte Kinder bindet,
Mein Name stirbt mit mir, mein Dasein endet.

Illo.

2005 Nicht eures Gelds bedarf's! Ein Herz wie euers
Wiegt Tonnen Goldes auf und Millionen!

Buttler.

Ich kam, ein schlechter Reitersbursch, aus Irland
Nach Prag mit einem Herrn, den ich begrub.
Vom niedern Dienst im Stalle stieg ich auf
2010 Durch Kriegsgeschick zu dieser Würd' und Höhe,
Das Spielzeug eines grillenhaften Glücks.
Auch Wallenstein ist der Fortuna Kind,
Ich liebe einen Weg, der meinem gleicht.

Illo.

Verwandte sind sich alle starken Seelen.

Buttler.

2015 Es ist ein großer Augenblick der Zeit,
Dem Tapfern, dem Entschloßnen ist sie günstig.
Wie Scheidemünze geht von Hand zu Hand,
Tauscht Stadt und Schloß den eilenden Besitzer.
Uralter Häuser Enkel wandern aus,
2020 Ganz neue Wappen kommen auf und Namen,
Auf deutscher Erde unwillkommen wagt's
Ein nördlich Volk, sich bleibend einzubürgern.
Der Prinz von Weimar rüstet sich mit Kraft,
Am Main ein mächtig Fürstenthum zu gründen;
2025 Dem Mansfeld fehlte nur, dem Halberstädter
Ein läng'res Leben, mit dem Ritterschwert
Landeigenthum sich tapfer zu erfechten.
Wer unter diesen reicht an unsern Friedland?
Nichts ist zu hoch, wonach der Starke nicht
2030 Befugniß hat die Leiter anzusetzen.

Terzky.

Das ist gesprochen wie ein Mann!

Buttler.

Versichert euch der Spanier und Welschen,
Den Schotten Leßly will ich auf mich nehmen.
Kommt zur Gesellschaft! Kommt!

Terzky.

                    Wo ist der Kellermeister?

2035 Laß aufgehn, was du hast! die besten Weine!
Heut' gilt es.   Unsre Sachen stehen gut.

(Sehen, jeder an seine Tafel.)

Fünfter Auftritt.

Kellermeister mit Neumann vorwärts kommend. Bediente gehen ab
und zu.

Kellermeister.

Der edle Wein! Wenn meine alte Herrschaft,
Die Frau Mama, das wilde Leben säh',
In ihrem Grabe kehrte sie sich um!
2040 Ja, ja! Herr Officier! Es geht zurück
Mit diesem edlen Haus. Kein Maß noch Ziel!
Und die durchlauchtige Verschwägerung
Mit diesem Herzog bringt uns wenig Segen.

Neumann.

Behüte Gott! Jetzt wird der Flor erst angehn.

Kellermeister.

2045 Meint Er? Es ließ' sich vieles davon sagen.

Bedienter (kommt).

Burgunder für den vierten Tisch!

Kellermeister.

Das ist
Die siebenzigste Flasche nun, Herr Lieut'nant.

Bedienter.

Das macht, der deutsche Herr, der Tiefenbach,
Sitzt dran.

(Geht ab.)

Kellermeister (zu Neumann fortfahrend).

Sie wollen gar zu hoch hinaus.   Kurfürsten
2050 Und Königen wollen sie's im Prunke gleich thun,
Und wo der Fürst sich hingetraut, da will der Graf,
Mein gnäd'ger Herre, nicht dahinten bleiben.

(zu den Bedienten)

Was steht ihr horchen? Will euch Beine machen.
Seht nach den Tischen, nach den Flaschen! Da!
2055 Graf Palffy hat ein leeres Glas vor sich!

Zweiter Bedienter (kommt).

Den großen Kelch verlangt man, Kellermeister,
Den reichen, güldnen, mit dem böhm'schen Wappen,
Ihr wißt schon welchen, hat der Herr gesagt.

Kellermeister.

Der auf des Friedrichs seine Königskrönung
2060 Vom Meister Wilhelm ist verfertigt worden,
Das schöne Prachtstück aus der Prager Beute?

Zweiter Bedienter.

Ja, den! Ten Umtrunk wollen sie mit halten.

Kellermeister.

(mit Kopfschütteln, indem er den Pocal hervorholt und ausspült)

Das gibt nach Wien was zu berichten wieder!

Neumann.

Zeigt! Das ist eine Pracht von einem Becher!

2060 Von Golde schwer, und in erhabner Arbeit
Sind kluge Dinge zierlich drauf gebildet.
Gleich auf dem ersten Schildlein, laßt 'mal sehn
Die stolze Amazone da zu Pferd,
Die über'n Krummstab setzt und Bischofsmützen!
2070 Auf einer Stange trägt sie einen Hut,
Nebst einer Fahn', worauf ein Kelch zu sehn.
Könnt ihr mir sagen, was das all bedeutet?

Kellermeister.

Die Weibsperson, die ihr da seht zu Roß,
Das ist die Wahlfreiheit der böhm'schen Kron'.
2075 Das wird bedeutet durch den runden Hut
Und durch das wilde Roß, auf dem sie reitet.
Des Menschen Zierat ist der Hut, denn wer
Den Hut nicht sitzen lassen darf vor Kaisern
Und Königen, der ist kein Mann der Freiheit.

Neumann.

2080 Was aber soll der Kelch da auf der Fahn'?

Kellermeister.

Der Kelch bezeugt die böhm'sche Kirchenfreiheit,
Wie sie gewesen zu der Väter Zeit.
Die Väter im Hussitenkrieg erstritten
Sich dieses schöne Vorrecht über'n Papst,
2085 Der keinem Laien gönnen will den Kelch.
Nichts geht dem Utraquisten über'n Kelch,
Es ist sein köstlich Kleinod, hat dem Böhmen
Teu'res Blut in mancher Schlacht gekostet.

Neumann.

 's die Rolle, die da drüber schwebt?

Kellermeister.

2090 Den böhm'schen Majestätsbrief zeigt sie an,
Den wir dem Kaiser Rudolph abgezwungen,
Ein köstlich unschätzbares Pergament,
Das frei Geläut' und offenen Gesang
Dem neuen Glauben sichert, wie dem alten.
2095 Doch seit der G r ä tz e r über uns regiert,
Hat das ein End', und nach der Prager Schlacht,
Wo Pfalzgraf Friedrich Kron' und Reich verloren,
Ist unser Glaub' um Kanzel und Altar,
Und unsre Brüder sehen mit dem Rücken
2100 Die Heimat an, den Majestätsbrief aber
Zerschnitt der Kaiser selbst mit seiner Schere.

Neumann

Das alles wißt ihr! Wohl bewandert seid ihr
In eures Landes Chronik, Kellermeister.

Kellermeister.

Drum waren meine Ahnherrn Taboriten
2105 Und dienten unter dem Prokop und Ziska.
Frieb' sei mit ihrem Staube! Kämpften sie
Für eine gute Sache doch! Tragt fort!

Neumann.

Erst laßt mich noch das zweite Schildlein sehn.
Sieh doch! Das ist, wie auf dem Prager Schloß
2110 Des Kaisers Räthe, Martinitz, Slawata,
Kopf unter sich herabgestürzet werden.
Ganz recht! Da steht Graf Thurn, der es befiehlt.

(Bedienter geht mit dem Kelch.)

Kellermeister.

Schweigt mir von diesem Tag, es war der drei
Und zwanzigste des Mai's, da man ein tausend

2115 Sechshundert schrieb und achtzehn. Ist mir's doch,
Als wär' es heut', und mit dem Unglückstag
Fing's an, das große Herzeleid des Landes.
Seit diesem Tag, es sind jetzt sechzehn Jahr,
Ist nimmer Fried' gewesen auf der Erden.

An der zweiten Tafel (wird gerufen).

2120 Der Fürst von Weimar!

An der dritten und vierten Tafel.

Herzog Bernhard lebe!

(Musik fällt ein.)

Erster Bedienter.

Hört den Tumult!

Zweiter Bedienter (kommt gelaufen).

Habt ihr gehört? Sie lassen
Den Weimar leben!

Dritter Bedienter.

Oestreichs Feind!

Erster Bedienter.

Den Lutheraner!

Zweiter Bedienter.

Vorhin, da bracht' der Deodat des Kaisers
Gesundheit aus, da blieb's ganz mäuschenstille.

Kellermeister.

2125 Beim Trunk geht vieles drein. Ein ordentlicher
Bedienter muß kein Ohr für so was haben.

Dritter Bedienter (bei Seite zum vierten).

Paß' ja wohl auf, Johann, daß wir dem Pater
Quiroga recht viel zu erzählen haben;
Er will dafür uns auch viel Ablaß geben.

Vierter Bedienter.

2130 Ich mach' mir an des Illo seinem Stuhl
Deßwegen auch zu thun, so viel ich kann;
Der führt dir gar verwundersame Reden.

(Gehen zu den Tafeln.)

Kellermeister (zu Neumann).

Wer mag der schwarze Herr sein mit dem Kreuz,
Der mit Graf Palffy so vertraulich schwatzt?

Neumann.

2135 Das ist auch einer, dem sie zu viel trauen,
Maradas nennt er sich, ein Spanier.

Kellermeister.

'S ist nichts mit den Hispaniern, sag' ich euch,
Die Welschen alle taugen nichts.

Neumann.

Ei, ei,
So solltet ihr nicht sprechen, Kellermeister.
2140 Es sind die ersten Generale drunter,
Auf die der Herzog just am meisten hält.

(Terzky kommt und holt das Papier ab, an den Tafeln entsteht eine Bewegung.)

Kellermeister (zu den Bedienten).

Der Generallieutenant steht auf. Gebt Acht!
Sie machen Aufbruch. Fort und rückt die Sessel!

(Die Bedienten eilen nach hinten, ein Theil der Gäste kommt vorwärts.)

Sechster Auftritt.

Octavio Piccolomini kommt im Gespräch mit Marabas, und beide stellen sich
ganz vorne hin auf eine Seite des Prosceniums. Auf die entgegengesetzte Seite tritt
Max Piccolomini, allein, in sich gekehrt und ohne Antheil an der übrigen Handlung.
Den mittlern Raum zwischen beiden, doch einige Schritte mehr zurück, erfüllen Butler, Isolani, Göß, Tiefenbach, Colalto und bald darauf Graf Terzky.

Isolani.
(während daß die Gesellschaft vorwärts kommt)

Gut' Nacht! Gut' Nacht, Colalto! Generallieut'nant,
2145 Gut' Nacht! Ich sagte besser, guten Morgen.

Göß (zu Tiefenbach).

Herr Bruder, prosit Mahlzeit!

Tiefenbach.

Das war ein königliches Mahl!

Göß.

Ja, die Frau Gräfin

Verstehl's. Sie lernt' es ihrer Schwieger ab,
Gott hab' sie selig! Das war eine Hausfrau!

Isolani (will weggehen).

2150 Lichter! Lichter!

Terzky (kommt mit der Schrift zu Isolani).

Herr Bruder! Zwei Minuten noch. Hier ist
Noch was zu unterschreiben.

Isolani.

Unterschreiben,

So viel ihr wollt! Verschont mich nur mit Lesen.

Terzky.

Ich will euch nicht bemühn. Es ist der Eid,
2155 Den ihr schon kennt. Nur einige Federstriche.
(wie Isolani die Schrift dem Octavio hinreicht)

Wie's kommt! Wen's eben trifft! Es ist kein Rang hier.
(Octavio durchläuft die Schrift mit anscheinender Gleichgültigkeit. Terzky
beobachtet ihn von weitem.)

Göz (zu Terzky).

Herr Graf! Erlaubt mir, daß ich mich empfehle.

Terzky.

Eilt doch nicht so! Noch einen Schlaftrunk! He!
(Zu den Bedienten.)

Göz.

Bin's nicht im Stand.

Terzky.

Ein Spielchen.

Göz.

Excusiert mich.

Tiefenbach (setzt sich).

1160 Vergebt, ihr Herr'n. Das Stehen wird mir sauer.

Terzky.

Macht's euch bequem, Herr Generalfeldzeugmeister!

Tiefenbach.

Das Haupt ist frisch, der Magen ist gesund,
Die Beine aber wollen nicht mehr tragen.

Isolani (auf seine Corpulenz zeigend).

Ihr habt die Last auch gar zu groß gemacht.
(Octavio hat unterschrieben und reicht Terzky die Schrift, der sie dem Isolani
gibt. Dieser geht an den Tisch, zu unterschreiben.)

Tiefenbach.

1165 Der Krieg in Pommern hat mir's zugezogen,
Da mußten wir heraus in Schnee und Eis,
Das werd' ich wohl mein Lebtag nicht verwinden.

Göz.

Ja wohl! der Schwed' frug nach der Jahrszeit nichts.
(Terzky reicht das Papier an Don Marabas; dieser geht an den Tisch, zu
unterschreiben.)

Octavio (nähert sich Buttlern).

Ihr liebt die Bacchusfeste auch nicht sehr,

2170 Herr Oberster, ich hab' es wohl bemerkt,
Und würdet, däucht mir, besser euch gefallen
Im Toben einer Schlacht, als eines Schmauses.

Buttler.

Ich muß gestehen, es ist nicht in meiner Art.

Octavio (zutraulich näher tretend.)

Auch nicht in meiner, kann ich euch versichern,
2175 Und mich erfreut's, sehr würd'ger Oberst Buttler,
Daß wir uns in der Denkart so begegnen.
Ein halbes Dutzend guter Freunde höchstens
Um einen kleinen, runden Tisch, ein Gläschen
Tokaierwein, ein offnes Herz dabei
2180 Und ein vernünftiges Gespräch, — so lieb' ich's!

Buttler.

Ja, wenn man's haben kann, ich halt' es mit.

(Das Papier kommt an Buttlern, der an den Tisch geht, zu unterschreiben.
Das Proscenium wird leer, so daß beide Piccolomini, jeder auf seiner Seite,
allein stehen bleiben.)

Octavio.

(nachdem er seinen Sohn eine Zeit lang aus der Ferne stillschweigend betrachtet,
nähert sich ihm ein wenig)

Du bist sehr lange ausgeblieben, Freund.

Max (wendet sich schnell um, verlegen).

Ich — bringende Geschäfte hielten mich.

Octavio.

Doch, wie ich sehe, bist du noch nicht hier!

Max.

2185 Du weißt, daß groß Gewühl mich immer still macht.

Octavio (rückt ihm noch näher).

Ich darf nicht wissen, was so lang' dich aufhielt?

(Listig) — Und Terzky weiß es doch.

Max.

Was weiß der Terzky?

Octavio (bedeutend).

Er war der einz'ge, der dich nicht vermißte.

Isolani.

(der von weitem Acht gegeben, tritt dazu)

Recht, alter Vater! Fall' ihm ins Gepäck!

2190 Schlag' die Quartier' ihm auf! Es ist nicht richtig.

Terzky (kommt mit der Schrift).

Fehlt keiner mehr? Hat alles unterschrieben?

Octavio.

Es haben's alle.

Terzky (rufend).

Nun? Wer unterschreibt noch?

Buttler (zu Terzky).

Zähl' nach! Just dreißig Namen müssen's sein.

Terzky.

Ein Kreuz steht hier.

Tiefenbach.

Das Kreuz bin ich.

Isolani (zu Terzky).

2195 Er kann nicht schreiben, doch sein Kreuz ist gut,

Und wird ihm honoriert von Jud und Christ.

Octavio (pressiert, zu Max).

Gehn wir zusammen, Oberst. Es wird spät.

Terzky.

Ein Piccolomini nur ist aufgeschrieben.

Isolani (auf Max zeigend).

Gebt Acht, es fehlt an diesem steinernen Gast,

2200 Der uns den ganzen Abend nichts getaugt.

(Max empfängt aus Terzkys Händen das Blatt, in welches er gedankenlos
hineinsieht.)

Terzky.

Das ist gesprochen wie ein Mann!

Buttler.

Versichert euch der Spanier und Welschen,
Den Schotten Leßly will ich auf mich nehmen.
Kommt zur Gesellschaft! Kommt!

Terzky.

Wo ist der Kellermeister?

2035 Laß aufgehn, was du hast! die besten Weine!
Heut' gilt es. Unsre Sachen stehen gut.

(Gehen, jeder an seine Tafel.)

Fünfter Auftritt.

Kellermeister mit Neumann vorwärts kommend. Bediente gehen ab
und zu.

Kellermeister.

Der edle Wein! Wenn meine alte Herrschaft,
Die Frau Mama, das wilde Leben säh',
In ihrem Grabe kehrte sie sich um!
2040 Ja, ja! Herr Officier! Es geht zurück
Mit diesem edlen Haus. Kein Maß noch Ziel!
Und die durchlauchtige Verschwägerung
Mit diesem Herzog bringt uns wenig Segen.

Neumann.

Behüte Gott! Jetzt wird der Flor erst angehn.

Kellermeister.

2045 Meint Er? Es ließ' sich vieles davon sagen.

Bedienter (kommt).

Burgunder für den vierten Tisch!

Kellermeister.

Das ist
Die siebenzigste Flasche nun, Herr Lieut'nant.

Bedienter.

Das macht, der deutsche Herr, der Tiefenbach,
Sitzt dran.

(Geht ab.)

Kellermeister (zu Neumann fortfahrend).

Sie wollen gar zu hoch hinaus. Kurfürsten
2050 Und Königen wollen sie's im Prunke gleich thun,
Und wo der Fürst sich hingetraut, da will der Graf,
Mein gnäd'ger Herre, nicht dahinten bleiben.

(zu den Bedienten)

Was steht ihr horchen? Will euch Beine machen.
Seht nach den Tischen, nach den Flaschen! Da!
2055 Graf Palffy hat ein leeres Glas vor sich!

Zweiter Bedienter (kommt).

Den großen Kelch verlangt man, Kellermeister,
Den reichen, güldnen, mit dem böhm'schen Wappen,
Ihr wißt schon welchen, hat der Herr gesagt.

Kellermeister.

Der auf des Friedrichs seine Königskrönung
2060 Vom Meister Wilhelm ist verfertigt worden,
Das schöne Prachtstück aus der Prager Beute?

Zweiter Bedienter.

Ja, den! Den Umtrunk wollen sie mit halten.

Kellermeister.

(mit Kopfschütteln, indem er den Pocal hervorholt und ausspült)

Das gibt nach Wien was zu berichten wieder!

Neumann.

Zeigt! Das ist eine Pracht von einem Becher!

185

Terzky.

Das ist gesprochen wie ein Mann!

Buttler.

Versichert euch der Spanier und Welschen,
Den Schotten Leßly will ich auf mich nehmen.
Kommt zur Gesellschaft! Kommt!

Terzky.

            Wo ist der Kellermeister?

2035 Laß aufgehn, was du hast! die besten Weine!
Heut' gilt es. Unsre Sachen stehen gut.

     (Gehen, jeder an seine Tafel.)

Fünfter Auftritt.

Kellermeister mit **Neumann** vorwärts kommend. **Bediente** gehen ab
und zu.

Kellermeister.

Der edle Wein! Wenn meine alte Herrschaft,
Die Frau Mama, das wilde Leben säh',
In ihrem Grabe kehrte sie sich um!
2040 Ja, ja! Herr Officier! Es geht zurück
Mit diesem edlen Haus. Kein Maß noch Ziel!
Und die durchlauchtige Verschwägerung
Mit diesem Herzog bringt uns wenig Segen.

Neumann.

Behüte Gott! Jetzt wird der Flor erst angehn.

Kellermeister.

2045 Meint Er? Es ließ' sich vieles davon sagen.

Bedienter (kommt).

Burgunder für den vierten Tisch!

Kellermeister.

Das ist
Die siebenzigste Flasche nun, Herr Lieut'nant.

Bedienter.

Das macht, der deutsche Herr, der Tiefenbach,
Sitzt dran.

(Geht ab.)

Kellermeister (zu Neumann fortfahrend).

Sie wollen gar zu hoch hinaus.　Kurfürsten
2050 Und Königen wollen sie's im Prunke gleich thun,
Und wo der Fürst sich hingetraut, da will der Graf,
Mein gnäb'ger Herre, nicht dahinten bleiben.

(zu den Bedienten)

Was steht ihr horchen? Will euch Beine machen.
Seht nach den Tischen, nach den Flaschen! Da!
2055 Graf Palffy hat ein leeres Glas vor sich!

Zweiter Bedienter (kommt).

Den großen Kelch verlangt man, Kellermeister,
Den reichen, güldnen, mit dem böhm'schen Wappen,
Ihr wißt schon welchen, hat der Herr gesagt.

Kellermeister.

Der auf des Friedrichs seine Königskrönung
2060 Vom Meister Wilhelm ist verfertigt worden,
Das schöne Prachtstück aus der Prager Beute?

Zweiter Bedienter.

Ja, den! Den Umtrunk wollen sie mit halten.

Kellermeister.

(mit Kopfschütteln, indem er den Pocal hervorholt und ausspült)

Das gibt nach Wien was zu berichten wieder!

Neumann.

Zeigt! Das ist eine Pracht von einem Becher!

Illo.

(vor Wuth stammelnd und seiner nicht mehr mächtig, hält ihm mit der einen
Hand die Schrift, mit der andern den Degen vor)

Schreib — Judas!

Isolani.

Pfui, Illo!

Octavio. Terzky. Buttler (zugleich).

Degen weg!

Max.

(ist ihm rasch in den Arm gefallen und hat ihn entwaffnet, zu Graf Terzky)

Bring' ihn zu Bette!

(Er geht ab. Illo, fluchend und scheltend, wird von einigen Commandeure
gehalten. Unter allgemeinem Aufbruch fällt der Vorhang.)

Fünfter Aufzug.

Scene: Ein Zimmer in Piccolominis Wohnung
Es ist Nacht.

Erster Auftritt.

Octavio Piccolomini. Kammerdiener leuchtet. Gleich darauf
Max Piccolomini.

Octavio.

Sobald mein Sohn herein ist, weiset ihn
Zu mir.   Was ist die Glocke?

Kammerdiener.

Gleich ist's Morgen.

Octavio.

2365 Setzt euer Licht hieher.   Wir legen uns
Nicht mehr zu Bette, ihr könnt schlafen gehn.
(Kammerdiener ab. Octavio geht nachdenkend durchs Zimmer. Max Piccolomini tritt auf, nicht gleich von ihm bemerkt, und sieht ihm einige Augenblicke schweigend zu.

Max.

Bist du mir bös', Octavio? Weiß Gott,
Ich bin nicht schuld an dem verhaßten Streit.
Ich sahe wohl, du hattest unterschrieben;
2370 Was du gebilliget, das konnte mir
Auch recht sein; doch es war — du weißt, ich kann
In solchen Sachen nur dem eignen Licht,

Nicht fremdem folgen.

Octavio.
(geht auf ihn zu und umarmt ihn)

Folg' ihm ferner auch,
Mein bester Sohn! Es hat dich treuer jetzt
2275 Geleitet, als das Beispiel deines Vaters.

Max.
Erklär' dich deutlicher.

Octavio.
Ich werd' es thun.
Nach dem, was diese Nacht geschehen ist,
Darf kein Geheimniß bleiben zwischen uns.
(nachdem beide sich niedergesetzt)
Max, sage mir, was denkst du von dem Eid,
2280 Den man zur Unterschrift uns vorgelegt?

Max.
Für etwas unverfänglich's halt' ich ihn,
Obgleich ich dieses Förmliche nicht liebe.

Octavio.
Du hättest dich aus keinem andern Grunde
Der abgedrungnen Unterschrift geweigert?

Max.
2285 Es war ein ernst Geschäft, ich war zerstreut,
Die Sache selbst erschien mir nicht so dringend.

Octavio.
Sei offen, Max. Du hattest keinen Argwohn?

Max.
Worüber Argwohn? Nicht den mindesten.

Octavio.
Dank's deinem Engel, Piccolomini!
2290 Unwissend zog er dich zurück vom Abgrund.

Max.

Ich weiß nicht, was du meinst.

Octavio.

Ich will dir's sagen

Zu einem Schelmstück solltest du den Namen
Hergeben, deinen Pflichten, deinem Eid
Mit einem einz'gen Federstrich entsagen.

Max (steht auf).

2295 Octavio!

Octavio.

Bleib sitzen. Viel noch hast du
Von mir zu hören, Freund, hast Jahre lang
Gelebt in unbegreiflicher Verblendung.
Das schwärzeste Complot entspinnet sich
Vor deinen Augen, eine Macht der Hölle
2300 Umnebelt deiner Sinne hellen Tag,
Ich darf nicht länger schweigen, muß die Binde
Von deinen Augen nehmen.

Max.

Eh' du sprichst,

Bedenk' es wohl! Wenn von Vermuthungen
Die Rede sein soll — und ich fürchte fast,
2305 Es ist nichts weiter — spare sie! Ich bin
Jetzt nicht gefaßt, sie ruhig zu vernehmen.

Octavio.

So ernsten Grund du hast, dies Licht zu fliehn,
So dringendern hab' ich, daß ich dir's gebe.
Ich konnte dich der Unschuld deines Herzens,
2310 Dem eignen Urtheil ruhig anvertraun;
Doch deinem Herzen selbst seh' ich das Netz

Verderblich jetzt bereiten.   Das Geheimniß,

(ihn scharf mit den Augen fixirend)

Das d u vor mir verbirgst, entreißt mir m e i n e s.

Max.

(versucht zu antworten, stockt aber und schlägt den Blick verlegen zu Boden.)

Octavio (nach einer Pause).

So wisse denn! Man hintergeht dich, spielt

2315 Aufs schändlichste mit dir und mit uns allen.

Der Herzog stellt sich an, als wollt' er die

Armee verlassen; und in dieser Stunde

Wird's eingeleitet, die Armee dem Kaiser

— Zu stehlen und dem Feinde zuzuführen!

Max.

2320 Das Pfaffenmärchen kenn' ich, aber nicht

Aus deinem Mund erwartet' ich's zu hören.

Octavio.

Der Mund, aus dem du's gegenwärtig hörst,

Verbürget dir, es sei kein Pfaffenmärchen.

Max.

Zu welchem Rasenden macht man den Herzog!

2325 Er könnte daran denken, dreißig tausend

Geprüfter Truppen, ehrlicher Soldaten,

Worunter mehr denn tausend Edelleute,

Von Eid und Pflicht und Ehre wegzulocken,

Zu einer Schurkenthat sie zu vereinen?

Octavio.

2330 So was nichtswürdig schändliches begehrt

Er keineswegs.   Was er von uns will,

Führt einen weit unschuldigeren Namen.

Nichts will er, als dem Reich den Frieden schenken;

Und weil der Kaiser diesen Frieden haßt,
2335 So will er ihn — er will ihn dazu zwingen!
Zufrieden stellen will er alle Theile,
Und zum Ersatz für seine Mühe Böhmen,
Das er schon inne hat, für sich behalten.

Max.

Hat er's um uns verdient, Octavio,
2340 Daß wir — wir so unwürdig von ihm denken?

Octavio.

Von unserm Denken ist hier nicht die Rede.
Die Sache spricht, die klaresten Beweise.
Mein Sohn! Dir ist nicht unbekannt, wie schlimm
Wir mit dem Hofe stehn; doch von den Ränken,
2345 Den Lügenkünsten hast du keine Ahnung,
Die man in Uebung setzte, Meuterei
Im Lager auszusäen. Aufgelöst
Sind alle Bande, die den Officier
An seinen Kaiser fesseln, den Soldaten
2350 Vertraulich binden an das Bürgerleben.
Pflicht= und gesetzlos steht er gegenüber
Dem Staat gelagert, den er schützen soll,
Und drohet, gegen ihn das Schwert zu kehren.
Es ist so weit gekommen, daß der Kaiser
2355 In diesem Augenblick vor seinen eignen
Armeen zittert, der Verräther Dolche
In seiner Hauptstadt fürchtet, seiner Burg;
Ja, im Begriffe steht, die zarten Enkel
Nicht vor den Schweden, vor den Lutheranern
2360 — Nein! vor den eignen Truppen wegzuflüchten!

Max.

Hör' auf! Du.ängstigest, erschütterst mich.
Ich weiß, daß man vor leeren Schrecken zittert;
Doch wahres Unglück bringt der falsche Wahn.

Octavio.

Es ist kein Wahn.   Der bürgerliche Krieg
2365 Entbrennt, der unnatürlichste von allen,
Wenn wir nicht, schleunig rettend, ihm begegnen.
Der Obersten sind viele längst erkauft,
Der Subalternen Treue wankt; es wanken
Schon ganze Regimenter, Garnisonen.
2370 Ausländern sind die Festungen vertraut,
Dem Schafgotsch, dem verdächtigen, hat man
Die ganze Mannschaft Schlesiens, dem Terzky
Fünf Regimenter, Reiterei und Fußvolk,
Dem Illo, Kinsky, Buttler, Isolan
2375 Die bestmontierten Truppen übergeben.

Max.

Uns beiden auch.

Octavio.

                Weil man uns glaubt zu haben,
Zu locken meint durch glänzende Versprechen.
So theilt man mir die Fürstenthümer Glatz
Und Sagan zu, und wohl seh' ich den Angel,
2380 Womit man dich zu fangen denkt.   ●

Max.

                        Nein! Nein!
Nein! sag' ich dir!

Octavio.
O öffne doch die Augen!

Weßwegen glaubst du, daß man uns nach Pilsen
Beorderte? Um mit uns Rath zu pflegen?
Wann hätte Friedland unsers Raths bedurft?
2385 Wir sind berufen, uns ihm zu verkaufen,
Und weigern wir uns — Geißel ihm zu bleiben.
Deßwegen ist Graf Gallas weggeblieben.
Auch deinen Vater sähest du nicht hier,
Wenn höh're Pflicht ihn nicht gefesselt hielt'.

Max.

2390 Er hat es keinen Hehl, daß wir um seinetwillen
Hieher berufen sind; gestehet ein,
Er brauche unsers Arms, sich zu erhalten.
Er that so viel für uns, und so ist's Pflicht,
Daß wir jetzt auch für ihn was thun!

Octavio.

Und weißt du,
2395 Was dieses ist, was wir für ihn thun sollen?
Des Illo trunkner Muth hat dir's verrathen.
Besinn dich doch, was du gehört, gesehn.
Zeugt das verfälschte Blatt, die weggelaßne,
So ganz entscheidungsvolle Clausel nicht,
2400 Man wolle zu nichts gutem uns verbinden?

Max.

Was mit dem Blatte diese Nacht geschehn,
Ist mir nichts weiter als ein schlechter Streich
Von diesem Illo. Dies Geschlecht von Mäklern
Pflegt alles auf die Spitze gleich zu stellen.
2405 Sie sehen, daß der Herzog mit dem Hof
Zerfallen ist, vermeinen ihm zu dienen,

Wenn sie den Bruch unheilbar nur erweitern.
Der Herzog, glaub' mir, weiß von all dem nichts.

Octavio.

Es schmerzt mich, deinen Glauben an den Mann,
2410 Der dir so wohlgegründet scheint, zu stürzen.
Doch hier darf keine Schonung sein.   Du mußt
Maßregeln nehmen, schleunige, mußt handeln.
Ich will dir also nur gestehn, daß alles,
Was ich dir jetzt vertraut, was so unglaublich
2415 Dir scheint, daß — daß ich es aus seinem eignen,
Des Fürsten Munde habe.

Max (in heftiger Bewegung).
                    Nimmermehr!

Octavio.

Er selbst vertraute mir — was ich zwar längst
Auf anderm Weg schon in Erfahrung brachte:
Daß er zum Schweden wolle übergehn,
2420 Und an der Spitze des verbundnen Heers
Den Kaiser zwingen wolle —

Max.
                    Er ist heftig,
Es hat der Hof empfindlich ihn beleidigt;
In einem Augenblick des Unmuths, sei's!
Mag er sich leicht einmal vergessen haben.

Octavio.
2425 Bei kaltem Blute war er, als er mir
Dies eingestand; und weil er mein Erstaunen
Als Furcht auslegte, wies er im Vertraun
Mir Briefe vor, der Schweden und der Sachsen,
Die zu bestimmter Hilfe Hoffnung geben.

Max.

2430 Es kann nicht sein! kann nicht sein! kann nicht sein!
Siehst du, daß es nicht kann! Du hätteft ihm
Nothwendig deinen Abscheu ja gezeigt,
Er hätt' sich weisen lassen, oder du
—Du ftündeft nicht mehr lebend mir zur Seite!

Octavio.

2435 Wohl hab' ich mein Bedenken ihm geäußert,
Hab' dringend, hab' mit Ernft ihn abgemahnt;
Doch meinen Abscheu, meine innerste
Gesinnung hab' ich tief verftectt.

Max.

              Du wärft
So falsch gewesen! Das sieht meinem Vater
2440 Nicht gleich! Ich glaubte deinen Worten nicht,
Da du von ihm mir Böses fagtest; kann's
Noch wen'ger jetzt, da du dich selbft verleumdeft.

Octavio.

Ich drängte mich nicht selbft in sein Geheimniß.

Max.

Aufrichtigkeit verdiente sein Vertraun.

Octavio.

2445 Nicht würdig war er meiner Wahrheit mehr.

Max.

Noch minder würdig deiner war Betrug.

Octavio.

Mein befter Sohn! Es ift nicht immer möglich,
Im Leben sich so kinderrein zu halten,
Wie's uns die Stimme lehrt im Innerften.

2450 In steter Nothwehr gegen arge List
Bleibt auch das redliche Gemüth nicht wahr.
Das eben ist der Fluch der bösen That,
Daß sie, fortzeugend, immer Böses muß gebären.
Ich klügle nicht, ich thue meine Pflicht;
2455 Der Kaiser schreibt mir mein Betragen vor.
Wohl wär' es besser, überall dem Herzen
Zu folgen; doch darüber würde man
Sich manchen guten Zweck versagen müssen.
Hier gilt's, mein Sohn, dem Kaiser wohl zu dienen,
2460 Das Herz mag dazu sprechen, was es will.

Max.

Ich soll dich heut' nicht fassen, nicht verstehn.
Der Fürst, sagst du, entdeckte redlich dir sein Herz
Zu einem bösen Zweck, und du willst ihn
Zu einem guten Zweck betrogen haben!
2465 Hör' auf, ich bitte dich! Du raubst den Freund
Mir nicht. Laß mich den Vater nicht verlieren!

Octavio.
(unterdrückt seine Empfindlichkeit)

Noch weißt du alles nicht, mein Sohn! Ich habe
Dir noch was zu eröffnen.
(nach einer Pause)
Herzog Friedland
Hat seine Zurüstung gemacht. Er traut
2470 Auf seine Sterne. Unbereitet denkt er uns
Zu überfallen, mit der sichern Hand
Meint er den goldnen Zirkel schon zu fassen.
Er irret sich. Wir haben auch gehandelt.
Er faßt sein bös' geheimnißvolles Schicksal.

Max.

2475 Nichts rasches, Vater! O, bei allem guten
Laß dich beschwören! Keine Uebereilung!

Octavio.

Mit leisen Tritten schlich er seinen bösen Weg,
So leis' und schlau ist ihm die Rache nachgeschlichen.
Schon steht sie ungesehen, finster hinter ihm,

2480 Ein Schritt nur noch, und schaudernd rühret er sie an.
Du hast den Questenberg bei mir gesehn,
Noch kennst du nur sein öffentlich Geschäft,
Auch ein geheimes hat er mitgebracht,
Das bloß für mich war.

Max.

Darf ich's wissen?

Octavio.

Max

2485 Des Reiches Wohlfahrt leg' ich mit dem Worte,
Des Vaters Leben dir in deine Hand.
Der Wallenstein ist deinem Herzen theuer,
Ein starkes Band der Liebe, der Verehrung
Knüpft seit der frühen Jugend dich an ihn.

2490 Du nährst den Wunsch — O laß mich immerhin
Vorgreifen deinem zögernden Vertrauen! —
Die Hoffnung nährst du, ihm viel näher noch
Anzugehören.

Max.

Vater!

Octavio.

Deinem Herzen trau' ich,
Doch bin ich deiner Fassung auch gewiß?

2495 Wirst du's vermögen, ruhigen Gesichts
Vor diesen Mann zu treten, wenn ich dir
Sein ganz Geschick nun anvertrauet habe?

Max.

Nachdem du seine Schuld mir anvertraut!

Octavio.
(nimmt ein Papier aus der Schatulle und reicht es ihm hin).

Max.

Was? Wie? Ein offner kaiserlicher Brief.

Octavio.

2500 Lies ihn.

Max (nachdem er einen Blick hineingeworfen).
Der Fürst verurtheilt und geächtet!

Octavio.

So ist's.

Max.
O, das geht weit! O unglücksvoller Irrthum

Octavio.

Lies weiter! Faß dich!

Max.
(nachdem er weiter gelesen, mit einem Blick des Erstaunens auf seinen Vater)
Wie? Was? Du? Du bist —

Octavio.

Bloß für den Augenblick, und bis der König
Von Ungarn bei dem Heer erscheinen kann,
2505 Ist das Commando mir gegeben.

Max.

Und glaubst du, daß du's ihm entreißen werdest?
Das denke ja nicht! Vater! Vater! Vater!
Ein unglückselig Amt ist dir geworden.
Dies Blatt hier, dieses willst du geltend machen?

2510 Den Mächtigen in seines Heeres Mitte,
Umringt von seinen Tausenden, entwaffnen?
Du bist verloren! Du, wir alle sind's!

Octavio.

Was ich dabei zu wagen habe, weiß ich.
Ich stehe in der Allmacht Hand; sie wird
2515 Das fromme Kaiserhaus mit ihrem Schilde
Bedecken, und das Werk der Nacht zertrümmern.
Der Kaiser hat noch treue Diener, auch im Lager
Gibt es der braven Männer g'nug, die sich
Zur guten Sache munter schlagen werden.
2520 Die Treuen sind gewarnt, bewacht die andern;
Den ersten Schritt erwart' ich nur, sogleich —

Max.

Auf den Verdacht hin willst du rasch gleich handeln?

Octavio.

Fern sei vom Kaiser die Tyrannenweise!
Den Willen nicht, die That nur will er strafen.
2525 Noch hat der Fürst sein Schicksal in der Hand.
Er lasse das Verbrechen unvollführt,
So wird man ihn still vom Commando nehmen,
Er wird dem Sohne seines Kaisers weichen.
Ein ehrenvoll Exil auf seine Schlösser
2530 Wird Wohlthat mehr als Strafe für ihn sein.
Jedoch der erste offenbare Schritt —

Max.

Was nennst du einen solchen Schritt? Er wird
Nie einen bösen thun. Du aber könntest —
Du hast's gethan — den frömmsten auch mißdeuten.

Octavio.

2535 Wie strafbar auch des Fürsten Zwecke waren,
Die Schritte, die er öffentlich gethan,
Verstatteten noch eine milde Deutung.
Nicht eher denk' ich dieses Blatt zu brauchen,
Bis eine That gethan ist, die unwidersprechlich
2540 Den Hochverrath bezeugt und ihn verdammt.

Max.

Und wer soll Richter drüber sein?

Octavio.

Du selbst.

Max.

O dann bedarf es dieses Blattes nie!
Ich hab' dein Wort, du wirst nicht eher handeln,
Bevor du mich, mich selber überzeugt.

Octavio.

2545 Ist's möglich? Noch — nach allem, was du weißt —
Kannst du an seine Unschuld glauben?

Max (lebhaft).

Dein Urtheil kann sich irren, nicht mein Herz.
(gemäßigter fortfahrend)
Der Geist ist nicht zu fassen, wie ein andrer.
Wie er sein Schicksal an die Sterne knüpft,
2550 So gleicht er ihnen auch in wunderbarer,
Geheimer, ewig unbegriffner Bahn.
Glaub' mir, man thut ihm Unrecht. Alles wird
Sich lösen. Glänzend werden wir den Reinen
Aus diesem schwarzen Argwohn treten sehn.

Octavio.

2555 Ich will's erwarten.

Zweiter Auftritt.

Die Vorigen. Der Kammerdiener. Gleich darauf ein Courier.

Octavio.

Was gibt's?

Kammerdiener.

Ein Eilbot' wartet vor der Thür.

Octavio.

So früh am Tag! Wer ist's? Wo kommt er her?

Kammerdiener.

Das wollt' er mir nicht sagen.

Octavio.

Führ' ihn herein. Laß nichts davon verlauten.

(Kammerdiener ab. Cornet tritt ein)

2560 Seid ihr's Cornet? Ihr kommt vom Grafen Gallas?
Gebt her den Brief.

Cornet.

Bloß mündlich ist mein Auftrag.
Der Generallieut'naut traute nicht.

Octavio.

Was ist's?

Cornet.

Er läßt euch sagen — Darf ich frei hier sprechen?

Octavio.

Mein Sohn weiß alles.

Cornet.

Wir haben ihn.

Octavio.

Wen meint ihr?

Cornet.

2565 Den Unterhändler, den Sesin!

Octavio (schnell).

Habt ihr?

Cornet.

Im Böhmerwald erwischt' ihn Hauptmann Mohrbrand
Vorgestern früh, als er nach Regensburg
Zum Schweden unterwegs war mit Depeschen.

Octavio.

Und die Depeschen —

Cornet.

Hat der Generallieut'nant

2570 Sogleich nach Wien geschickt mit dem Gefangnen.

Octavio.

Nun endlich, endlich! Das ist eine große Zeitung!
Der Mann ist uns ein kostbares Gefäß,
Das wicht'ge Dinge einschließt.   Fand man viel?

Cornet.

An sechs Pakete mit Graf Terzkys Wappen.

Octavio.

2575 Keins von des Fürsten Hand?

Cornet.

Nicht, daß ich wüßte.

Octavio.

Und der Sesina?

Cornet.

Der that sehr erschrocken,
Als man ihm sagt', es ginge nacher Wien.
Graf Altring aber sprach ihm guten Muth ein,
Wenn er nur alles wollte frei bekennen.

Octavio.

2580 Ist Altringer bei eurem Herrn? Ich hörte,
Er läge krank zu Linz.

Cornet.

Schon seit drei Tagen
Ist er zu Frauenberg beim Generallieut'nant.
Sie haben sechzig Fähnlein schon beisammen,
Erles'nes Volk, und lassen euch entbieten,
1585 Daß sie von euch Befehle nur erwarten.

Octavio.

In wenig Tagen kann sich viel ereignen.
Wann müßt ihr fort?

Cornet.

Ich wart' auf eure Ordre.

Octavio.

Bleibt bis zum Abend.

Cornet.

Wohl.

(Will gehen.)

Octavio.

Sah euch doch niemand?

Cornet.

Kein Mensch.   Die Kapuziner ließen mich
1590 Durchs Klosterpförtchen ein, so wie gewöhnlich.

Octavio.

Geht, ruht euch aus und haltet euch verborgen.
Ich denk' euch noch vor Abend abzufert'gen.
Die Sachen liegen der Entwicklung nah,
Und eh' der Tag, der eben jetzt am Himmel
1595 Verhängnißvoll heranbricht, untergeht,
Muß ein entscheidend Loos gefallen sein.

(Cornet geht ab.)

Dritter Auftritt.

Beide Piccolomini.

Octavio.

Was nun, mein Sohn? Jetzt werden wir bald klar sein,
Denn alles, weiß ich, ging durch den Sesina.

Max.
(der während des ganzen vorigen Auftritts in einem heftigen innern Kampf
gestanden, entschlossen)

Ich will auf kürzerm Weg mir Licht verschaffen.

2600 Leb' wohl!

Octavio.
Wohin? Bleib da!

Max.

Zum Fürsten.

Octavio (erschrickt).

Was?

Max (zurückkommend).

Wenn du geglaubt, ich werde eine Rolle
In deinem Spiele spielen, hast du dich
In mir verrechnet. Mein Weg muß gerad' sein.
Ich kann nicht wahr sein mit der Zunge, mit

2605 Dem Herzen falsch; nicht zusehn, daß mir einer
Als seinem Freunde traut, und mein Gewissen
Damit beschwichtigen, daß er's auf seine
Gefahr thut, daß mein Mund ihn nicht belogen.
Wofür mich einer kauft, das muß ich sein.

2610 Ich geh' zum Herzog. Heut' noch werd' ich ihn
Auffordern, seinen Leumund vor der Welt
Zu retten, eure künstlichen Gewebe
Mit einem g'raden Schritte zu durchreißen.

Octavio.

Das wolltest du?

Max.

Das will ich.   Zweifle nicht.

Octavio.

2615 Ich habe mich in dir verrechnet, ja!
Ich rechnete auf einen weisen Sohn,
Der die wohlthät'gen Hände würde segnen,
Die ihn zurück vom Abgrund ziehn, und einen
Verblendeten entdeck' ich, den zwei Augen
2620 Zum Thoren machten, Leidenschaft umnebelt,
Den selbst des Tages volles Licht nicht heilt.
Befrag' ihn! Geh'!. Sei unbesonnen g'nug
Ihm deines Vaters, deines Kaisers
Geheimniß preiszugeben.   Nöth'ge mich
2625 Zu einem lauten Bruche vor der Zeit!
Und jetzt, nachdem ein Wunderwerk des Himmels
Bis heute mein Geheimniß hat beschützt,
Des Argwohns helle Blicke eingeschläfert,
Laß mich's erleben, daß mein eigner Sohn
2630 Mit unbedachtsam rasendem Beginnen
Der Staatskunst mühevolles Werk vernichtet.

Max.

O diese Staatskunst, wie verwünsch' ich sie!
Ihr werdet ihn durch eure Staatskunst noch
Zu einem Schritte treiben — Ja! ihr könntet ihn,
2635 Weil ihr ihn schuldig wollt, noch schuldig machen.
O! das kann nicht gut endigen, und mag sich's
Entscheiden wie es will, ich sehe ahnend
Die unglückselige Entwicklung nahen.

Denn dieser Königliche, wenn er fällt,

2640 Wird eine Welt im Sturze mit sich reißen,
Und wie ein Schiff, das mitten auf dem Weltmeer
In Brand geräth mit einemmal, und berstend
Auffliegt und alle Mannschaft, die es trug,
Ausschüttet plötzlich zwischen Meer und Himmel,

2645 Wird er uns alle, die wir an sein Glück
Befestigt sind, in seinen Fall hinabziehn.
Halte du es, wie du willst! Doch mir vergönne,
Daß ich auf meine Weise mich betrage.
Rein muß es bleiben zwischen mir und ihm,

2650 Und eh' der Tag sich neigt, muß sich's erklären,
Ob ich den Freund, ob ich den Vater soll entbehren.

(Indem er abgeht, fällt der Vorhang.)

COMMENTARY.

[For explanation of allusions to history, see Introduction; to persons or places, see Index. For abbreviations. Introd. ix, x; Wh. stands for Whitney's German Grammar.]

PERSONEN.

Generallieutenant. In the modern German service, the commander of an army-corps. In the 30 Y. W., however, and as S. uses the term, the *locum tenens*, the generallisimo's chief executive officer for the entire army, Introd. lxv.—**Chef.** The term does not exist in the American service. It designates the honorary head of a regiment; not the acting colonel, but a person of distinction, upon whom has been conferred the privilege of wearing the uniform, and, on state-occasions, of assuming the command. Thus, in the present Prussian *Garde-corps*, the first regiment of grenadiers is called the *Kaiser-Alexander Regiment*, the *Chef* is the emperor of Russia, while the colonel in command is Oberst v. Wassow. Terzky, it will be observed, as a person of great prominence in W.'s army, is *Chef* of several regiments. In 30 Y. W. the title was conferred more freely than at present day.—**Kürassier,** from French *cuirassier*, from *cuir*, leather. The *cuirassiers* wore originally a breast-piece of leather, now of steel.—**Feldmarschall** designates now the highest rank in the service. But in 30 Y. W. used rather loosely to designate a rank between our brigadier and major-general. The term was not used in its present sense before the 18th century, in France, after the ancient office of *connétable* had been abolished. In the German army of to-day, the Crown-Prince, Prince Frederick Charles, Wrangel, v. Moltke, and one or two others are field-marshals.

—**Rittmeister,** in French, *chef d'escadron*, captain of cavalry.
—**Adjutant,** aide-de-camp.—**Oberst,** colonel.   In form, the
superlative of *ober*, and should be declined as an adjective.
But as a military term, generally declined nom. s. *der Oberst*,
gen. s. *Obersts* or *Obersten*, dat. s. *Oberst ;* pl. *Obersten.*   The
usage varies.   S. has nom. s. *Oberster*, v. 2170 ; also in several
places the archaic forms *Obrist, Obristen.*—**Prinzessin.**   The
word *Fürst* designates a sovereign ruler, which W. was as Duke
of Mecklenburg, and perhaps even as Duke of Friedland,
Introd. xiv, xviii.   *Fürstin*, the wife of such ruler.   *Prinz* and
Prinzessin, the children of a *Fürst*, or persons of the blood
royal, not actually rulers, or persons of the highest rank
below royalty, *e.g.*, Prince Bismarck.—**Cornet,** standard-
bearer of cavalry.—**Kellermeister,** head-butler.—**Hoboisten,**
often spelled *Oboisten.*   From French *hautbois*, Ital. *oboe*, a
wind instrument somewhat similar to clarionet.   H. designates
here military musicians in general (see heading to Act IV.).

ANALYSIS OF ACT I.

Scene 1. Merely introductory.   The reader is to understand
that Illo has been in Pilsen already some time, while Isolani has
just arrived from a cavalry raid far behind the Swedish lines
at Ratisbon, and Buttler has also come from some place, not
mentioned, but evidently Frauenburg (Introd. lii, and Index).
—**Scene 2.** The action of the drama really begins with the
appearance of Octavio Piccolomini and Questenberg.   The
sharp repartees that pass between Questenberg on one side, and
Illo, Buttler, and Isolani on the other, serve to reveal the
temper of the army and its scarcely concealed contempt for the
court and the emperor's ministers.—**Scene 3.** Octavio and
Questenberg being left alone, the latter gives vent to his
astonishment.   He regards the army as wholly lost for the
emperor, and a mere tool in the hands of Wallenstein.   Octavio
seeks to comfort him, assuring him that things are not so bad
as they seem, and explaining the unbounded confidence placed
in him (Octavio) by W., so that the latter could not take the
first step towards an insurrection without his knowledge.—

Scene 4. The appearance of Max serves to reveal the temper of the army from still another point. The young colonel symbolizes the nobler spirits among the officers, he regards the policy of the court as dictated by envy of Wallenstein's greatness and by unwillingness to accede to a peace which all Germany longs for. Max's beautiful apostrophe to Peace must be understood as having direct reference to the general European war consequent upon the French Revolution and present to Schiller's mind while writing. By the warmth of his outburst, and his allusion to the blessings of wedded life, Max betrays his love for Thekla, whom he has just escorted to Pilsen.—**Scene 5.** Questenberg and Octavio are thunderstruck, the former by Max's devotion to his general, the latter by the dangerous complications which may arise from this sudden love. Questenberg, who does not suspect Max's relations to Thekla, is unable to comprehend Octavio's confused ejaculations.

SCENE I.

[1] *Der weite Weg.* From Donauwörth to Pilsen, not far from 150 m. This raid by Isolani seems to be an invention of Schiller's, and rather improbable. The Swedes had complete control of the upper Danube.—[5] *Sei*, 'was;' subj. of indirect speech, Wh. § 333.4.*a.*—[6] *An die*, 'as many as.'—[7] *Mir*, dat. of "interest," Wh. § 222, III.—[7] *Noch* expresses either continuance or addition. Here it may denote either, while we were 'still' en route, or, not only did we cut our way through safely, but we 'also' captured this booty.—[8] *Grad zu Pass*, 'just in time,' 'à propos.'—[14] *Behilft sich*, does not mean 'helps himself to whatever he can find,' but *sich behelfen* and *sich schicken* mean about the same, *i.e.*, to adapt one's self to circumstances. [22] *Stutzt*, 'is startled,' taken aback.—[24] *Zehen.* The battle at Dessau bridge was April, 1626, consequently only eight years before.—[26] *Sprengen*, 'to make jump,' causative from *springen.* Dependent on *seh'*, v. 24.—[30] *Fertig*, 'finished,' *i.e.*, a hero complete in every respect.—*Soll sein*, 'is said to be,' Wh. § 257.3.—[31] *Sollt*, here implying a promise, 'you shall' see. Wh. § 257.1.—[32] *Fürstin, Prinzessin*, see PERSONEN.— [39] *Ergetze*, subj. of purpose or desire, Wh. § 332.5.*b.d.*— [40] *Aussen*, for *weg*, 'away.'—[41] B's answer implies that G. had not only resolved to keep away from Pilsen himself, but had

also sought to detain B. Consequently B. and Illo must know that G. is unfavorably disposed. Compare Introd. lii–liv.— [44] *Noch kürzlich*, 'only recently.'—[45] *General-Major*, now used to designate the commander of a brigade. How Schiller came to make B. a general, when all accounts represent him as merely colonel of a regiment, would be difficult to explain. Probably the term was used in a different sense in 30 Y. W.— [47] *Geschenkt, i.e.*, made him *Chef*. See PERSONEN.—[48] *Reiter*, a simple cavalryman.—*Er.* This use of the pronoun of 3d pers. s. for 2d was very common in 30 Y. W.—[50] *Macht einmal.* The inversion has the force of ' if,' 'when.' Wb. § 443.5.—[53] *Bestätigung.* We do not know the full extent of W.'s powers, but it is quite certain that he had the right of appointing colonels, Introd. xxxii, and highly probable that he had also the right of creating *Chefs.* The emperor's confirmation, therefore, was scarcely necessary.—[57] *So gar bedenklich*, 'so very doubtful, apprehensive.' The student should learn to distinguish between *gar*, which intensifies the following adjective, and the compound *sogar*, which usually means 'indeed, even.' —[61] *Contentieren.* Isolani is given to using foreign words. Characteristic of the soldiery in 30 Y. W., which was a period of dire confusion of speech, *Sprachenmengerei.* The *Lager* is full of such expressions.—[63] *Zu einem ordentlichen Mann, i.e.*, make a respectable man of me once more. Herchenhahn relates, II. 16 : "Isolani once brought in two flags captured from the Swedes. Wallenstein gave him 2,000 thalers, and the next day as many more, because Isolani had gambled away the first sum over night." Schiller seems to have invented this third donation.—[66] *Zu Ehren bringen*, here, to restore to honor, credit. *Ehren* is probably not dat. pl., but archaic dat. sing.— [68] *Schenkte*, condit. ' would give.'—*Leut'*, *i.e.*, the vassals, serfs attached to the feudal estates.—[69] *Nicht*, used frequently in the German exclamational phrase, but superfluous in English. —[71] *Da !* Here, and in several other places, an ejaculation of contempt or impatience.—*Sauber*, 'nice,' used ironically. For Q.'s demands, see Act II., sc. 7.—[77] *Vom Platze*, from his position as generalissimo, *i.e.*, resign.

SCENE 2.

[82] *Der Gäste mehr.* In early German *viel, mehr, wenig, genug*, and similar words, governed regularly the genitive case.

But this government is almost extinct in modern German (such
words being treated in apposition with the following noun)
and occurs only in poetry or very elevated style. It also occurs
in such expressions as *unser viel*, many of us.—[83] *Es brauchte*,
used impersonally, Wh. § 292.3. The sense is best given by
the rather colloquial expression 'it took' such a war to collect
so many great generals in one camp.—[88] *Hätte*, subj. with
suppressed condition, Wh. § 332.2.e, 'I could almost have for-
gotten the evils of war (had I not recollected myself in time),
when (*da*) I perceived' the perfect order and discipline, &c.—
[93] *Reihen, der*, formerly (and still in poetry) spelled *Reigen*.
Originally a dance (in a circle). Hence, a circle or round of
persons. Not to be confounded with *die Reihe*, a row or line.
—[96] Buttler, as colonel of heavy dragoons, impersonates
strength; Isolani, commander of the lighter armed and
mounted Croats, impersonates quickness.—*Questenbergen*. The
en is the remains of declension of proper nouns, now almost
obsolete, Wh. § 105. Schiller is not consistent in use of it, see
v. 1007, 1089.—[106] *Znaim*. (See Introd. xxx, xxxii, lxix.)—
[107] *Von-wegen*, on behalf of. *Wegen* is really dat. pl., but the
two words together have force of preposition, like the single
word *wegen*.—[110] *Dass ich wüsste*, so far as I know, remember.
The subj. has force of softening a positive assertion, Wh.
§ 332.3a.—[113] *Aufs Haupt geschlagen*, 'routed.' For anachronism, Introd. lxix. The object of this anachronism is to
heighten the dramatic effect of Illo's description of circumstances under which W. resumed command.—[118] *Ungnade*, see
zwingen, v. 111. H. W. II. 131 relates that Eggenberg intimated to W. that if he (W.) should presume to resign the command (Introd. xxxii) the emperor might feel induced to use
harsh measures (probably confiscation of his estates). The
statement is of no authority.—[119] *Erbarme*, 'would take com-
passion,' subj. of indirect speech, quoting Q.'s words on the
occasion, Wh. § 333.3d, 333.4a.—[122] *Just*, compare *contentieren*, v. 61.—[123] *Soll*, I am to, it is my mission to, Wh. § 257.2.
Q.'s obligation arises from the emperor's command.—[131] *Soll*.
The phrase has the force of: if it (the country) is not to be
considered as having.—[132] *Freund*, for *Freundes*. A poetic
license.—*Gleich*, 'alike,' both friend and foe.—[133] *Ei was*,
O pshaw!—[138] *Drauf gehen*, 'come to grief.' The peasants,
after being ruined, will turn soldiers. For inversion, see v. 50,

macht einmal.—**146** *Blutigel* refers to the court-parasites, like
Q., who ostensibly deplore the war, but in reality grow rich on
confiscations and fat salaries.—*Saugten.* The verb is more cor-
rectly inflected strong: past *ich sog*, condit. *ich söge*, p. part.
gesogen.—**147** *So arg*, to be connected with *arm*, v. 143. Q. has
just said that the emperor was impoverished, to which Isol.
replies that it can not be 'so bad,' there is still plenty of gold
uncoined, v. 148, alluding to the massive gold chain and key
worn by Q. as imperial chamberlain, see v. 1290.—*Ja*, has here
the force of the interjection 'why!'—**151** *Da*, see v. 71.—
Verses 151–160 exhibit change of construction; *der S.* and *der
M.* are in nomin. Then the construction is altered and the *die*,
v. 158, is put in accus. 'There now! This S. and this M.,
who get all the emperor's favors, &c., let them pay for the war.'
—**163** *Benefiz*, probably used here in technical sense of 'land-
gift' in the conferment of the emperor.—**165** *Das Brot vorschneiden*, measure the soldier's rations.—*Die Rechnung streichen*,
as a strict mercantile expression, means to cancel an account as
paid. But probably used here loosely for *das Geld in die
Tasche streichen*, 'pocket the money.' The emperor's ministers
and favorites are described as curtailing the soldiers' rations,
but charging full prices for the army supplies and pocketing
the difference.—**167** *Remonte*, a French term, a supply of new
horses.—**172** *Gnadenbrot*, alms, pension.—**173** *Kapuziner*,
either Quiroga himself, or one of his subordinates.—**177** *Unverrichteter Dinge*, without accomplishing anything. Gen. of
manner, Wh. § 220.2.—This episode narrated by Isolani seems
to be an invention of Schiller's, but it tallies with what we
know of the Vienna court.—**180** *Der Posten*, the item. Q.'s
suggestion is, that W., being in haste, paid an exorbitant price.
—**183** *Auskommen*, here, to accomplish anything, succeed.—
187 *Durchgegriffen*, past. part. for imperat., Wh. § 359.3.—
Mitten is dat. pl. of adj. *mitte*, used adverbially. The phrase
reminds us of the Latin *in medias res.*—**195** *Stand*, here, 'class
or order of society.'—**198** *Schaf* is about as sarcastic as the
English 'calf' would be. Q. retorts by saying: In likening
me to a *Schaf*, you liken yourself to a wild beast.—**208** See
König von Ungarn.—**209** *Pflicht*, your duties as an officer; *Name*,
the name of the general under whom you serve.—**210–240** This
superb description is applicable to the year 1629, but scarcely
to 1634. W. may have had as many regiments, but they were

not complete, many were disorganized, Ratisbon had been
captured by Bernhard of Weimar, and the army had all it could
do to hold its own against the Swedes and Saxons. The detachment in Westphalia, v. 214, had been cut to pieces in
summer of 1633, at Hameln. ' Schiller has introduced the
passage to give an idea of W.'s power in general, and the
character of his army.—212 *In diesem Königreich*, Bohemia.—
235 *Die Fremde*, foreign countries.—238 *Uns* for *zu uns*,
Deserted to our banners. Characteristic of the freedom with
which the soldiers of 30 Y. W. changed masters. After battle
of Steinau, in 1633, nearly all the privates of the captured
Swedish army enlisted under W. (R. W. 328).—*Doppeladler,
Löwe, Lilien*, the arms of Austria, Sweden, and France, respectively.—239 *Schilderhaus*, guard-house.—240 *Kaiserburg*, the
Hofburg, emperor's palace in Vienna.—244 *Ersten besten*, the
first-comer.—258 *Es ist nur zur Erinnerung*, let me remind you.
—262 *Eins geht ins andre drein*, one involves the other.—
264 *Sich in ihrem Ziel nur vergriff*, only mistook its object or
aim, was misapplied.—This act attributed to B. seems to have
been invented by Schiller.

SCENE 3.

280 *Finden*, infinitive in absolute constr., Wh. § 347.—
Gleich, straightway. Contrast v. 132.—286 *Zu bannen*, infin.
passive, Wh. § 343.III.*b*, 'to be exorcised.'—This allusion to
B. is fully explained in *Tod*, Act II. sc. 6.—297 *Amt.* Explained in v. 2505, where Octavio reveals himself as commander in W.'s stead.—299 *Wie misslich die Person*, what a
ticklish, hazardous part.—302 *Beginnen*, act, proceeding. See
editor's Glossary to *Hermann u. Dorothea.*—306 *Schlimmver-
wahrt*, poorly guarded. W.'s heart, by reason of his ambition,
is represented as open to the temptation of abusing the powers
entrusted to him.—308 *Dem bessern*, a better.—314 *Umsonst*,
without a purpose.—317 *Kaisers Landen.* Carinthia, from
which country the duchess is represented as having just come,
was one of the unquestioned hereditary possessions of the
Habsburgs. Whereas the title to the crown of Bohemia had
often been in dispute, and had been directly involved in the
origin of the 30 Y. W. See G. T. W. chap. 2. Bohemia,
therefore, although subjected to the emperor, is regarded here

as not being a *Kaisers Land* by eminence, but rather as a precarious possession.—[319] *Stehen*, withstand, meet. For form, see *finden*, v. 280.—[321] *Der Reichsfeind*. The Swedes, as foreigners in Germany, are represented as enemies of the German empire, from the Austrian-point of view. Masters of the Upper Danube in consequence of capture of Ratisbon.—[323] *Im inneren Lande*. The *Grenzen* refer to the frontier of the Austrian possessions; the present phrase, to the interior, especially to the duchies of Upper and Lower Austria, where peasant insurrections, encouraged by the Swedes, were not infrequent.—[324] *Alle Stände schwierig*, may mean, 'all classes of society are restive' (see v. 195), or may be used in a technical sense, 'all the estates are indisposed to vote supplies of money and men.' The *Stände*, or landed nobility, of the Austrian provinces constituted local parliaments, as it were.—[335] *Findet ein Herz*, literally, 'will pluck up heart;' whereas O.'s idea is rather, 'will come to his senses,' *kommt zur Besinnung*.—[336] *Spricht man aus*. Compare *macht*, v. 50.—[337] *Zudem*, 'besides.'—[350] *Gleich*, for *obgleich*, 'although.'—[362] *Der Morgen vor*, 'the morning of' the battle.—[367] *Bedenken*. See *bedenklich*, v. 57.—This episode between W. and O., an invention of Schiller's, is fully explained in *Tod*, II. 3. v. 900–942.—[375] *Befinde*, subj. of indirect speech, Wh. § 333.1.—[378] *Freiheit*, here, absence of restraint arising from knowledge of a dangerous secret.—[379] *Sicher*, confident.—O.'s idea is this. Knowing Max's fondness for W., but still unaware of its intensity, he says: So long as Max knows nothing, he will preserve his freedom of thought and action, and W. will remain in delusion. But if Max were to receive the least intimation, he would betray his knowledge by a change of manner, even without intending to do so, and W. would be put on his guard. —[382] *Bedenken*, here, 'consider.' Somewhat different sense from v. 367.

SCENE 4.

[384] *Ja*, see v. 147.—[392] *Von meinetwegen*, comp. v. 107, 'on my own account.' In form, *meinet* is dat. pl. agreeing with *wegen*. The phrase was originally *von meinen wegen*, then *meinent wegen*, finally *meinet wegen*.—[394] *Beide Hände*. The usual Cotta editions have *beider Hände*, i.e., the hands of both father and son, which accords better with the following line. But the

H. K. A. has *beide.*—[399] A stage-expression, 'you are straying
from your part.'—[402] 'I will not have any advantage over the
other officers,' I am ready to take my share of the scolding.—
[408] 'And so also it will remain,' *i.e.,* you can not help it.—
[411] *Ihm wider die Natur,* 'it is contrary to his character,'
Wh. § 222, III.—[412] The sense is best rendered by: he was born
to command, Wh. § 222, II.*d.*—[420] *Mag,* expressive here both of
ability and of willingness. Wh. § 255 gives but an imperfect
idea of the functions of this verb.—[421] *Taugte,* inversion, as
v. 50. Conditional mood. Connected etymologically with
Tugend, which denoted originally 'excellence,' 'fitness,' in general.—[423] *Frommen,* 'to avail.' Derived from Old German
fram, frum (Greek προμος, English 'from'), in the sense of 'for-
wards.' The fundamental meaning of the verb, therefore, is
to further a person or cause. The present meaning of the adj.
fromm, 'pious,' *i.e.,* promoting the glory of God, is a com-
paratively modern limitation.—[424] *Lust.* Supply 'to see.'—
W. is described as so magnetic that one has only to approach
him to feel one's own latent talents awakening.—[431] *Sei,* see
ergetze, v. 39.—[433] *Vermögen,* talent, capacity.—The general
sense of 430–434 is that W. does not check or diminish one's
individuality, but only takes care that it shall manifest itself
in the proper place and time.—[435] *Ueber'm Herrscher,* 'in the
master,' *i.e.,* in acting as a master.—[437] An allusion to W.'s
birth, as a simple nobleman. Max retorts by saying that W.
was born with every capacity for his present dignity.—[440] To
carry out his character, his innate tendencies, down to the
veriest tittle, *buchstäblich.*—[443] *Ueberall,* in sense of *überhaupt,*
'in general, in any case, anyhow.'—[446] *Die Proben geben es,*
i.e., the experiments that we have already made with W. show
that he will indeed fix upon a goal to suit himself. Ironical.
—*Sie,* they at court, the emperor's satellites.—[449] *Sich in*
gutem ergeben, to give up with a good grace.—[450] *Fertig*
werden, here, to get the better of.—[452] *Grauet,* supply *es,*
Wh. § 292.2.*a.*—[453] *Soll geschehen,* they wish it to be per-
formed, see v. 125.—[455] *Da dringt die Gegenwart,* the needs
of the moment are urgent.—*Persönliches,* the personality of
the leader must have sway, *eigenes Auge,* his own eye must see
and measure the emergency. The sense is : You can not direct
his movements by instructions from a distance, at home.—
[458] *Gönnen,* best rendered by the negative 'do not grudge.'

Natur, used here in the sense of 'nature' in general. *In den grossen Verhältnissen der Natur leben* means to move in an exalted, ample sphere, be free from dwarfing restrictions.— **461** *Ordnungen*, combines here the idea of 'custom, usage,' and 'decree,' *Verordnung;* in general, that which has been established by authority of long standing.—**465** *Gewicht*, in the sense of check.—*Bedrängen*, and *Dränger*, have the force both of pressing hard and oppressing.—**468** *Der Weg der Ordnung*, time-honored routine, 'law and order.'—*Krümmen*, poetic for *Krümmungen*.—**469** *Umweg*, here wide detour, suggestive of loss of time.—**470** *Kanonball*, commonly *Kanonenkugel.*—**472** *Macht sich Platz*, 'makes for itself a path.'—**476** *Reben-hügel*, poetic for *Weinberg.*—**482** *Fünfzehnjährig*, designating the 30 Y. W. in general as it then appeared to O., 1618–1634, and not Max's connection with it, which was only since 1625. Compare v. 24 and note, and *Tod*, Act III. sc. 18, v. 2143.— **485** *Das letzte*, the final object.—**496** *Saat*, young growing grain.—**499** *Es ist gethan um*, it is all over with.—**500** *Friede machen.* In this phrase the noun seems, in poetry at least, to remain undeclined, as if part of a compound verb, *friede-machen.* Compare v. 505.—**501** *Freuden*. Dat. sing., Wh. § 95. —**504** *Wie wird dir*, what is the matter with you, Wh. § 222, II.*f.*—**508** *Länder*, viz., Carinthia.—**520** *Hätte gezeigt*, 'has revealed,' subj. of qualified assertion, see *wüsste*, v. 110, or subj. of indirect speech, with ellipsis, 'I am to regard you then as having said that the journey had revealed this.'—**539** *Maien*, green twigs and branches, especially of beech, willow, and birch. So called because abundant in month of May.— **543** *In die Lüfte grüssen*, bowing *into* the air, swinging their hats.—**545** The war is likened to a day; peace, to the repose of evening.—**549** Glad that he has lived to see the day.—**554** *Zur Gerte*, as a mere sprout.—**564** *Presste mir das Innerste zusammen*, serried my inmost soul.—**567** *Sauer*, bitter, painful.— **569** *Grossem besten*, public weal. The *gross* contrasts Europe in general with Austria in particular.—**570** *Ein paar*, indeclinable, two or three; *ein Paar*, declined, a pair.—*Hufe* Low German, *Hube* High German, a measure of land, about 80 acres. Origin obscure; probably connected with *haben.* Analogous in meaning, but not in etymology, with the Old English, 'hide' of land.—**576** The sense is: if we do not suspend hostilities, as the preliminary to peace.

SCENE 5.

585 *Dahingehen,* simply 'go away.' The *da* is not demonstrative.—587 O. means that he has detected Max's love for Thekla, which is betrayed by the whole tenor of 505–558, especially by the last line.—592 *Will,* is on the point of, Wh. § 258.b.—593 *Zu ihr, i.e,* to Thekla.—593 *Mir,* see v. 7.— 597 *Es* denotes here the possibility of Max's falling in love.— 599 *Es,* here our secret, *i.e.,* the revelation of the dangerous nature of W.'s plans.—600 *Ich musste,* it was my duty.

ANALYSIS OF ACT II.

Scene 1. Serves to introduce the astrologer Seni, and to prepare the reader for the further exhibition of Wallenstein's astrological fancies in Scene 6, and Act III. sc. 4.—**Scene 2.** Introduces Wallenstein and the Duchess. The latter, in describing her reception at the court in Vienna, on her way from Carinthia to Pilsen, gives the general an inkling of the disfavor with which he is now regarded, and intimates the possibility of his being dismissed from the command.—**Scene 3.** Enter the evil genius and the good genius of the drama, the Countess Terzky and the Princess Thekla. The latter is welcomed by her father, whom she has not seen since she was a child.— **Scene 4.** The family group is interrupted, first by Max, who comes to remonstrate with Wallenstein for having rewarded with princely munificence his trifling services as the Duchess's escort, next by Terzky, bringing important letters.—**Scene 5.** Wallenstein and Terzky are left alone. The general admits that the court has resolved upon his deposition. Terzky reproaches him with procrastination, and urges him to take decided steps.—**Scene 6.** They are joined by Illo, who describes the temper of the officers. Wallenstein insists upon it that the officers must give him a written pledge of unconditional fidelity. This Illo and Terzky promise to procure. Illo urges the general to take a decided stand. Wallenstein replies that the stars do not indicate that the right time has come. He indulges in his astrological rhapsody, likening Illo to one born under the domination of Saturn, and therefore incapable of penetrating into the secrets of nature.—**scene 7.** In the presence of Wallenstein and the assembled officers, Questenberg delivers his instructions, first, that the army shall immediately evacuate Bohemia, second, that Wallenstein shall detach a force to co-operate with the Cardinal Infant. These demands cause an explosion of rage on the part of all the officers, and bring the action to a crisis.

Scene 1.

Doctor, not necessarily M.D. The highest grade in any of the four faculties: law, medicine, theology, or philosophy. The three grades were formerly baccalaureus, magister, and doctor.—**603** *Ruft ins Gewehr.* An officer of the lower grades is saluted only by the sentry posted outside the guardhouse. But when a general officer passes, here Wallenstein himself, the sentry calls out the entire guard to present arms.—**609** *Erkerstube*, a room with projecting or bow window. *Erker*, from mediæval Lat. *arcora*, from *arcus*, a bow.—**611** *Mathematicus*, here astrologer, one who calculates the position of the heavenly bodies. For use of double accus. after *fragen*, see Wh. § 227.3a.—**613** That is what I call humbugging people.—**618** Do not have anything to do with him.—**631** *Mancherlei denkt sich*, many a thought suggests itself. Wh. § 281.

Scene 2.

636 Technical phrase for a formal audience.—**639** *Führt an*, I alleged, gave as the reason.—**640** *Hätten bestimmt.* Wh. § 333.4e. Introd lxiii.—**645** *Lätherisch.* S has followed here the vernacular accentuation. Whereas the cultivated class s pronounce the word—in the sense of ‘Lutheran’—*Luthérisch.*—**648** *Sonst*, ‘in other respects.’ In v. 651, ‘formerly.’—**672** *Muhme*, strictly ‘aunt,’ but extended to other degrees of relationship, or even mere friendship.—**682** *Ambassador*, may designate either Oñate or Castañeda, Introd. xxxviii, xl. The allusion has point when connected with events of 1630, Introd. xix.—**687** *Wäre es an dem, was* etc., ‘could there be anything, any truth in what is whispered at court,’ etc.—**690** *Wink*, here ‘hint.’—**691** *Zeihe*, see *sei*, v. 5. The student should learn to discriminate readily between this verb *zeihen*, and the verb *ziehen*, v. 696.—[698] Introd. xix.—[706] The sense is best rendered by: Prevail upon your pride to yield. Literally, 'win it from your pride.'—[710] *Verhasst*, in the sense of that which hates, 'invidious.'—[713] *So*, for *so wie so*, 'as it is,' 'at the best.'—*Wenig*, see *mehr*, v. 82.

SCENE 3.

[721] *Beugen, i.e.*, for purpose of kissing it.—[725] Introd. xvi. —[727] *Aus Pommern*, probably refers to siege of Stralsund, in 1628.—*Stift*, here, 'convent-school.'—[737] This line, connected with 725, fixes T.'s present age at nearly seventeen.—[739] *Doch*, to be connected with *nicht erkannt*. A polite form of contradicting a negation; very common in German, and has here the directness, without the rudeness, of the English : Yes, I should (have recognized him).—[741] For purposes of his own, Schiller has represented W. as still in the flower of manhood. In reality, the general was a hopeless victim to the gout.— [742] *Fein*, scarcely to be rendered by 'beautifully;' perhaps, by 'acutely.'—[747] *Weiter leiten*, in sense of 'perpetuate.'— [751] *Es*, used rather loosely for *ihn, i.e., Kranz*, the logical antecedent.—[752] *Königlichen Schmuck, i.e.*, a coronet. By making T. the wife of a king. Compare v. 640, note; also *Tod*, III. 4. v. 1513. The appositeness of W.'s allusion to a coronet is brought out by the circumstance that Thekla is to be regarded as appearing in this scene with a wreath of diamonds. This is shown by Schiller's MS., which has in the heading of the scene the words—erased before printing—*reich mit Brillianten geschmückt*, see also v. 1538. Wallenstein, accordingly, expresses the hope that he may convert this diamond wreath into a coronet.

SCENE 4.

[757] T. is represented by W. as his *Lebenssonne*. In escorting her to the camp, Max is likened to the morning-star heralding the approach of the sun.—[768] *Jagdzug*, a carriage and four horses, for driving to the hunting-ground.—[772] *Volles Herzens*, Wh. § 121.3, § 220.—[776] *Es steht Ihnen an*, it is befitting in you.—[780] See note to v. 752.—[783] *Nicht*, see v. 69.—[785] *Soll ich*, not 'I shall,' but 'I am to be,' it is the tendency of W.'s

conduct to make me a captive.—[794] *Des Herrn.* Uncertain whether this refers to Terzky, or to the emperor.—[795] *Versammlung.* Refers to Scene 7.

SCENE 5.

[796] *Sie* refers to the duchess, and her words in scene 2.— Contrary to history, W. is represented here as having full knowledge of plan for his deposition. Furthermore, the king of Hungary is mentioned as the new commander. He was not appointed until after W.'s death.—[803] They think that they have done with me.—[805] *Verloren,* see *durchgegriffen,* v. 187. —[806] 'Begs to be excused.'—[813] *Kürzlich,* see v. 44.—[816] The Halberstadt Convention was called by Oxenstjerna, early in Feb., 1634, to bring about a league among the Protestant princes of North Germany, similar to that established by the Heilbronn League for South Germany, in 1633. See G. T. W. 164.—[824] *Land,* viz., Pomerania, which the Swedes demanded as their recompense, Introd. xxxvii, lviii.—[825] *Wir,* we Germans.—[828] *Gönn',* see v. 458.—*Ja,* see v. 147.—[832] It shall not be said of me.—[836] *Reichsfürstlich,* allusion to Mecklenburg, or its equivalent. Introd. xviii, xxxii.—[840] *Gothen.* Schiller seems to have borrowed the application of this term to Swedes from an inscription quoted by M. B. 363. As here used, the term conveys a sneer, the Swedes being likened to the Goths and Vandals.—[844] *Fischen,* compare phrase 'to fish in troubled waters.'—[849] *Werden irr' an dir,* do not know what to make of you.—[854] This statement is borne out by history. Nothing has yet been discovered in W.'s handwriting bearing directly on the plot.—[860] *Zum besten haben,* 'fooling.'—[864] *Wüsste,* see v. 110.

SCENE 6.

[877] *Pharobank,* see v. 63, note.—[882] *Zudem,* see v. 337.— [889] This is borrowed from H. W. III. 175; also T.'s suspicions in v. 885.—[890] *Bewenden.* There is more in it than may appear, "thereby hangs a tale." See note to v. 367.—[891] *Gut sagen,* answer for, guarantee.—[917] *Regimenter,* see v. 1231.—[918] *Zum S. stossen lassen,* 'let them join.' As military terms, *stossen zu jemanden* means 'to join,' with a view to co-operation; *stossen auf,* 'to encounter,' as an enemy.—[925] *Zuvorkommen,* to anticipate.—[928] *Wahrnehmen,* here, to seize, avail one's self of.—

931 Illo's speech is best rendered by paraphrasing: To the accomplishment of a decisive result there must be a happy co-operation, a coincidence of many single circumstances. Scattered here and there are the threads of fortune, the opportunities, which, if they can only be concentrated in one point, make up a fruitful knot.—**941** *Deinen Wink*, a sign from you.—**947** Each one's spirits rise.—**951** *Der gemeine Geist*, esprit de corps, *zerstreut sich*, 'will be frittered away.'—*Eigen* is the antithesis to *gemein*; each one begins to think of his own petty interests.—**956** *Gemeine Pflicht*, not used in the sense of v. 951, but designates every-day, routine duty.—**957** *Wohlbehalten*, 'safe and sound.' This violent separation of *wohl* from the adj. part. is scarcely justifiable, even in Schiller.—**958** W.'s own words, according to quotations from Scsyma's MS., H. W. III. 40, 60.—**964** *Venus*. The ascendency of this planet at a given conjunction was believed, in astrology, to betoken good fortune, see v. 1613.—*Maleficus, i.e.*, Saturn or Mars, see v. 1610.—This speech has been transferred by Schiller from Terzky to Illo.—**967** *Jupiter*. Those persons born at the moment when Jupiter was in the ascendant were supposed to be endowed with peculiar insight into the mysteries of nature and life. The ascendency of Saturn (*der Unterirdische*, v. 971), on the other hand, prognosticated dulness of insight and a disposition to be content with mere earthly, trivial things. Saturn is called *der Unterirdische* because he rules over the subterrestrial forces, as distinguished from the heavenly.—**970** *Finster*, 'in obscurity of vision.'—**972** *Bleifarben*. In the language of alchymy, 'Saturn' designated 'lead.'—*Dir ins Leben geleuchtet*, 'lighted you into life.' Compare Macbeth's phrase: "lighted fools the way to dusty death."—**974** Clever in perceiving the connection between things not remote from one another.—**978** *Geisterleiter*, an allusion to Jacob's ladder, Gen. xxviii. 12, which played an important part in mediæval mysticism.—**993** *Häuser*. The astrologers divided the plan of the heavens into twelve compartments, called *mansiones, domicilia*. In the intersection-point, *Ecke*, formed by the crossing of any two of the lines, a star (planet) might be hid, thereby escaping the notice of a careless observer.—**996** Supply *um zu sehen* before *ob*. *Verberge* is put in subj. to denote object of one's thoughts and apprehensions, Wh. § 333.3.

Scene 7.

1013 *Den nichts mehr ändert.* With reference to W.'s inconsistency in announcing his resolve and then taking it back, he is styled in the *Perduellionis Chaos*, Introd. lxi, the *exorabiliter inexorabilis*. The epithet is pronounced by Ranke 'not bad' (R. W. 499).—**1023** *Ihren*, 'his.' The possessive adj. relating to *Majestät* takes commonly a capital.—**1027** Introd. xxxiii. —**1030** *Diese Länder*, *i.e.*, Bohemia, Silesia, Moravia, etc.— **1032** *Strömen.* The strategy of the Swedes in 30 Y. W. was to get control of the rivers.—**1036** *Hier*, used in sense of 'there.' —**1039** *Geist*, *i.e.*, in the Austrian army.—**1041** *Hellgeschieden*, clearly defined, orderly battle-array, in place of the previous irregular butchery.—**1046** *Als gält' es*, 'as if his object were.' —**1055** *Glücklich*, fortunate in not having had occasion to witness such slaughter before.—This description of Gustavus's attack on the Old Fort is greatly overwrought.—**1064** *Den Ruhm.* Gustavus did *not* lose his fame at Nuremberg. W. gained only a slight advantage, if any. But Schiller has made Q. exaggerate W.'s generalship, to contrast more forcibly the present unsatisfactory state with past triumphs.—**1066** *Wie ein Besiegter.* W. was indeed crippled by this battle. Introd. xxxiv.—**1071** *Mit einemmal.* Bernhard is represented here as marching all at once against R. But the capture of R. was a year later than Lützen. *Macht sich reissend Bahn.* Compare v. 472.—**1075** *Sieben Reitende.* So narrated by H. W. III. 125. —W.'s hatred of Duke of Bavaria dated from his deposition in 1630, Introd. xix. He is represented here as actuated by this hatred in not hastening to relief of Bavaria. See Introd. xxxix. —**1090** The reader must bear in mind that this campaign in Silesia was *before* the capture of Ratisbon.—**1096** *Arnheim.* This depreciation of A.'s generalship is not warranted by history. Thurn was undoubtedly a poor general.—**1098** Allusion to peace-negotiations. See Introd. xxxv.—**1115** *Ohne Schwertstreich*, not strictly true.—**1125** The cart upon which a condemned criminal (*armer Sünder*) is driven to execution.— **1126** *Mögen*, Wh. § 255.1.—**1133** See Introd. xxxix.—**1140** *Sterblich*, as mortals, as men.—**1146** *Generals*, for *Generale*, on account of metre. Not very elegant in a word so thoroughly Germanized.—**1149** In *Lager*, v. 55, we learn that some of the troops had been paid that very day, which statement is again contradicted in v. 882.—**1150** *Werden*, see v. 412, note.—*Sold*, *Soldat*, from the Latin *solidus*, a coin.—The *Soldaten* were hired troops, as distinguished from the feudal vassals of the Middle Ages, who were obliged to serve.—**1157** *Deut*, 'farthing,' small coin now out of use.—**1164** The other two were Dietrichstein and Liechtenstein.—**1165** *Fürstentag*. Introd. xix. Schiller speaks of the conference in 1630 first as a *Fürstentag*, then, v. 1174, as a *Reichstag*. It was neither one nor the other, but a *Churfürstentay*, or meeting of the seven princes, *Churfürsten*, who had the right of electing the emperor or his presumptive successor.—**1169** *Fürstenknecht*. Not to be connected with the *Fürsten* in v. 1171, but used in a general sense: I, a faithful servant of my master.—**1178** *Dem Thron, i.e.*, the emperor.— **1185** *Fürs erste*, 'in the first place.' Introd. lxix, lxx. *Wollen* for *will*, plural of deference.—**1191** *Lutherisch*, see v. 645.— **1199** *Er rückte vor*. For dramatic effect, to cause an explosion of W.'s, anger, and to give color to subsequent proceedings, Schiller has deliberately reversed the facts. Suys was ordered three times by the War Department in Vienna to cross the Inn, but refused, F. W. B. III. 135, pleading peremptory orders from W. This was in Dec., 1633. It was part of the real Questenberg's mission to settle this dispute, and it was regarded as settled in early part of January. W. ordered Suys to Pilsen, where he remained some time, but finally joined conspiracy against W., Introd. lii.—**1203** *Kriegsstand*, in sense of discipline, well regulated army.—**1231** *Acht*. All authorities, even those followed by Schiller, represent the Cardinal as asking for *six* regiments (6,000 cavalry), Introd. xlii, lxx.— **1242** *Haschen*, to clutch at. Altogether different is *erheischen*, v. 1247, 'to demand;' *heischen* (in mediæval German *eischen*) is identical with English 'ask.'—**1257** *Gerad heraus (damit)*, 'out with it.' Slightly different from *grad aus*, 'straight ahead,' v. 469.—**1262** Introd. xliii.—**1267** *Sonsten*, secondary form for *sonst*, v. 848.—**1268** *Stammbaum*, pedigree.—*Catechismus*, confession. W. says: When I found an officer to be serviceable, I did not care whether he was noble or not, whether Catholic or Protestant. This was strictly true — **1271** *Für* used for *vor*, 'God forbid.'—**1275** Almost *Illo's* very words at the first conference of officers, Introd. xliii. They were: *Ihr seid ruinirte Cavaliere*, H. W. III. 198. Schiller has put in W.'s mouth the substance of Illo's speech as recorded

in H. W.—^{1278} *Desswegen doch*, 'for all that.'—^{1284} *Dir Vorstellungen gethan*, have presented you our views, *i.e.*, our
remonstrances. The verb commonly used in this connection
is *machen*.—^{1290} See *Gold*, note to v. 147.

ANALYSIS OF ACT III.

Scene 1. Illo and Terzky plot to draw up a declaration to
be shown to the officers, in which they all pledge themselves
to Wallenstein, "saving and reserving their allegiance to the
emperor." After the banquet, when the wine has taken effect,
a false copy, from which this clause has been omitted, is to
be passed around for signatures.—**Scene 2.** Terzky and the
Countess speak of the love between Max and Thekla, looking
upon it as a means of securing Max.—**Scene 3.** In this interview between Max and the Countess, the latter elicits from the
young lover a full confession of his state of mind. Just as he
is describing the circumstances under which he made his declaration that morning, Thekla herself enters, unseen by him,
and overhears him.—**Scene 4.** After speaking of their meeting
at Wallenstein's quarters (Act II. Sc. 4), Thekla narrates an
interview she has just had with a remarkable old man, namely,
the astrologer Seni. The conversation turns upon the charms
of the belief in unseen spirits and planetary influences. Max
hopes that the Duke will retire to his estates and devote himself to the profitable and gladsome pursuits of peace.—
Scene 5. The Countess being called away by the din proceeding from the banquet-hall, Thekla puts Max on his guard
against the Terzkys, whom she suspects of some ulterior, selfish
object.—**Scene 6.** The Countess, returning, insists upon Max's
joining the banquet, his absence having already been com-
mented upon.—**Scene 7.** Thekla, being left alone, sings her
celebrated song.—**Scene 8.** The Countess, on her return, up-
braids Thekla for having made herself too cheap. She even
intimates that the Duke may have other and higher designs for
his daughter. Thekla displays a goodly share of her father's
temper and resolution. The Countess declares that in any case,
if Max is to win Thekla, it can only be through some great

sacrifice on his part.—**Scene 9.** Again alone, Thekla soliloquizes on the trials that beset her love. Her suspicions are confirmed by what the Countess has just said. She fears that they are all threatened with dire calamity. [The scene of this Act is laid in Terzky's house.]

SCENE 1.

1305 *Sich verschreiben*, literally, to write one's self away, to pledge one's self in writing.—**1314** *Trübe.* Effect for cause. The wine is called *trübe*, because it 'dims' the perceptions of the drinker. *Trüber Wein* would be 'cloudy, discolored wine.'—**1316** *Unterschoben*, spurious. Introd. xliv. —**1321** *Immer*, for *immerhin*, 'for all that.'—**1327** *Lieb*, in sense of *gleich*.—**1328** *Von der S. rücken*, 'make some progress,' in general sense.—**1335** I can not understand him.—**1338** *Geht heraus*, 'comes right out,' see v. 1257, expresses himself freely to S.—Terzky was present at many of the interviews between W. and S., and knew of W.'s offer to Gustavus. Introd. xlvi. The reader should not connect events of 1631, however, with those of 1633 and 1634, as Schiller has done here, Introd. xlviii.—**1362** *Karten*, arrange matters.—**1374** *Nicht.* This use is rhetorical rather than idiomatic, see v. 69.—**1378** *Weil*, 'while.' This use is archaic, and confined now to poetry or proverbial sayings.

SCENE 2.

1384 *Sie*, Thekla.—*Ihn*, Max, who—as we are to understand —has been kept waiting in another room. The lovers, no longer able to meet so freely as on the journey, are obliged to have recourse to T.'s apartments for a rendezvous.—**1391** The Countess addresses her 'aside' to W. as if he were present.— **1396** *Bräutigam*, see v. 641.—**1399** *Feinheit*, see v. 742.—**1403** *Den Kopf warm machen*, heat his fancy.—**1405** *Bedenke*, see *ergetze*, v. 39.—**1411** *Alten*, i.e., Max's father.

SCENE 3.

1412 *Base*, aunt or cousin (*cognata*). Subsequently, verse 1416 and elsewhere, Max uses the word *Tante*. He has probably caught up these words from Thekla, thereby making her

relatives his own, as it were, in token of his affection.—**1419**
'How I think and feel.' *Muth* has here something of the
force of the mediæval *Muot*. See editor's Glossary to *Herm.
u. Dorothea.*—**1425** *Ueberall*, see v. 443.—**1443** *Selig*, 'blessed,'
in the sense of departed from this life, 'translated.'—**1464**
Ob, this use as a prepos., with force of *über*, is archaic and
confined to poetry or to certain geographical expressions, *e.g.,
Oesterreich ob der Ens.*—**1462** *Zur Himmelspforte*, the name
(dedication) of the cloister.—**1480** *Ueberselig*, here simply
'over-blessed.'—**1485** *Entdecken*, here 'to disclose.'—**1491**
Erker, see v. 609.—**1491** *Den Blick*, Wh. § 230.3.—**1493** *Ritten auf*, 'drew up in a line.'—**1507** *Trifft*. The student will
observe the frequent change of tense, which is perfectly ad-
missible in German, and which imparts enhanced life to the
narrative. *Fiel, zitterte, sah* are past; *trifft, beherrscht, fasse,
berührt* are present; *rauscht', trennte* and the following again
are past.

SCENE 4.

1525 *Aendern*, I can not 'help' being myself happy.—**1537**
Edelsteine, see note to v. 752.—**1545** *Mummerei*, this parade of
ornament.—**1548** *Schwer*, 'heavy-spirited.'—**1554** *Wär's durch
Neuheit nur*, to be placed after *reizt :* which delights your
eye, and were it only by reason of its novelty.—**1557** Allusion
to what she had seen, as a child, of her father's first army, v.
724, 737.—**1558** *Mir*, dat. of interest, 'makes for me a living
reality.'—**1566** *Sieht sich heiter an*, 'is fair to look upon.' Wh.
§ 288.2.—**1570** *Nicht*, v. 69.—**1591** *Nicht eben*, 'not altogether,
not exactly.'—An intimation of the misfortune to overtake
her.—**1594** *Muth*, see v. 1419.—**1599** *Bild*, here not 'picture'
but 'image, effigy.'—**1605** *Gebildet*, 'represented.'—For explanation of astrological allusions, see v. 960–997. Saturn, it
may be observed, is here described as of a pale yellow, in v.
972 of a dull leaden hue.—**1608** *Von ihm über* for *ihm gegenüber*. Mars is at one end of the semicircle, Saturn at the
opposite, so that they confront each other.—**1621** *Stolz* has
here the force of 'ambition.'—*Den Raum*, space in general,
the unoccupied universe.—**1632** *Fabel*, 'fairy-lore.'—**1633** *Sie*,
i.e., 'love.'—**1635** *Fabelwesen*, fabulous beings, *i.e.*, the gods,
goddesses, nymphs, etc., of ancient mythology.—**1640** *Mit*,
used adverbially, 'kept company with men.'—**1646** *Da wir*

erst wurden, 'in the very moment of our birth.'—**1686** *Prächtig schaffend*, that which creates splendid things.—This spirited passage, for Max the utterance of an earnest hope, is strictly applicable to what the general had already accomplished, Introd. xxi–xxv.—**1677** The Countess takes up Max's idea, but converts the future to which he has alluded into the present; hence the present itself is thrown back into the past. She says: Consider me (*ich will*), with reference to that future, as having advised you (*gerathen haben*).

Scene 5.

1688, *Was hätten sie davon*, 'what advantage would they get by,' etc.—**1693** *Ueberall*, see v. 443.—**1705** *Zehen*. See note to v. 482.—**1727** *Also will's die Sitte*, conventional etiquette wishes it thus.—**1729** *Findest*. We should naturally expect here *fändest*, corresponding to *wäre*, Wh. § 332.1 But, aside from the aversion which all poets seem to have for this particular form *fände*, Schiller evidently uses the Indic. pres. here to make the connection with the present circumstances more direct. Thekla says: If you do not now, in this emergency, find the truth and the whole truth in me, where could you look for it.—**1730** *Wir haben uns gefunden, i.e.*, each has recognized in the other a mate.

Scene 6.

1738 'My husband sends (and says) that it is high time; he must come to the banquet.' *Sei*, denoting Terzky's message, is put in subj. of indir. speech, although the verb on which it depends is omitted, Wh. § 333.3.*d*. The *soll* is not put in subj., because it conveys of itself the idea of an order, see v. 125.—**1742** *Es eilt nicht*, there is no hurry.—**1745** *Ueberall*, see v. 443.—**1746** *Sein Umgang nicht*, it is no company for him.— *Mögen*, a logical concession, Wh. § 255.1. *Möchtet*, v. 1749, denotes desire, § 255.2.—**1753** *Bedingungen*, see v. 1424, 1474.

Scene 8.

1778 The Piccolominis were a celebrated family in Italian history. • Æneas Sylvius, Pope Pius II., was of that name.

Octavio P. married (Introd. lxv) the daughter of Henry Julius of Lauenburg (Introd. xliv, note to v. 2156).— [1782] *Sich nicht auszusetzen*, expose one's self to the risk of a refusal.—[1789] *Gut*, here 'kind.'—[1793] *Er*, Wallenstein.— [1796] *Lager*, here, 'couch.'—[1799] *Stift*, see v. 727.—[1818] *Reihen*, 'dance,' see v. 93.—[1826] *Fremdes Schicksal*, happily rendered by Coleridge "alien destinies," *i.e.*, the fate of another, father or husband. *Weib* in the line above denotes 'woman' in general, not necessarily 'wife.'—[1828] *Mit Wahl*, not intended to convey the idea of 'selecting,' which would be inconsistent with the Countess's argument, viz., that woman can *not* select her own fate. The phrase has the force of *willig*, v. 1836, 'cheerfully.' She is the best woman, who accepts another's fortunes of her own accord, without waiting to be forced.—[1864] *Er hätte besiegt*, see v. 520.—[1868] *Zorn*. W.'s explosions of ungovernable rage were notorious (R. W. 347). On such occasions he would behave like one demented.

SCENE 9.

[1898] *Wink*, see v. 690. The hint, namely, that Max is to be called upon to make some great sacrifice. It confirms her previous suspicions, v. 1687.—[1894] *Sie*, *i.e.*, the Countess.— [1895] *Leuchten*, see v. 972.—[1896] *Das*, for 'this.' Contrast *hier*, v. 1036.—[1900] *Haus*, probably in sense of 'family.' We are under the spell of an evil spirit.—[1902] *Freistatt*, 'place of refuge,' referring to *Stift*, v. 727, 1799.—[1903] *Muss*, *i.e.*, in accordance with fate.—It is to be observed that v. 1900-1913 are in rhyme. Düntzer (D. W. 198) thinks that S. borrowed the hint of v. 1908-1913 from a passage in Æneid, Book II., which he had previously translated. Possibly S. had also in mind the destruction of the family of Korah, Num. xvi. The idea of the last two lines is that when a family is doomed to destruction, not only do the demons of the upper and the lower world fall upon it, but even the god of pleasure lends a helping hand. That is, what would have been, under ordinary circumstances, a pleasure, now only aggravates the ruin. Whether this refers to the officer's revelry or to her love, is not altogether clear.

ANALYSIS OF ACT IV.

Scene 1. The banquet is in full blast. Max is welcomed by Isoluni, and, at Terzky's request, reads the officers' declaration. The copy contains the salvatory clause. The declaration is unanimously approved.—**Scene 2.** Terzky gets from Neumann the false copy, and orders the true one to be burned.—**Scene 3.** Illo and Terzky congratulate each other on their success so far.—**Scene 4.** They are interrupted by Buttler, who gives them to understand that he has seen through their artifice, but is willing, for reasons of his own, to co-operate with them.—**Scene 5.** The *Kellermeister* and Neumann speak of the banquet. Terzky sends for the celebrated *Pocal*, which gives the *Kellermeister* the occasion for displaying his knowledge of Bohemian history, some of the episodes of which are depicted on the goblet.—**Scene 6.** The company is about to break up. The false declaration is passed around and signed by all, except Max.—**Scene 7.** Illo comes on the scene, intoxicated. Max declines to sign. He has no suspicions, but is averse to what looks like transacting business amid such confusion. Illo becomes furious, denouncing those timid spirits who seek to save their consciences by 'a clause.' This excites suspicion. Illo even draws his sword upon Max, but is disarmed. The company breaks up in confusion.

[H. W. III. 205 gives the following account of the banquet: —At the close Ilow presented the declaration for subscription, thinking that no one would read it. For he had prepared a false copy omitting the clause '*so lange der Friedländer in seiner kaiserlichen Majestät Dienst verbleiben, oder diese zu Ihrer Dienste Beförderung ihn gebrauchen werde.*' Some of the officers noticed the omission. Ilow, Trzka, and some generals signed, others refused. These Ilow tried to persuade that it was all right, assuring them that mention had been made of the emperor in the heading of the declaration. Trzka drew his sword and denounced all who refused to sign as cowardly traitors to the duke. The other officers who had signed did the same. Those who had objected were coerced into signing, but wrote their names so as to be scarcely legible. Piccolomini, who had drunk deep, staggered to the table and, picking up a large goblet in his left hand, while he held his drawn sword in the right, drained the goblet to the health of the emperor. But by reason of his peculiar state, this was regarded more as jest than earnest.—This passage, which agrees substantially with the *Gründlicher Bericht*, will explain many of the 'motives' in Schiller's representation. Why the dramatist has reversed the parts played by Ilow and Trzka, it would be difficult to say, unless he wished to show how the abler man of the two, as he had portrayed them, might, under the influence of liquor, lose his head completely. Furthermore, not only is Octavio Piccolomini's drunken freak suppressed, but he is represented as self-possessed and abstemious. The change was necessary to make his character in the drama consistent, as that of an elderly man and a consummate diplomatist. Herchenhahn's description is an interesting revelation of the real Piccolomini, still a hot-blooded young Italian. All authorities agree in speaking of the banquet as an orgie.]

SCENE 1.

Nach der Tiefe, towards the background of the stage.— *Credenztisch*, buffet, sideboard.—**1914** *Was wir lieben*, a toast to our loves. A jesting allusion to Max's love for Thekla, which Isolani has detected.— *Wo steckt Er*, where have you been.—**1926** *Ob*, see v. 996 note.—**1929** The Latin words are taken from one of Ilow's speeches, M. B. 243.—[In the Declaration. *Als*, for *also*, 'so, therefore.' This form of the word, as well as *alse*, recurs incessantly in documents of the period.— Schiller probably adopted it from the *Gründlicher Bericht*.— *Wieder*, 'in our turn.'—*Körperlicher Eid*, in Latin *juramentum corporale*, so called from the mediæval practice of touching the *corporale*, or cloth that covered the consecrated elements.— The Declaration is reproduced by Schiller almost word for word from the *Gründlicher Bericht*, M. B. 247. Introd. xliv.] —**1933** *Gewillt*, not from *wollen*, but from *Wille*, Wh. § 405. I.1, § 416, 2.*a.*—**1934** *Was*, 'why,' Wh. § 176.3.—**1936** *Lass gut sein*, let it be, wait.

SCENE 2.

Winkt, see v. 941.—**1943** *Schenktisch*, same as *Credenztisch*. —Neumann is mentioned, H. W. III. 201, as having prepared the original declaration; he is not mentioned in connection with the spurious one, H. W. III. 205.

SCENE 3.

1949 *Warm*, see v. 1403.—**1950** *Cordial*, 'favorably disposed.'
—**1954** *Meint*, here, 'says.'

SCENE 4.

1972 'I do not offer to sell (*feil bieten*) my allegiance.' To
Terzky's allusion to W.'s generosity, B. replies that it is not love
of gain that induces him to desert the emperor.—**1793** And I
should not have advised you to (attempt to) get from me, only
six months ago, by haggling, what I now volunteer to do.
This construction is the counterpart of v. 1677. There the
present was thrown into the future. Here it is thrown into the
past; hence, what is anterior to the present, viz., B.'s hypothe-
tical assumption, is made anterior conditional, *ich wollte nicht
gerathen haben* having the force of *ich hätte nicht gerathen, i.e.*,
assuming that you did attempt it then, I should not like to be
considered as having advised it.—**1981** *Meinen*, expresses both
'believing' and 'saying.'—As has been stated in Introd., the
full analysis of B.'s character must be reserved for a subsequent
volume. Suffice it to say that Schiller's Buttler differs radically
from the Butler of history, and that, according to Schiller's
representation, he has been insulted, as he believes, by the
emperor, and therefore joins Illo and Terzky in order to better
gratify his revenge, see *Tod*, Act II., sc. 6.—**1990** *Noch leichte
Ursache sonst*, nor any other trivial motive.—**2007** *Schlecht*,
archaic for *schlicht*, 'simple.' Both forms are identical in
origin.—**2018** Supply here *so*.—**2022** *Ein nördlich Volk*, the
Swedes. Comp. v. 824.—**2032** *Welsch*. From Old German *wala-
hisc*, itself a corruption of Latin *Gallicus* (from Gallus, Gallia).
Applied by eminence to Italians, as in this line; also, by exten-
sion, to all nations of Romance origin, as French, Spaniards,
etc. But not applied to other foreigners, such as Swedes,
Russians, Poles, Hungarians.—**2035** *Lass aufgehen*, etc. Don't
spare anything.—**2036** *Heute gilt es*, we must do it, it is our
right and duty to do it to-day.

SCENE 5.

2039 *Frau Mama*, Introd. lxvii.—**2044** *Behüte Gott*, intended
to contradict the butler's last assertion.—'The prosperity of
this family is just beginning.'—**2045** *Meint*, see y. 1981.—'A

good deal might be said on that point.'—**2047** *Lieutenant.*
Inconsistent with *Personen*, where Neumann is given as *Ritt-meister.*—**2048** *Das macht*, 'that's because.' Logically, *das* is
object, and the subject of *macht* is the following clause.—
Deutsch. A slight hit by Schiller at his countrymen for their
love of drink.—**2049** *Sie wollen gar zu hoch hinaus,* they, *i.e.,*
the Terzkys, are becoming altogether too ambitious.— **2053**
Why do you stand here listening? See v. 1934, and Wh.
§ 343, I. 6.—**2059** This repetition of poss. adj. with noun in
poss. is colloquial.—**2062** *Mit*, colloq. for *damit.*—*Umtrunk,*
drinking a toast, v. 2120, where the goblet is passed from
man to man.—**2065** *Erhaben*, embossed.—**2067** *Schildlein,*
panel, quarter.—**2069** *Setzt*, makes her horse leap, comp.
sprengen, v. 26.—**2074** The Bohemian Estates claimed that
the succession to their throne was not necessarily hereditary in
the House of Habsburg, but that each king had to be elected
by them and held of them. The exercise of this claim in the
deposition of Ferdinand II. and election of Frederick of Palatinate precipitated 30 Y. W.—**2086** The followers of Huss
were called Utraquists because they demanded both bread and
wine, communion in each form, *sub utraque specie.*—**2098**
Um, in full, *um K. u. A. gekommen,* 'has lost,' viz., right of
public worship, *K. u. A.*—**2104** *Drum*, 'that's why,' for
'that's because.' Effect for cause. Compare *das macht*, v.
2048.—**2125** *Geht vieles drein*, 'much must be overlooked.'—
2130 *Des Illo seinem*, see v. 2059.—**2132** *Dir*. This use of
the ethical dative is altogether superfluous for English.—**2133**
Schwarz, here 'swarthy.'—**2138** *Welschen*, see v. 2032.

SCENE 6.

In sich gekehrt, 'absorbed in thought.'—**2146** *Prosit*, from
prodesse, used in various connections, but chiefly in drinking
to a person's health; 'may it profit you.' Compare *Prosit
Neujahr.* The usual phrase, in rising at the end of a meal, is
gesegnete Mahlzeit. *Prosit*, in connection with *Mahlzeit*, sounds
student-like.—**2156** *Kein Rang.* Neither Herchenhahn nor
the *Gründlicher Bericht* say anything about the order in which
the *Revers* was signed. But we know that it was first presented to Henry Julius of Saxe-Lauenburg, in deference to his
high rank, not as an officer but as a prince of the German

Empire, R. W. 378.—**2157** *Mich empfehlen*, a stereotype formula for saying good-bye.—**2160** *Sauer*, see v. 567.—**2161** *Generalfeldzeugmeister*, now one of the very highest grades in the German and Austrian service; in 30 Y. W., the term, like *Feldmarshall*, had scarcely a fixed value.—**2166** *Pommern*, referring to Gustavus's first campaign, in winter of 1630–1.—**2181** *Mit*, see v. 1640.—**2189** *Fall' ihm ins Gepäck, schlag' ihm die Quartiere auf*, military terms, 'capture his baggage, beat up his quarters.'—*Es ist nicht richtig*, 'there's something wrong.' Isol. perceives that Octavio is taking Max to task, and he connects it with Max's love and tardiness, see v. 1914. —**2193** *Dreissig*. The number has been stated variously at fifty and at forty-two.—**2196** *Honoriert*, 'honored' in sense of advancing money.—**2199** *Es fehlt an*, i.e., his signature is wanting.

SCENE 7.

2202 *Das bring' ich dir*, 'this to your health.'—**2207** *Dass ihr's wisst*, spoken to the others, 'know, you fellows.'— **2208** *Schilt*, 'speaks of him abusively,' see Wh. § 227.3.*b*.— **2218** *Unterschrieben*, see *durchgegriffen*, v. 187.—**2223** *Bedeutet*, 'instruct.'—**2231** *Gesinnt*, from *Sinn*, not from *sinnen*, see *gewillt*, v. 1933.—**2232** *Der Fratzen*, gen. sing., see *Freuden*, v. 501. Do not translate here by 'grimace,' but by 'caricature, scrawl,' meaning the declaration. Etymology obscure; possibly connected with Gothic *fratvjan*, An. Sax. *frätvan*, Engl. 'to fret,' i.e., to ornament by tracing lines. According to this, the fundamental meaning of the word would be 'to mark.' By a shifting of use, the word came to mean 'to ornament,' and then just the opposite, 'to distort.'—**2234** *Welschen*, see v. 2032.—**2237** This application of the phrase is borrowed from M. B. 330. The original, of course, is Matt. xii. 30.—**2245** *Verderbest*, see Wh. § 272.2.—**2247** *Was ficht das mich an*, 'what's that to me.'—**2255** *Sich verclausuliert*, protected himself by 'ifs' and 'ands.'—**2257** *Lieferungen*, contracts for supplying the army.—*An*, see v. 6.—**2258** *Tragen*, for *eintragen*.

ANALYSIS OF ACT V.

Scene 1. At this interview, which takes place immediately after the banquet in Act IV., Octavio discloses to Max the full extent of W.'s conspiracy. He is forced to the disclosure by the events that have taken place at the banquet. Max refuses to believe in the treasonableness of the general's designs. Octavio shows him the danger that may arise from his love for Thekla, and produces the emperor's letters-patent, in which Wallenstein is deposed and he himself created provisional commander.—**Scene 2.** The cornet, who enters, brings the startling news from Gallas (in Frauenburg), that Wallenstein's secret agent, Sesin, has been captured, with important letters, in Terzky's handwriting, to the Swedish commander in Ratisbon.—**Scene 3.** Octavio demands of his son if he still refuses to believe in W.'s guilt. Max announces the intention of going to W. in person and calling upon him to clear himself of the imputation of treason. Octavio, fearing that this may defeat his plans, by compelling him to break with W. before the time, is in despair.

SCENE 1.

2267 *Böse,* here 'angry.'—**2269** *Sahe,* Archaic or provincial for *sah* —**2273** *Fremd,* that which comes from another, comp. v. 1826.—**2281** *Unverfänglich,* 'harmless.'—**2282** *Dieses Förmliche,* this way of putting a thing into set words.—**2283** *Hättest,* see v. 520.—**2284** *Der abgedrungnen U.,* for *der Unterschrift, die man dir abdringen wollte.*—**2300** A Schilleresque redundancy. Translate: the clearness of thy perceptions.—**2308** *Dringendern.* This balancing of positive (v. 2307) with comparative is not uncommon in German, but is scarcely permissible in English.—**2309** To bring out the point of this line, supply *früher, i.e.,* before this late journey of thine. The allusion to Thekla is confirmed by v. 2313.—**2318** *Es wird eingeleitet,* the first steps are being taken.—**2334** What a madman they make him out.—**2352** *Gelagert,* in his encampment, as a besieger. *Belagert* is 'besieged.'—**2357** *Burg,* see v. 240. According to H. W. III., 217, there was a great panic in Vienna about this time. The report was circulated that W.

had ordered Scherffenberg, the officer in command of duchy
of Lower Austria, to have the city set on fire in several places
at once, by his emissaries, to march upon the city during the
confusion, to plunder it, and to murder the emperor, the King
of Hungary, and the entire imperial family.   The report was
utterly without foundation.—**2364** *Der bürgerliche Krieg*,
commonly *der Bürgerkrieg.*—**2373** *Fünf.*   According to H.
W. III. 190, T. had five regiments of cuirassiers, two of dragoons, and one of infantry.   Ranke says the same, R. W. 448.
—**2375** *Best montiert*, the best equipped.—**2378** According to
H. W. III. 192, W. promised to Gallas the principalities of
Glogau and Sagan; to Piccolomini, Glatz.—**2390** *Er hat es
keinen Hehl*, he makes no secret of it.—**2396** *Muth*, mood, fit,
see v. 1419.—**2402** *Ein schlechter Streich*, a poor trick.—**2403**
Mäklern, fault-finders.—**2404** *Auf die S. stellen*, carry things
to the extreme.—**2421** *Zwingen.*   See Introd. xxxvii.   In H.
W. III. 54, there is a confused account of this conference,
where the same verb *zwingen* is used.—**2433** *Sei's*, I grant you,
Wh. § 331.1.*d.*—**2433** *Sich weisen lassen*, he would have lis-
tened to reason.—**2438** *Wärst.* see *hätte*, v. 520.—**2446** *Deiner*,
'of thee.'—**2454** *Klügle*, indulge in nice distinctions.— **2461**
Ich soll dich nicht verstehen, it does seem as if I am not to understand you.—**2463** *Du willst*, you say that you have, Wh. §
258.*a.*—**2470** *Unbereitet*, qualifies *uns.*—**2472** *Goldenen Zirkel*,
Bohemian crown.   Introd. xlvii.—**2494** *Fassung*, self-posses-
sion.—**2499** *Offen*, not 'an opened' letter, but letters-patent.
—**2508** *Geworden*, see v. 412.—**2518** See *mehr*, v. 82.— **2519**
Schlagen zu, 'join.'   See *stossen*, v. 918.—**2526** *Lasse*, Wh.
§ 331.1.*d.*—**2548** His spirit is not to be comprehended by the
ordinary rules.

SCENE 2.

2562 *Generallieutenant.*   Schiller makes here a slip, in
ascribing to Gallas his real rank, which elsewhere in the drama
has been assigned to Octavio.—**2574** *An*, see v. 6. — **2576**
That sehr erschrocken, 'he acted as if much alarmed.'   Not to
be confounded with the colloquialism *thät erschrecken*, 'he
did fear,' which colloquialism, corresponding to the English
auxiliary use of the verb 'to do,' occurs frequently in the
Lager, e.g., v. 32, *thät pochen*, 'did knock,' Wh. § 242.3.— **2577**
Nacher, Bavarian and Austrian for *nach.*   Borrowed by

Schiller from the *Gründlicher Bericht*, where it occurs frequently.—*Es ginge*, 'he must go.'—[2581] Introd. li, lii.—[2584]
Fahnlein, company.   Literally, a body of men united under
one set of colors, *Fahne*.

SCENE 3.

[2605] *Zusehen*, to look on, in sense of being a mere specta-
tor, letting things take their course.—[2611] *Leumund*, good
name, honor.   Not connected etymologically with *Mund*, but
derived from old German *hliumunt* (Gothic *hliuma*, ear).   The
primitive meaning was 'that which strikes the ear.'—[2625]
Laut, here in sense of 'open.'—[2630] *Beginnen*, see v. 302.—
[2647] *Halte du es*, conduct thyself.

INDEX OF PERSONS AND PLACES.

Altringer, better spelled *Aldringen.* Johann v. Introd. li–liii. Son of poor parents, but rose rapidly to distinction. First, as captain of volunteers. Active at battle of Dessau Bridge, 1626, see v. 25, and at capture of Mantua, 1629. Had command of W.'s forces that accompanied Feria from Italy through So. Germany to Rhine, 1633. At time of W.'s conspiracy, was Count and Field Marshal, see PERSONEN. Subsequently made Lt. General.

Arnheim, better *Arnim,* Johann Georg v. Brandenburg nobleman. Served with great distinction under W. Had command at siege of Stralsund, 1628. Sent, 1629, with 10,000 troops, to co-operate with King of Poland against Gust. Ad., but resigned that same year, being disgusted with Polish maladministration. Appointed commander of forces of Electoral Saxony, 1631, to co-operate with Gust. Ad. Present at Breitenfeld, and subsequently invaded Bohemia. Driven out by W. in spring of 1632. Introd. xxix, xxxi, xxxiii. In constant communication with W. on subject of peace, Introd. xxxvii, xli, liii. His correspondence with W., covering many years, published in F. W. B. Arnim was throughout life a staunch Lutheran.

Baiern, Bavaria. Smaller in 30 Y. W. than at present. Annexation of Upper Palatinate, *i.e.,* country around Nuremberg, confirmed in 1648, Introd. lviii. Created a kingdom, by treaty of Pressburg, 1805. Maximilian of B. was persistent enemy of W., the most energetic Catholic prince in Germany, and leader of the League. Introd. xv, xix, xxix, xxxviii, xxxix, l.

Banner, (Swed. Banér). Trained under Gust. Ad., and one of the most distinguished Swed. generals. Noted for victory over Austro-Saxons at Wittstock, 1636, and his forays through Silesia, Bavaria, and Bohemia, 1637-1641. Died 1641. Sent, it is said, 600 flags and ensigns as trophies to Sweden.

Belt, name given to channels leading from Baltic to Catte-gat. Little B. between Jutland and Fünen ; Great B. betw. Fünen and Seeland. The *Scheren d. B.*, v. 1160, tall cliffs (Swed. skära, comp. Engl. 'sheer'). Schiller seems to have had in mind a passage in H. W. I. 206, where it is narrated that W., on overrunning Jutland, Introd. xvii, and forcing the last Danish detachment to surrender at Aalborg, was so enraged at the Belt for arresting his progress—he was unprovided with ships—that he ordered red-hot shot to be fired into the waves, in token of defiance.

Bernhard of Weimar, Introd. xxxiii, xxxiv, xxxix, lvii. See *Franken*. Most celebrated general on Prot. side, after Gust. Ad. Captured Rheinfeld and Breisach, 1638. Died 1639, of poison, as was asserted at time. G. T. W. 192. Set out to join W. at Eger, after news of loss of Prague, R. W. 432.

Böhmen, also spelled by S. *Böheim*, Bohemia. The Slavonic inhabitants call themselves Czehs (pr. Tschech). *Böhmerwald*, a chain of hills separating B. from Bavaria, Introd. xxxix.

Cardinal, see *Infant*.

Caraffa. Name of a celebrated Italian family that counted among its members one pope (Paul IV.), several cardinals and princes. Only two connected with German affairs : Pietro Luigi, Cardinal, sent by Pope Urban VIII. as envoy to Germany, 1623, was on friendly terms with W., but returned to Italy about 1628, R. W. 100 ; Geronimo, Marquis of Montenegro, who served in army of Ferd. II. at battle of White Mt., was subsequently appointed by Philip IV. capt. general of Aragon, and died 1633. The mention, v. 1006, is therefore unhistorical.

Colalto, Count Rambold. Figures in the drama as one of W.'s generals. C. had been Minister of War during W.'s first command, and warm friend of the general. Commanded imperial army in Italy, 1629, captured Mantua, but died, 1630, at Coire, on his way back to Germany. S. has probably confounded him with Colloredo, Introd. l, lii.

Frederick, Elector of Palatinate.   Married Elizabeth, daughter of James I. of England.   Elected King of Bohemia by the insurgents, 1619.   Defeated at White Mt., near Prague, 1620, and dispossessed not only of Bohemia but of Palatinate. Because of briefness of reign, called the 'Winter King.' After wandering in exile, died Nov. 1632, at Menz.   His son, Charles Lewis, restored to Lower Palatinate, 1648, Introd. lviii.

Friedland, W.'s principality, Introd. xiv.   Covered immense tract of land in Bohemia, skirting borders of Silesia and Lusatia.   Capital, Gitschin.   F. was also name of a small town in the district.

Gallas, Introd. xlix–lii, lxv.   Lt. Gen. and Count.   More successful as politician than as general, and lost more than one battle after W.'s death.

Gitschin, Introd. xiv, xx, xxii–xxiv.   50 m. n. e. of Prague.

Glatz, town in Silesia, on the Neisse, 15 m. s. e. of Braunau. In 30 Y. W. an Austrian, now Prussian fortress, and important strategic point.

Götz, Introd. lii.   Active against W., and president, in 1635, of court-martial that tried Schaffgotsch.

Gratz, capital of Styria.   Large, handsome city, on the Mur, about 100 s. w. of Vienna.   Ferd. II. called the *Grätzer*, because duke of Styria, Carinthia, and Carniola, before becoming emperor, and had G. as his residence.

Gustavus.   Introd. xxi, xxix, xxxiii, xxxiv, xlv–xlvii.

Halberstadt, capital of import. bishopric of that name, adjoining Magdeburg.   Originally Catholic, it was converted to Protestantism, and the chapter elected Christian of Brunswick 'administrator,' or secular head of the diocese, in 1616, G. T. W. 11, 12, 52.   Christian was the 'fighting bishop' of those days, a thorough man of the world, devoted to Frederick of Palatinate, and especially to Frederick's wife, whose glove he wore on his helmet.   After taking part in most campaigns in early part of 30 Y. W., but without much success, died 1626, soon after Mansfeld's defeat at Dessau.   Called *der Halberstädter.*

Harrach, Count Charles.   Introd. xiii.   Father of Duchess W. and Countess Trzka, Introd. lxvii.

Heidelberg, well-known town in Grand Duchy of Baden, on the Neckar.   In 30 Y. W. belonged to Palatinate.   Was captured and plundered by Tilly, 1622. The celebrated wine-cask, the largest in the world, was drained by his soldiers. It held many thousand gallons. The castle, the most renowned in Germany, was begun in 1400, and finished 1620, by Frederick. Blown up by army of Louis XIV., in 1689.

Hinnersam, also spelled Hennersam and Hinderson. Mentioned, H. W. III. 199, M. B. 328, as one of committee of five (the others were Ilow, Morwald, Breda, Loisy) to wait upon W. Introd. xliii. The name suggests that H. was an Englishman or a Scotchman.

Huss, Johannes. Professor at Univ. of Prague. Led by study of Wycliffe's writings to preach against Papal infallibility and to demand both bread and wine at communion, *sub utraque specie.* His followers in Bohemia were called Hussites, or Utraquists. He was condemned by Council of Constance, and burned at stake, 1415. This led to Hussite wars. See *Procop, Tabor,* and *Ziska.*

Infant, Don Fernando, younger brother of Philip IV. of Spain. Although cardinal in Roman Catholic church, his talents were rather literary and military than ecclesiastical. Introd. xl, xlii. Took part in battle of Nördlingen, Sept. 1634, Introd. lvii. See also *Königin v. Ungarn.*

Kürnthen, Carinthia. See note to v. 317. A highly picturesque mountainous region; by reason of its central position, little exposed to the hostilities raging all around it, hence v. 508. For real residence of W.'s wife and daughter, Introd. lxvi.

Kinsky, Count William. Introd. xlvii–xlix, lxvii. Mentioned, v. 2374, as one of W.'s officers. Such was not the case. K. was in Pilsen, still plying his negotiations, when the news came of loss of Prague, liii. Accompanied W. to Eger and was killed there.

König v. Ungarn, son of Emperor Ferdinand II., and subsequently himself emperor, as Ferdinand III., 1637–1657, Introd. lviii, lx, lxi. At time of the drama (1634) only 25 years old. Hence spoken of as the *Kind,* v. 208. The *Königin v. Ungarn,* his wife, was the Infanta Maria Anna, sister of Philip IV. of Spain and of Cardinal-Infant. She had been the destined bride of Charles I. of England.

Lamormain, French for Lämmermann, native of Luxemburg, and father-confessor of Ferd. II., over whom he had great influence. Introd. xxxvi. A Jesuit, and instigator of the Edict of Restitution, Introd. xxx.

Lech, in 30 Y. W., the boundary betw. Bavaria and Bishopric of Augsburg. In April, 1632, Gust. Ad. forced a passage at Rain, some distance n. of city of Augsburg, and defeated Tilly. The latter was mortally wounded and died a few days later, at Ingolstadt.

Liechtenstein, Count and Prince Charles. One of Ferd. II.'s Privy Councillors, *Statthalter* of Bohemia, after the battle of White Mt. L. was one of the clique that raised W. to power in 1623. See note to v. 1164. In v. 1920 mentioned as still alive; such was not the case. Perhaps S. has confounded the prince with another member of same family.

Linz. Capital of duchy of Upper Austria, on Danube, 100 m. w. of Vienna. Introd. li, note.

Lützen. Not far from Leipsic. Introd. xxxiv.

Mähren. Moravia. Inhabitants chiefly of Slavonic race, speaking Czechish, see *Böhmen.* They were, for most part, Protestants, until restoration of Catholicism by force of arms, Introd. xii-xv. Settlements of the Moravian Brethren (closely related to Bohemian Brethren, Introd. xi) are to be found in U. S. The one best known is at Bethlehem, Pa.

Mailand, Milan. Well-known city of northern Italy. In 30 Y. W., M. was the seat of a Spanish principality, Introd. xl, xlii. Subsequently passed into possession of Austria, and was annexed by Victor Emmanuel, 1859.

Main, one of principal rivers of Germany. Rises in northern part of Bavaria, flows w. in extremely tortuous course, and empties into Rhine opposite Menz. See *Franken.*

Mansfeld, Count Ernst. Illegitimate son of Peter Ernst v. M., a celebrated general in Austro-Spanish service. Young Ernst, dissatisfied with treatment he received from the Austrians, espoused Protestant cause and was for many years its foremost champion. His career and death sound more like romance than history. After participating in Bohemian insurrection in 1619, he overran Upper Palatinate and Alsace, also Lorraine, and cut his way through Spanish Netherlands to relieve Bergen-op-Zoom. He co-operated with Christian of Denmark against Tilly and Wallenstein. Defeated by the latter at Dessau, 1626, he marched through Silesia to Hungary, to join Bethlen Gabor, prince of Transylvania, and attack

Austria from E. Baffled by W.'s generalship, and disappointed by Bethlen, he set out for Venice to obtain subsidies, but died on the way. Perceiving that his end was near, he dressed in full uniform, buckled on his sword, and, leaning on the arms of his servants, awaited the summons. M. was a soldier and little else, reckless of life and money, fertile in expedients, indomitable, quick to see the enemy's weak points. Like B. of Weimar, he was never so dangerous as just after a reverse. Before rise of Wallenstein, he was regarded as the captain of his age, and the *condottiere* by eminence.

Maradas, better spelled Marrados, Count Balthasar. General in command of troops in Bohemia. Spaniard by birth, and inimical to W. Introd. lii.

Martinitz, Jaroslav v. M. and Slavata were members of Ferdinand's provincial regency for Bohemia at breaking out of insurrection, 1618. Having made themselves very obnoxious to the Protestant insurgents, they were thrown from window of council-chamber in the castle on the Hradschin (at Prague) into the Hirschgraben, a dry moat sixty or seventy feet deep. Falling on a pile of loose rubbish, they escaped with a few bruises, v. 2109–2119.

Mohrbrand. Mentioned, v. 2566, as having captured Sesina. Inasmuch as the capture itself is an invention of Schiller's, it would be difficult to locate the name. Not to be confounded with Morwald (Mohr v. Waldt, see Introd. lii, and *Hinnersam*). See also Mohra, Lt.-Col., Introd. liii.

Montecuculi, Count Ernst. One of W.'s officers for many years. It may be doubted whether he ever sympathized so warmly with W., as intimated v. 1954, or, indeed, that he took a prominent part on either side. His son, General Raymond M., far surpassed him in renown.

Nepomuk, small town, 20 m. s. of Pilsen. Celebrated as birth place of John of N., the patron saint of Bohemian Catholics. The Protestants venerated, if they did not canonize, Jerome of Prague and Huss.

Niederlande, Netherlands. The N. mentioned in the drama are the Spanish N., comprising what is now known as Belgium; capital, Brussels. Introd. xv, xlii. Seven provinces that had once belonged to Spain, revolted in 16th century, and declared themselves independent, as United Provinces, then Dutch

Republic; now, the kingdom of the Netherlands; capital, the Hague.

Nürnberg, Nuremberg. In 30 Y. W. a Free City (*Reichsstadt*), and most important city in South Germany. Now in Bavaria. Strongly Protestant, and scene of many important events, see v. 1036, Introd. xxxiii. The old walls, towers, and mediæval architecture of the city are still preserved, and attract tourists from all parts of the world.

Oder, principal river of Silesia. See *Steinau*.

Oesterreich, Austria. The student should bear in mind that in 30 Y. W., and even in Schiller's day, there was no Empire and no Emperor of Austria. The head of the House of Habsburg was ruler of the Duchies of Upper and Lower Austria, Bohemia, Hungary, Styria, Tyrol, etc., either in person or through his heir apparent. These several countries were united in what is called a "personal union," each having its own capital, local parliament (*Stände*, note to v. 324), and customs, etc. They did not constitute a homogeneous empire. In fact, they scarcely do, even at present day. The head of the Habsburg dynasty was, almost invariably, *elected* by the German *Churfürsten* to be head also of the German Empire (in legal phraseology, *das heilige römische Reich deutscher Nation*), and as such held the title *Deutscher Kaiser*. It was not until 1806, at the dissolution of this old German Empire, that Franz I. assumed the title Emperor of Austria. But Ferdinand II., 1619–1637, was *Deutscher Kaiser;* hence his influence over German affairs, Introd. xvii–xx.

Oñate, Introd. xl, xlii, xliv, l, lxx.

Oxenstirn, in Swedish, Axel Oxenstjerna. The renowned Chancellor of Gust. Ad., and regent of Sweden after death of latter. O. was noted for imperturbable coolness, sagacity, and persistency of purpose. The greatest Continental statesman of his day, next to Richelieu, and scarcely inferior even to the Cardinal. He was in Germany from 1630–1636. At time of W.'s death he was either in Halberstadt, see v. 816 note, or in Stendal, 40 m. n. of Magdeburg.

Palffy. Count and Palatin of Hungary. Ment. v. 2055, 2134. It is somewhat surprising that S. has failed to introduce among the 'motives' of the drama a statement in the *Gründlicher Bericht*, M. B. 242, viz., that W. had won over Isolani by falsely representing to him that the emperor intended to take from him, Isolani, the command of the Croats and Hungarians and give it to Palffy.

Pfalz, the Palatinate. Divided into Upper and Lower. The former conferred on Duke of Bavaria, 1621, Introd. xviii. The latter restored to Frederick's son, Introd. lviii. The lower Palatinate is now merged in Baden, Hesse-Darmstadt, Rhenish Prussia, and Rhenish Bavaria.

Pfalzgraf, Palsgrave, see *Frederick*.

Pilsen, scene of *Piccol.* and *Tod* I–III., small town (now 15,000), at confluence of Mies and Radbusa. In 30 Y. W. a fortified place. Had been besieged many times in Hussite wars, and was stormed by Mansfeld, 1618. Prague is 50 m. n. e., Eger about 40 m. n. w. Now an important railroad centre, and noted for its beer-breweries.

Pommern, Pomerania. In 30 Y. W. an independent duchy. The dynasty dying out with Boguslav, P. was divided, 1648, between Sweden and Brandenburg, the former getting West, the latter East P. Introd. lviii. West P. was wrested from the Swedes by the Great Elector, 1675, through battle of Fehrbellin. P. was scene of Gust. Ad.'s first campaign in Germany, Introd. xxi, xxix.

Prag, Prague. Capital of Bohemia, on the Moldau, a branch of the Elbe, 52 m. n. e. of Pilsen. Introd. liii.

Procop, the Elder, or Greater. The Council of Basel, convened 1431, to allay the religious conflict in Bohemia, made certain concessions which were accepted by the more moderate Utraquists but rejected by the more fanatic. These latter, the Taborites, led by Procop, and aided by the wildest sect of all, the *Waisen*, under another Procop, called the Younger, continued the war. They were utterly defeated near Prague, 1434, and both Procops killed.

Quiroga. Capuchin monk, father-confessor of king of Hungary. Introd. xxxii, xlii, lxx.

Regensburg, Ratisbon. Important city of Bavaria, at confluence of Danube and Regen. Taken and retaken repeatedly in 30 Y. W. Introd. xviii, xxxix.

Reichenberg, a town in W.'s principality of Friedland, 58 m. n. e. of Prague.

Rheingraf, Otto Ludwig v. Salm. Mentioned, v. 1034, as present at siege of Nuremberg. Such was not case, D. W. 192. note. See Index to *Tod*.

Riesenberge, more usual, Riesengebirge. Chain of mts. separating Bohemia from Silesia. The highest point is the Riesenkoppe, 5,400 ft., near Hirschberg. The R. is noted in German fairy-lore.

Rudolph, German Emperor, 1576-1612. At same time king of Bohemia and Hungary (see *Oesterreich*). A cousin of Ferd. II. R. granted to Bohemian Estates a royal charter (*Majestätsbrief*), 1609, guaranteeing to Lutherans and Utraquists right of public worship. This charter was cancelled by Ferd. II., 1620, after battle of White Mt.

Sachsen, Saxony. Important to discriminate the varying applications of the word. It may denote, *a.* The Electorate (now kingdom) of S. *b.* The small principalities scattered through Thuringia. *c.* The so-called circle of Lower Saxony, comprising Brunswick, Mecklenburg, Lüneburg, etc. In this drama, S. refers usually to *a.* In one place, v. 1158, to *c.*

Sagan. Introd. xv. About 50 m. n. e. of Bautzen.

Schaffgotsch, Count Ulrich. A Protestant, and zealous partisan of W. General of cavalry, and took decisive part at battle of Steinau. In Silesia at time of events in drama. After W.'s death, arrested, tried for treason and mutiny, put to the rack, and executed, July. 1635, at Ratisbon.

Schlesien, Silesia. In 30 Y. W., an Austrian province. Wrested almost entirely from Maria Theresa by Frederick the Great, in war of Austrian Succession, 1740-1748, and has remained Prussian ever since.

Schwaben, Swabia. That district of s. w. Germany comprised in Württemberg and parts of Baden and Bavaria.

Sesin. Introd. xlvi. S. was not captured, as narrated v. 2565. He had been sent to Oxenstjerna, at Halberstadt, in early part of February, probably by Kinsky, Introd. xlviii. On his way back he learned at Zwickau the news of W.'s death, just in time to avoid capture. H. W. III. Preface, 222, 225. Schiller was probably led to invent S.'s capture by the circumstance that Schlieff was captured, in Prague, with dispatches to Schaffgotsch, D. W. 153, note. The dramatic effect of the invention is obvious.

Slavata. Name of a number of prominent Bohemians. The one alluded to in drama is Wilhelm v., see *Martinitz.* Sl. was an uncle of W.'s, but the two hated one another thoroughly (R. W. 349, 505, Introd. lxi). The Slavatas were

Tilly, one of most celebrated generals in 30 Y. W.   A Walloon by birth, in command of armies of Catholic League. Gains victory of White Mt., Introd. xiv, overruns Bohemia, Upper and Lower Palatinate, defeats Danes and Mansfeld. See Introd. xvii, xxi. Overruns Electoral Saxony, and plunders Magdeburg. Introd. xxix, see also *Lech.* T. was not a politician, but an able general, and regarded as invincible until the rise of Gust. Ad.   He has been described as a monster of cruelty, but this is to be doubted.   It is also questionable if he is responsible for all the excesses committed at Magdeburg.

Tokai, town in northern Hungary, about 150 m. s. e. of Cracow.   Entrepot for celebrated Tokay wines grown in neighborhood.

Ungarn, Hungary.   It should be borne in mind that in 30 Y. W. a large portion of H. was in subjection to Turkish Sultan, and that even the Austrian Hungarians were anything but constant in loyalty to Habsburgs, and intrigued repeatedly with Bethlen Gabor, Introd. xv, xxxviii.   See also *Mansfeld.*

Weimar, see Bernhard.   **Werdenberg,** Introd. xx, xxxii, lxix.

Weser, formed by confluence of Fulda and Werra at Münden, near Cassel.   See note to v. 214.

Wien, Vienna.   The name usually supposed to be corruption of Latin Vindobona, the town having been founded as a Roman military post by Vespasian.   At one time on banks of Danube; now, about three miles south (although the river has recently, April, 1875, been brought to the suburbs by a new artificial channel, ten miles long, the *Donauregulirung*).   The city is intersected by a small stream, the Wien.   Residence of the Habsburgs, and capital of Lower Austria.

Ziska, born 1360.   Page and chamberlain at court of Emperor Wenzel at Prague.   Served in various wars, and was officer in English army at Agincourt.   At breaking out of Hussite wars took prominent part, and on death of Hussinecz was made leader of the Bohemians, 1421.   Founded Tabor, and led his troops to victory after victory until his name became a terror.   Lost, as a boy, his right eye, and subsequently the other, in battle, but continued to lead his army. Died of the pest, 1424.

Znaim. Introd. xxx, xxxii, lxix.   Pron. '*z*' as in 'zone.'

Important Announcement to Teachers, Students, and Readers of German Literature.

G. P. PUTNAM'S SONS *have the pleasure of announcing that they have commenced the publication of a series entitled*

GERMAN CLASSICS

FOR

AMERICAN STUDENTS.

EDITED BY

JAMES MORGAN HART, LL.D.,

Author of " German Universities," Graduate of the College of New Jersey, and the University of Göttingen, and formerly Assistant Professor of German in Cornell University, etc., etc.

The series will be issued in neat 16mo volumes, carefully printed, and handsomely bound, and will form not only a set of text-books for the student of German, but an attractive collection for the Library of the Masterpieces of German Literature. It will present the following important features:

The utmost pains will be taken to ensure textual accuracy, a point hitherto neglected in the preparation of text-books in the modern languages.

Each volume will contain:

I. An Introduction, setting forth the circumstances and influences under which the work—(or in the case of selections, each part)—was composed, the materials used by the author, or the sources from which he derived his inspiration, and the relative standing of the work in German literature.

II. A Running Commentary, explaining peculiarities in the use of words and difficulties in the grammatical structure of

170

the sentence, and discussing allusions to the personages and events of history, to the author's contemporaries, to national or provincial peculiarities of manner, customs and opinion.

By thus placing at the disposal of teacher and pupil all the helps needful to the complete understanding of the original, the present series will, it is hoped, supply a long-felt want of the school and college curriculum. It will also commend itself to the more advanced scholars who purpose entering upon a course of private reading.

It is at present proposed to include in the series the following volumes, which are believed to be fairly representative of classical German literature:

Schiller.—Wilhelm Tell. Maria Stuart. Jungfrau von Orleans. Wallenstein (3 vols.). Selections from the Minor Poems. Selections in Prose. **Lessing.**—Nathan der Weise. Minna von Barnhelm. Selections.	**Goethe.**—Hermann und Doro- thea. Egmont. Iphigenie. Tasso. Selections from the Mi- nor Poems. Selections in Prose. **Herder.**—Selections. **Wieland.**—Selections.

Should the German classics for American students meet with the favor that is anticipated, they will be followed by a supplemental series, embodying the best pieces of the minor lights of German literature, such as Arndt, Körner, Uhland, the Schlegels, Tieck, Heyne, Immermann, Platen, Rückert, &c.

The editor will be pleased to receive from practical teachers any suggestions in regard to such further additions as might be found desirable.

The first volume of the series will be "HERMANN UND DORO- THEA," which will be issued early in March. Price $1.00. It will be speedily followed by "THE PICCOLOMINI," price $1.25, &c.

Specimen copies will be sent prepaid to teachers for examination on receipt of half the price, and liberal terms will be made for introduction.

G. P. PUTNAM'S SONS,

4th Avenue and 23d Street, New York.

180

BRIEF BIOGRAPHIES. First Series. Contemporary Statesmen of Europe. Edited by Thomas Wentworth Higginson.

These volumes are planned to meet the desire which exists for accurate and graphic information in regard to the leaders of political action in other countries. They will give portraitures of the men, and analyses of their lives and work, that will be vivid and picturesque, as well as accurate and faithful, and that will combine the authority of careful historic narration with the interest attacking to anecdote and personal delineation.

The volumes are handsomely printed in square 16mo, and attractively bound in cloth extra. Price per vol., $1.50.

Vol. I.—English Statesmen. Now ready. By T. W. Higginson.

"Gives in a very compact and readable form just the information needed. . . Leaves little to be desired."—*N. Y. Nation.*
"A practical idea well carried out."—*Springfield Republican.*

Vol. II.—French Leaders. By Edward King.
Vol. III.—English Radical Leaders. By R. J. Hinton.

G. P. PUTNAM'S SONS

Have commenced the publication of a series of 12mo volumes, entitled,

"BRIEF BIOGRAPHIES."

The first issue is devoted to the Contemporary Statesmen of Europe, and will include eight or ten volumes, under the editorship of Thomas Wentworth Higginson.

The series will begin with the publication of two volumes, entitled respectively "English Statesmen" and "English Radical Leaders." The first will be under the immediate charge of the Editor of the series, and will include sketches of such men as Gladstone, Disraeli, John Bright, Earl Russell, Earl Granville, W. E. Forster, the Duke of Argyle, Lord Derby, Lord Cairns, and others. The second volume will treat of Professor Fawcett, Sir Charles Dilke, Jacob Bright, Peter A. Taylor, Arthur Mundella, Thos. Hughes, and others, and will be prepared by Col. R. J. Hinton, of Washington, D. C. The volume on the French Leaders will be prepared by Edward King. Succeeding volumes will treat of statesmen and political leaders in Germany, Austria, Italy, Spain, Russia, and other countries of Europe. Each work will be complete in itself, will receive the careful revision of the Editor, will be corrected to the latest dates, and will be properly indexed. It is proposed that the whole series shall be attractive to the transient reader, and at the same time shall be thoroughly to be relied upon in every statement of fact. Should the public patronage justify the completion of the work, it will certainly fill an important gap, as no similar series is believed to exist in any language. Each volume will be handsomely printed in square 16mo and attractively bound in cloth extra, and will sell for $1.50.

181

HART. German Universities. A Record of Personal Experience, and a Critical Comparison of the System of Higher Education in Germany with those of England and the United States. By James Morgan Hart. 12mo, cloth, $1.75.

"Admirable in conception and execution."—*Prof. Moses Coit Tyler.*
"The book is evidently the result of the closest personal observation under the guidance of high culture."—*N. Y. Independent.*

BRISTED. Five Years in an English University. By Charles Astor Bristed, late Foundation Scholar of Trinity College, Cambridge. Fourth edition. Revised and amended by the author. 12mo, cloth extra, $2.25.

A new edition of this standard work, for some years out of print, has long been called for. With its facts and statistics corrected, and brought down to recent date, the volume conveys to the college graduate or undergraduate information of special value and importance, while the vivid and attractive record of a personal experience contains much to interest the general reader.

"It is characterized by most excellent taste, and contains a great deal of most novel and interesting information."—*Philadelphia Inquirer.*

PUTNAM. The World's Progress. A Dictionary of Dates; being a Chronological and Alphabetical Record of Essential Facts in the History of the World and the Progress of Society, from the Creation to the Present Time. By G. P. Putnam, A.M. A new edition, continued to 1872. In one large volume, 12mo, cloth, $3.50; half calf, gilt, $5.50.

"A more convenient literary labor-saving machine than this excellent compilation can scarcely be found in any language."—*N. Y. Tribune.*
"It has been planned so as to facilitate access to the largest amount of useful information in the smallest possible compass."—*Buffalo Courier.*
"The best manual of the kind that has yet appeared in the English language."—*Boston Courier.*
"An exceedingly valuable book; well-nigh indispensable to a very large portion of the community."—*N. Y. Courier and Enquirer.*
"It is absolutely essential to the desk of every merchant, and the table of every student and professional man."—*Christian Enquirer.*
"It is worth ten times its price. . . . It completely supplies my need."—*S. W. Riegart, Principal of High School, Lancaster, Pa.*

BEST READING, THE. A Classified Bibliography for Easy Reference. With Hints on the Selection of Books; on the Formation of Libraries, Public and Private; on Courses of Reading, etc.; a Guide for the Librarian, Bookbuyer, and Bookseller. The Classified Lists, arranged under about 500 subject headings, include all the most desirable books now to be obtained either in Great Britain or the United States, with the published prices annexed. Revised Edition. 12mo, paper, $1. Cloth, $1.50.

"The best work of the kind we have seen."—*College Courant.*
"We know of no manual that can take its place as a guide to the selection of a library."—*N. Y. Independent.*

182

Just Published:

Druck:
Customized Business Services GmbH
im Auftrag der KNV-Gruppe
Ferdinand-Jühlke-Str. 7
99095 Erfurt